BAD INFLUENCE

ALSO BY BRANDON MASSEY

Thunderland

Dark Corner

Within the Shadows

The Other Brother

Vicious

The Last Affair

Don't Ever Tell

Cornered

Covenant

In the Dark

Frenzied

Nana

The Quiet Ones

No Stone Unturned

The Exes

The Landlord

BAD INFLUENCE

A PSYCHOLOGICAL THRILLER

BRANDON MASSEY

DARK CORNER PUBLISHING

Copyright © 2024 by Brandon Massey

All rights reserved.

No part of this book may be reproduced in any form or by any electronic or mechanical means, including information storage and retrieval systems, without written permission from the author, except for the use of brief quotations in a book review.

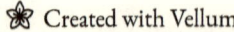 Created with Vellum

BEFORE

Trouble had arrived.

On that golden Saturday morning in June, Karen Newport sat in the parlor of her palatial home, filling out a crossword puzzle and sipping warm peach tea, when she glanced out the big front window and saw the girl trespassing on her property.

At first, Karen thought she was imagining the sight. Only last week, she had warned this child to stay away from her home, or else she would contact the police.

But already, the girl had returned. Brazen in her misbehavior.

She was a striking African American kid, beige-skinned and willowy, with the face of a model and long auburn hair; at only ten years old, she was already as tall as Karen. After last week's encounter, Karen had asked a fellow neighbor about this child's presence in their community. Her friend confirmed not only the child's legitimate residency in their prestigious suburban Atlanta neighborhood but also her age and name.

Scarlett.

While Karen watched, Scarlett pedaled her shiny bicycle into Karen's driveway and hopped off. She wore white shorts and a pink

T-shirt that declared *Princess* in glittery silver letters above an image of a golden tiara.

Scarlett dug into a book bag slung over her shoulder and removed a small pair of garden shears.

Karen's mouth puckered into a scowl.

What's the girl here for this time? She's undoubtedly up to no good.

Scarlett approached the large flower bed. Karen's prized rosebushes danced in the summer breeze.

Twisting around on the sofa, Karen reached for her walker.

Karen was eighty-three years old and lived alone, much to the consternation of her children. She cherished her lifestyle far too much to move into some lackluster, senior-living community. She had outlived two husbands, the last of whom had purchased this wonderful residence for her, and she intended to enjoy the remainder of her days in her luxurious haven.

But her mobility wasn't what it used to be. Using her walker, she shuffled to the front door. She opened it; she rarely engaged the lock. Security in their community was so rigorously managed that Karen believed such measures were unnecessary.

The girl knelt beside the roses. Using the shears, the child ruthlessly severed the blooming flowers. As each precious one dropped to the ground, the girl picked them up and tossed the flowers over her shoulder as if they were no more valuable than rotted apples.

Last week, the girl had taken several of Karen's roses without permission. This time, she was destroying them.

"Scarlett!" Karen's voice crackled with fury. "Stop it! Stop it right now!"

Scarlett turned toward her. She grinned with a malicious delight that lifted the hairs at the nape of Karen's neck.

What was wrong with this child? Karen found this girl's pleasure while performing this destructive act deeply unsettling.

Straightening as her anger mounted, Karen said: "I warned you, little girl. I warned you to stay off my property. Now, I'm calling the authorities!"

Karen made a dramatic show of brandishing her mobile phone in front of her.

Scarlett flipped her middle finger at Karen and stuck out her tongue.

Karen gasped.

"Get off my property!" Karen screamed.

Scarlett flung the shears to the grass and took her time walking back to her bicycle, obviously unconcerned with the punishment Karen had in mind.

Well, she would learn better, Karen thought. She would realize this was a world of rules and laws, and she'd better abide by them—or she would suffer the consequences.

Karen called the police.

Later that night, Karen snapped awake, convinced she heard someone in the house.

She lay in bed listening, her heart knocking at a rapid pace. The blurry, blood-red numerals on the nearby clock read 2:23. Blackness filled the spacious master bedroom, the darkness broken only by the faint bluish glow of a night-light near the bathroom.

Muffled voices came from downstairs. She couldn't discern what they were saying, but more than one person was speaking.

A home invasion? Here? That seemed like an absurd idea. The community was so secure she didn't need to lock her doors.

But earlier, she'd summoned the authorities to handle a lawless child, hadn't she? The world was changing, and even gated neighborhoods with million-dollar homes might no longer be secure.

Karen pushed herself upright and fumbled for her bifocals. She picked up her phone and dragged her walker toward her.

She always slept with the bedroom door open. A faint light illuminated the second-floor corridor, but from where she sat on the bed, no one appeared to be in the hallway.

But the voices grew louder as she shuffled across the room and entered the hall.

At the grand spiral staircase, a custom-designed chairlift allowed safe transport between the floors of her home. The padded seat rested in position at the top of the stairs.

She heard gunfire echoing below, but she only shook her head. By then, it was apparent to her that the noises came from the television in the parlor. Not intruders.

The disturbing thought, in fact, was that she had left the television on at a high volume and was only then aware of it. How had that happened? Was her memory failing despite her best efforts to keep her mind active?

She would need to go down there and shut off the TV. Otherwise, she'd never get back to sleep.

She moved toward the chairlift.

"Old snitch bitch," someone whispered behind her.

Karen turned.

Scarlett stood in the hallway. She wore dark pajamas and sneakers, her long hair knotted in a ponytail.

Instinctively, Karen knew the girl wasn't there for another go at the roses. Pure malice smoldered in the child's beautiful eyes.

"Stay back." Voice quavering, Karen lifted her phone. "I'll call the police again!"

"Snitches get stitches," Scarlett said.

A scream flew up Karen's throat, and she raised her hands defensively, but the girl pounced like a panther. She shoved Karen hard.

Her arms flailing, Karen plummeted down the long staircase.

By the time her twisted, broken body thudded to the bottom, she was already dead.

1

Several years later.

When Adrian Wall's thirteen-year-old daughter climbed into his Kia SUV that Friday after school, she was beaming.

"Someone's in a good mood," Adrian said. "How are you, Harp?"

After the rough day he'd experienced at work, he was relieved to see Harper smiling. According to his good friend and colleague, a company reorganization loomed. As a contract employee with the financial services firm for only the past six months, Adrian wasn't confident that the corporate reshuffle would include a spot for him, and a nagging anxiety dogged him.

"Hey, Daddy." Harper climbed into the passenger seat, buckled her seat belt, and pulled out her iPhone. She smiled as she swiped and tapped. They had gifted her the smartphone, her first ever, for her thirteenth birthday that past May, and she and the device were inseparable.

Harper's appearance was a balanced mosaic of both her parents. She'd inherited Adrian's warm, reddish-brown complexion and dark brown eyes. She had her mother's heart-shaped face, thick, lustrous black hair, and full lips. *She's gonna be a heartbreaker*, relatives often said, and Adrian tended to agree.

Seeing Harper in an upbeat mood gave him hope for their upcoming weekend together. This weekend was his scheduled visitation. The idea of scheduled time with his child still felt foreign to Adrian, but that was one condition included in his legal separation agreement with his wife, Stephanie. Although he was nine months into it, he continued to feel as though he were living someone else's life.

He pulled away from the carpool line at the front of Carver Middle School. The August afternoon was clear and humid, typical Georgia weather. Still, some students he passed were attired as though for a day at the beach. Dress code standards for school had changed since his youth.

"Did you have a good day at school?" he asked. "The way you're grinning, I wonder if you scored an A on that math test."

"I got a C," she said, but that didn't dim her smile.

"Okay." He tried not to show his concern. During one of their monthly family counseling sessions, Harper disclosed that he focused too much on her academic performance, as if he used her grades as a yardstick to determine whether she was "worth loving." That reveal had stunned him, and since he'd found out, he had tried to curb his obsession with her academic scores.

It was tough, though. He hadn't fulfilled his own potential in school, and he believed it was partly responsible for the lackluster state of his career.

"I've got a new friend," Harper said.

"That's exciting." Adrian steered from the school's massive parking lot to the adjoining road, where traffic breezed back and forth. "Boy or girl?"

Harper made a disgusted sound. "Why would I want to be friends with a boy?"

Thank God you aren't yet, Adrian thought.

"Her name's Scarlett. She's new at our school. She's in my

Science class, and she sits behind me. We started talking this week when we had to do a lab project."

"Scarlett, huh? That's great, sweetheart."

Making new friends had long proved a challenge for Harper. As an only child, she was more socially isolated than many peers. For the past couple of years, making new friends had become an obsession of hers. Steph had assured him that their daughter's social aspirations were normal: *It's what girls do. Don't worry about it.*

"Can you please go home first, Daddy?" Harper asked. "I need to get some clothes."

For Harper, "home" meant the three-bedroom house in Alpharetta where she and her mother lived, not the two-bedroom apartment that Adrian rented ten minutes away.

He was about to remind her she already had clothes at his place, but he worried that might annoy her, and he was determined to keep things running smoothly.

"Sure, I'll swing by the house," Adrian said.

Five minutes later, Adrian turned into the neighborhood he and Stephanie had moved into a decade ago, Valley Mills. It was a mid-sized community of about a hundred properties, all of them three- or four-bedroom houses sitting on modest-sized lots. It was a respectable neighborhood of starter houses.

He missed living there. Sometimes, when driving back from work, he took the route to the house and wouldn't realize his misstep until he had turned into the community.

Their place stood at the edge of a cul-de-sac. Steph's Toyota Camry was parked in the driveway.

"Your mother's home," Adrian said, more to himself than to his daughter.

Harper ignored him, her attention riveted on her iPhone. Adrian parked in the driveway beside his wife's car.

Harper opened the door and got out, but Adrian clutched the steering wheel. Steph wasn't expecting him to visit; she was expecting him to pick up Harper from school and take her to his apartment for the weekend.

But he wanted to see Steph. He felt as if he were on the brink of a tsunami at work, and during such times in the past, Steph had always been a valued confidante, a voice of reason amid the chaos. He craved her perspective.

"Are you coming?" Harper asked, pausing at the passenger door.

"Do you think it's okay?" he asked.

"Of course it is." Harper's face screwed into a frown. "It's *your* house, too, Daddy—if you want it to be."

"It's not that simple, Harp."

Her frown deepened.

He knew Harper hated the current situation; she always tried to force them back together. He understood. His parents had divorced when he was only eight, his father leaving the state altogether to start anew in Texas, and the aftermath of that breakup had wounded Adrian for years.

Sighing, he climbed out of the car and followed Harper to the door. She used her key to unlock it, and he went inside after she did.

It had been a couple of weeks since Adrian had last entered the house. Each time he stepped inside, it was marginally different, as if it were slowly transforming into a new environment that excluded him. This time, he noticed the big, framed photo of Steph wearing her wedding dress, a memorable picture taken on the day of their marriage, which had long hung in a prominent position in the entry hall, was gone. A generic piece of African-themed art hung in its place.

The observation hit him like a blow to the chest. What did this mean? Was she disgusted by the memory of their marriage? Had she given up on their chances of reconciliation?

He hadn't given up on them.

As Harper hurried along the hallway, heading toward the staircase, Adrian slowly moved into the house. He worried about what other changes he might discover.

He heard voices upstairs. A man laughing, and Steph laughing, too.

His heart knocked. Who was Steph talking to? Was someone in the house? Did she have a boyfriend already?

While dating wasn't disallowed per their separation, he hadn't been on any dates or even looked at any dating apps. That felt like giving up hope.

But perhaps Steph had moved on.

"Steph?" Adrian charged forward and reached the staircase.

"Oh, hey," Steph said from the stairs. "What are you doing here?"

"Is someone else in here?" he asked. "Harper said she needed some clothes."

"I'll be down in a minute."

She stepped away from the staircase, out of view, but he heard her talking mutedly. His jaws clenched.

When Steph came downstairs, he noticed two things about her: she had a new hairstyle and was wearing a new outfit, too. Her dark hair had been trimmed in a stylish bob that flattered her heart-shaped face. She wore a summery green blouse with a peek of cleavage and a white skirt showcasing her figure. Light makeup complemented her rich brown skin.

Steph had probably shed fifteen pounds since their separation began, as if she were ramping up for the dating market. She was forty-one, a year younger than he, and looked fantastic.

"Are you going out?" he asked. He despised the jealous tone in his voice.

She frowned but didn't answer. She strolled past him into the kitchen. She looked so good to him that it took all his willpower to avoid touching her shoulder and leaning in to kiss her.

"You look great," he said to clean up for his prior comment.

"Thanks." Leaning against the counter, she sipped water from a bottle. "If you must know, I'm meeting a friend for an early dinner in Buckhead."

"Who?" he asked.

Her face tightened.

"Never mind," he said. "Hey, so at my job, there's a reorg coming. Trevor heard it through the grapevine."

Trevor was a longtime friend. He had also helped Adrian land the contracting gig at the company.

"Sounds like you better look for a new job, Adrian. Contractors don't fare well in restructuring. That happened to me, remember?"

"That was a crazy time for us, wasn't it?" He liked that she mentioned a shared experience of theirs. "I've got to figure out my plan."

"We can chat about it some other time," she said, her attention shifting to her phone. "I've got to finish getting ready."

"For your date?" He couldn't help coming back to it.

"I'm not getting into this with you right now."

"We're supposed to be working things out, Steph. Not moving on."

At that moment, Harper burst into the kitchen carrying her overnight bag.

"Is everything okay?" Harper asked. Her gaze shifted from her mother to Adrian. "What are you guys arguing about?"

"We're not arguing," Steph said. "Your father was asking inappropriate questions, but I'm sure he regrets doing that."

Steph directed a barbed look at Adrian, and Harper turned to glower at Adrian, too. Adrian raised his hands in a defenseless posture.

"Forget it," he said. "Harp, let's go. I don't want your mother to be late for her date."

"You're going on a date, Mom?" Harper's mouth dropped open.

Adrian grinned inwardly, pleased at the blow he had landed, but knew he had made a wrong move. How was putting their child in the middle of their marital woes helping?

Steph's face was a stone mask, but Adrian saw the anger simmering in her gaze.

"I'm only meeting a friend for dinner," Steph told Harper. "I'll see you on Sunday, sweetheart. Have fun with your father."

Steph said nothing to Adrian as he and his daughter left the house. Still, he felt her eyes firing arrows into his back. As he walked to the door, he noticed another of their marriage photos that had hung in the hallway was gone, too, but she hadn't replaced it with anything.

The spot was empty.

2

Adrian had planned what he'd thought would be an enjoyable weekend for him and Harper, but on Saturday, his daughter derailed his plans.

His original itinerary: lunch at the Cheesecake Factory, one of Harper's favorite restaurants, and then a matinee for them to catch a new sci-fi thriller that had recently hit theaters. Harper had always loved watching genre flicks with him and Steph, and he was looking forward to taking her to see the film, just the two of them.

But halfway through lunch, Harper hit Adrian with a curveball.

"Scarlett invited me to hang out with her," she said.

"Scarlett?" Adrian was about to bite his turkey cheeseburger sans the bun. Seeing how good Steph looked these days had inspired him to drop a few pounds, too. "And Scarlett is . . ."

"Wow, you really don't listen to me at all." She stirred her raspberry lemonade with a straw. "My new friend. I told you about her yesterday."

"I'm sorry, peanut. I should have remembered." He chewed his burger. "So. Scarlett invited you to something?"

"She's having a party today at Main Event."

Main Event was an entertainment complex that featured a bowling alley, an arcade, laser tag, and other games. Once, during happier times, Adrian and Steph had thrown Harper a birthday party there.

"Today?" he asked. "When?"

Harper glanced at her phone, where he assumed she was checking a text message. "Three o'clock, I guess? She's invited a bunch of her friends."

"But I bought movie tickets for us. I thought you wanted to see this one."

"We can stream it at home in probably a month or something. No one ever invites me to parties." Her lips drew into a pout. "*Please, Daddy?*"

How could he say no to her? She would never forgive him if he denied her this opportunity to spend time with a new friend.

"You can go," he said. Kiss twenty dollars for those movie tickets goodbye. He wished he could get a refund.

"Yeah!" She grinned. "Oh, I've gotta change clothes before I go."

She wore a pink T-shirt, jeans, and white Chuck Taylor sneakers.

"I don't get it," he said. "What's wrong with what you're wearing now? Is this a black-tie affair or something?"

"Can we just go back to your place, please?"

He saw no point in questioning her further. The teenage girl party attire rules were as baffling to him as ancient Sanskrit.

After they finished lunch, they went back to his apartment. Harper changed into a tank top and shorts that, in his opinion, revealed too much skin. She applied dramatic makeup and let her silk-pressed hair cascade freely to her shoulders.

"You look eighteen," he said unpleasantly. "Or older."

"You should see Scarlett," Harper said.

He drove them to Main Event. The entertainment venue was an immense brick building, and the parking lot was packed. Saturday was the big day for birthday parties, he recalled.

"You can drop me off, Daddy," Harper said. "I'll text you later when it's over."

"I want to meet your new friend and her parents. I'm not dropping you off to spend time with total strangers."

"You're going to embarrass me."

"They have a good bar here. I promise I'll say a quick hello and then hang out at the bar and watch sports."

"Whatever. Please don't hang around and be annoying."

Adrian got lucky and found a parking spot near the entrance, beside a black Mercedes-Benz G-class SUV flaunting a vanity plate that declared: HOTMOM.

It was a mob scene inside, with a long line of adults and kids of various ages waiting for their parties to begin. Noise assaulted his ears—pure sensory overload. He wished he had brought his headphones.

According to Harper, her friend's crew was already there. He followed his daughter through the throngs of people to the bowling alley section. Once there, Harper pointed out a group of teenage girls who apparently had reserved alleys six and seven.

He could immediately see why Harper had wanted to change clothes. The other teenagers followed a similar dress code: high-cut shorts and midriff-baring crop tops. They wore makeup and jewelry and had elaborately styled hair. He assumed they were all thirteen or fourteen years old, but they looked older to him.

Adrian didn't see any adults in the group. Were these kids on their own?

"Don't follow me, please," Harper said between clenched teeth.

Adrian hung back as Harper shyly approached the children. The tallest girl there—she had to be Scarlett—embraced her as if she and Harper had been friends for years.

The girl he assumed was Scarlett stood out. She was beige-skinned, with big sparkling eyes, a slender frame, and long, dark auburn hair. She also wore the skimpiest outfit in the group, set off by an opulent platinum necklace.

Adrian was appalled that the girl's parents allowed her to dress like this, but maybe he was old-fashioned. He found he didn't *want* to be near this group for fear of appearing to be a perv.

He started to turn away, but the girl waved at him and grinned. Then she strode toward him.

"Mr. Wall!" she said, her voice cutting through the din. "I'm Scarlett."

She offered her hand. Surprised at this girl's confidence in addressing an adult, he shook it. She met his gaze forthrightly.

"Nice to meet you, Scarlett," he said. "Thanks for inviting my daughter to your party."

"Oh, Harp is awesome. I love her. She's *so* smart, but she's chill. She's my girl."

Adrian thought that was excessive praise for two children who had only recently connected, but what did he know?

"Are your parents here?" Adrian asked. "I'd like to meet them."

"My mom's at the bar getting smashed." Scarlett giggled, sounding like a teenager then. "I'll text her and let her know you're here."

"Thanks. Have fun."

Scarlett flitted back to her entourage. Harper glanced at him and seemed relieved that Adrian hadn't humiliated her.

The U-shaped bar occupied the center of the vast indoor space. About a dozen gigantic televisions hung in the area, each tuned to some type of sporting event. Patrons crowded the counter, drinks in hand.

Adrian had no idea what Scarlett's mother looked like, so he grabbed the first empty seat. He tried to flag down a bartender, waving his hand like a commuter trying to hail a cab in Manhattan.

While he was trying to snare a drink, someone wearing a luxurious, feminine fragrance slid beside him at the counter. Manicured fingers lay across his bare forearm, startling him.

He pivoted to discover an exquisite Black woman pressing against him. Her perfect teeth flashed in a dazzling, dimpled smile.

"I've got you, honey," she said in a smoky voice. "You're Harper's father, right? Adrian? I'm Gina, Scarlett's mom."

The day had suddenly become a lot more intriguing.

3

With a casual snap of her fingers, Gina summoned the bartender. The man arrived promptly as if he were her personal assistant. Adrian had been trying to get the same guy's attention for the past two minutes.

"What are you having, honey?" Gina asked Adrian.

"A club soda with lime," Adrian said.

Gina wrinkled her nose, looked about to question him, then shrugged. The bartender nodded and got to work.

Gina's hand still lay on Adrian's forearm. He noticed she had candy apple red fingernails and wasn't wearing a wedding band.

Adrian swallowed. Gina was sheathed in a pastel V-neck romper that clung to her toned physique, which resembled that of a fitness model, likely sculpted from countless hours in a gym. The outfit also revealed a generous glimpse of her cleavage, and with her in such tantalizing proximity, Adrian had to summon all his willpower not to ogle.

He guessed she was in her mid-thirties. She conducted herself like a woman accustomed to getting whatever she wanted, and with her looks, he imagined she bent people to her will as quickly as blades of grass in a breeze.

"Enjoying the party?" Gina asked him.

She wore red lipstick that matched her nails. She still had not taken her hand off his forearm, either.

"It looks like fun for the kids," Adrian said. "I'm not usually a fan of these venues, all the noise and whatnot."

"Honey, tell me about it." Gina grinned. "My baby wanted to come here today, though, for a little fun with her girls, and you know she always gets what she wants."

"Doting parents," Adrian said.

"What can I say? I love my little princess. She's my heart."

The bartender brought Adrian's beverage. Adrian reached for it, which gave him a reason to finally extract his arm from Gina's hand.

"Come join me at my table." Gina paused. "Is your wife here?"

"It's only me and Harper."

Her light brown eyes glimmered as if she liked this answer. "We're right over there, at the high-top. You can put your soda on my tab."

Before he could respond, she took his free hand and tugged him along with her. Adrian let her lead him. Her hand was satiny and soft, and she strutted with a confident swing of her hips, clearly aware that she attracted admiring glances and reveling in it.

What would Stephanie think if she had spotted him walking with a beautiful woman then? Would she be jealous? Would she care?

Gina brought him to a high-top table on the edge of the dining area. A forty-something, blonde-haired woman sat there, scrolling on her phone.

"Hey, girl, this is Adrian," Gina announced. "He's Harper's father. She's the new girl in the gang. Adrian, meet Candy."

Candy fluttered her fingers in greeting, and Adrian waved back—the gesture allowed him to extricate his hand from Gina's. He grabbed the stool next to Gina.

Gina eased onto her chair and sipped her drink. It looked like she had a cocktail with a brown liquor base; Adrian thought he caught a whiff of cognac. He sipped his club soda.

Now that he had met the daughter's mother, he decided that he needed to get a handle on the family.

"Scarlett is new to the school, so I hear," Adrian said. "Did you guys recently move into the area?"

"My baby is new to *public* school," Gina said. Her lips curled. "We'd been sending her to Queen's Academy since kindergarten until those pretentious assholes pissed us off."

Adrian knew of the school; it was a private institution with tuition that cost as much as an exclusive college.

"They don't deserve our money anymore," Gina said, flicking her auburn hair over her shoulder. "Besides, we're paying taxes on the public schools anyway, right? Why not let our baby go there? It's a good school from what I hear."

"It's highly rated," Adrian said. "Where do you guys live?"

"We live in St. Martin's Country Club."

Adrian blinked. The posh, gated golf community housed many local celebrities and executives. Homes started at seven figures.

"I went to a wedding reception there once," he said. "It's beautiful."

"It had better be for what we paid. We'll have y'all over sometime soon. Do you golf?"

"I've played a few times, but I'm no Tiger Woods."

"Honey, as long as you're willing to pick up the sticks, that's all my husband needs to hear. That's where he is now, on that damn course." She shook her head.

So she *was* married. Relief washed over him. He had been uncomfortable with all the touching, but if she was married, he expected that she would maintain some boundaries, that perhaps she was only affectionate, and that explained her behavior toward him.

"What do you do for fun?" Gina sipped her drink through the straw, her gaze fastened on him with an intensity that made his heart throb a little faster. "I *know* you don't come to places like this."

"I like going to the movies," he said. "I'm a movie buff, mostly sci-fi and thrillers. Harper and I were going to hit a matinee this afternoon until she told me she was invited to your daughter's party."

"It was sort of a last-minute thing," Gina said with a throaty laugh. "I love going to the movies, but my husband hates sitting still. There's nothing like getting that huge bag of popcorn and snuggling down in the seat, watching that enormous screen. I mean, we have a theater in the house, but it's nothing like the real thing, you know? I haven't been in ages."

"It's the best way to watch a flick," Adrian said.

"Maybe we could go sometime."

He wasn't sure how to respond to the comment, so he let it pass without an answer. Did she mean to bring his wife to a movie with her and her husband, like a double date? Or did she mean just the two of them? If that was what she meant, why did she think that was appropriate since they were both married?

"I need another cocktail," Gina said, plunking her glass on the table. She straightened on the stool and thrust her buxom chest forward. "Do you want a drink, honey?"

"I'm still working on my club soda, thanks."

"You should try what I'm having. Do you like Hennessy?"

"I don't drink anymore, Gina. Long story."

"Oh." She pursed her lips. "I can respect that. But I'm gonna need you to loosen up, honey, if you're gonna hang with me. You're *way* too uptight right now, sitting over there with your boring little club soda and looking at me like you're scared I'm gonna hop onto your lap."

"I can cut loose when you get to know me," he said. As soon as he said it, he could have kicked himself. Why did he say that?

"Get a couple more drinks in me, and I *might* hop onto that lap." Gina snickered. Her friend, Candy, looked up from her phone and grinned.

"My wife probably wouldn't like that." He tried to deliver his message in a humorous tone while making it clear that lap-hopping would be prohibited.

"My baby says you and your wife are separated," Gina said.

"Excuse me?" Adrian stammered. "Harper told her that?"

"You know how kids are, gossiping about all their families' business." Gina caught their server's attention and ordered another cocktail and a round of appetizers.

He would need to have a pointed conversation with Harper about oversharing. Some things didn't need to be divulged outside of their family unit. She had just met this girl, Scarlett.

"We're working things out," Adrian said.

"Sounds like your wife is back on the market, from what I hear."

Adrian was speechless.

"I mean, good for her, right?" Gina said. "Maybe your girlfriend needs to see what's out there before she can appreciate you. All I know is that a real asshole wouldn't have brought his daughter to a last-minute party at a place he doesn't want to be."

"I wanted to make her happy," Adrian said. "Harper's going through a lot right now, considering the separation. It was the least I could do."

The server arrived with a new round of drinks, which included another club soda for Adrian. Gina sipped her cocktail greedily.

"You're a sweetheart," Gina said. "But who wants to make *you* happy, hmm?"

Her question caught him off guard; this entire line of discussion, in fact, had thrown him off kilter.

"I'll be fine," he said. "I'm good."

"Are you seeing anyone new? Your baby says you aren't."

"I'm going to work things out with my wife."

"Who's back on the market, as we've established."

Put in such blunt terms, he realized he sounded pathetic, like he was clinging to false hope. But he shrugged.

"Like you said, maybe she'll figure out what she's missing," he said.

"We're gonna exchange numbers, honey, all right? I'll be checking in on you." She reached across the table, took his hand, and squeezed, and he didn't pull back. "Our daughters are friends; that means we're gonna be friends, too—and I've got a feeling you could use a friend right now."

She squeezed his hand again, her gaze locked onto his, and he felt a delicious warmth spreading throughout his body. After a beat, she let him go and picked up her drink, but the sensation of her hand against his lingered.

He loved Steph, and he was determined to reconcile with her. Still, was having a female friend—a platonic friend, obviously—such a terrible thing? Perhaps he could use a woman's perspective on his situation. These days, he felt like a man floating alone on a broken raft in a vast ocean, and Gina could be the lifeline he needed.

Yeah, he thought, trying not to stare at Gina's luscious lips as she sipped her drink. *I'm going to make it work with Steph, but there's nothing wrong with having a friend. Nothing at all.*

4

On Monday morning, an ominous email directed Adrian and his coworkers to report to the FiPro company cafeteria at ten o'clock for a cryptically titled "business update" meeting.

"I told you," Trevor said as he and Adrian walked to the bank of elevators. "Heads about to roll, bruh. This is how they do it."

He had known Trevor for over a decade. They had been cube neighbors at a prior job and had kept in touch over the years via social media and their fantasy football league. Last Friday, Trevor had whispered a rumor about a seismic company shakeup on the horizon; Adrian dreaded this meeting would confirm those whispers. He had toiled at FiPro for six months as a contract treasury analyst, garnered stellar marks on his performance evaluation, and never feigned illness or snatched an unapproved vacation day—but would any of that matter now?

His stomach roiled like choppy waters. He didn't want to think about losing his job, but with the prospect of getting terminated on the table, he had no choice but to consider his alternatives. None of them looked good.

He had about a thousand bucks in savings; better than nothing, but not enough to cover his rent. Some money sat in his 401(k), but he was far from being on track for an eventual retirement, and he would tap into that money only in a dire emergency. They had a modest college fund for Harper, and he was the administrator of that account. Steph would eviscerate him if he ever touched it.

He could call his employment agency, but they weren't helpful. He only got his current job because Trevor, a longtime employee at FiPro, had put in a good word for him with HR. If he lost this position, it could take months for him to land another one.

He needed an executive in his corner to shelter him from the fallout. Trevor had those connections and had introduced Adrian to a couple of folks. Still, Adrian doubted he had made enough of an impression for those people to intercede on his behalf. He had never been good at networking—one of those professional shortcomings that explained his current predicament.

The bottom line? He was vulnerable. His distress must have been etched on his face because Trevor eyed him with concern as they rode down in the elevator.

"You'll be safe, bruh. I've got a hunch."

"Have you heard any gossip about contractors?" Adrian asked.

"Well." Clearing his throat, Trevor pushed up his glasses on his nose. "You got a strong review. That matters here. Keith is a fan, too. I'm sure he made a case for you."

Keith was Adrian's direct supervisor, but he was only a manager, not an executive of their division. If Adrian's name was on a list, Adrian doubted he could intervene.

The elevator dinged, and they shuffled to the large cafeteria. About a dozen people had already claimed seats, with more streaming in by the second.

At one end of the café, a projection screen had been set up. A towering, slender Black man wearing a tailored charcoal gray suit waited nearby, big hands clasped before him. Perhaps in his mid-fifties, he reminded Adrian of Rick Fox, the former NBA star and sometime actor; he had a chiseled, classically handsome face.

"That's Lamont Washington," Adrian said.

"Mr. CEO himself," Trevor said as they settled into their seats at a table. He grimaced. "Shit just got real, bruh."

"If he's here talking to us . . ."

"It ain't good news for the home team." Trevor shifted in his chair. Perspiration beaded his receding hairline.

During his six months at FiPro, Adrian had spotted Washington only in fleeting moments and had never spoken to the man. Like the rest of the company executives, Washington worked on the tenth floor, the "baller suite," as Trevor liked to call it, an area off-limits to underlings unless you were summoned.

Adrian Googled the guy on his smartphone and found Lamont Washington's LinkedIn profile. Washington held an MBA from Harvard Business School and had attended Morehouse for undergrad. After stints at elite financial firms, he founded FiPro twenty years ago. He built the company into a fintech corporation that employed four thousand people and exceeded $1.6 billion in annual revenue.

Whenever Adrian encountered men of outstanding achievement like Washington, he couldn't help comparing the course of his life to theirs. Washington, like him, was a Black man, but he had ascended to the top of the corporate ladder while Adrian was barely clinging to the bottom rung. Where had he faltered in his own climb?

At precisely ten o'clock, the room brimmed at capacity, a hubbub issuing from the crowd. Washington started the meeting by briefly introducing himself—Lamont Washington III—and then launched a PowerPoint presentation. He spoke in a resonant baritone that would have been well-suited to narration for a nature documentary, each word crisply enunciated; he marched through the bullet points on the slides that detailed company performance over the past several quarters: cratering profit margins, a sinking stock price, the rising costs of doing business, increased global competition, the need to invest in "key" initiatives such as artificial intelligence and other "vehicles to accelerate efficiency and innovation."

More mind-numbing corporate mumbo jumbo followed, and Adrian struggled to stay focused. *Get to the point, man.*

About twenty minutes into the presentation, Washington finally dropped the bomb: "Company leadership has determined that for FiPro to meet the needs of an increasingly challenging, more complex global business environment, a fifteen percent reduction in force is going to be necessary."

Adrian stiffened, and groans rose from the audience. Beside him, Trevor bounced his knee like a child who needed to urinate. When he and Adrian locked gazes, Trevor only shook his head.

"This is a difficult message to hear," Washington said, "and I understand all of you are justifiably concerned. We haven't made this decision lightly. But for FiPro to thrive, we must take these painful steps."

An older woman beside Adrian had begun crying, wiping tears from her cheeks.

"Before the close of business today, your direct manager will contact you with details on the future of your role here at FiPro," Washington said. He clasped his big hands. "Thank you all for your hard work and sacrifice . . ."

Washington ended the meeting and abruptly strode out of the room, not hanging around to take questions. Adrian hadn't noticed before but saw multiple broad-shouldered men wearing black suits standing along the area's perimeter: corporate security in case someone went ballistic. One of the goons trailed Washington out of the meeting like a personal bodyguard.

The rest of the audience filed out of the cafeteria like mourners leaving a wake. Adrian and Trevor didn't speak as they rode the elevator back upstairs.

"See you," Trevor said when they reached the ninth floor. "We'll get through this, bruh. Keep me in the loop."

"You do the same," Adrian said.

They shared a fist bump, and Adrian trudged to his seat on the other side of the floor near a wall of windows. Instead of old-school cubes, it was an open layout intended to spark collaboration, but no one was talking. Gloom had settled over the office.

Adrian settled in front of his laptop. He had multiple pressing tasks that day but was not motivated to do any of them.

He texted Steph: *Hey, the rumors are true. They're doing a RIF. Will find out today if I make the cut.*

Steph responded about five minutes later: *Good luck.*

Adrian felt like flinging his phone through the window. That was all she could say? *Good luck.* Like he was some distant acquaintance, not the man who had shared her bed for over a decade.

His head pounded.

Another text message arrived, but it wasn't from Steph as he had hoped. It was from Gina.

Hey there. I'm checking in. Wassup with you?

This was a surprise. When Gina had insisted on exchanging numbers at Main Event on Saturday, he hadn't wanted—or expected—to hear from her, and he hadn't planned to reach out, either. The truth was that he was so attracted to her that he didn't entirely trust himself. He meant what he said to her about his intention to reconcile with Steph.

Still, they could be friends, he reasoned, like their daughters were. Besides, she was married, anyway, probably to some hotshot executive or pro athlete, and she wouldn't be remotely interested in him.

Got some potential bad news at work, he replied. *I'll know more later today, but job at FiPro might be on the line.*

Oh, no! she replied. *So sorry to hear that, honey. I'll be praying for you.* She sent a steepled hands emoji.

Why couldn't his own wife respond like that?

I appreciate that, he typed.

Lemme know how it goes, okay?

Can you talk to my wife for me, please? Adrian wanted to say. *Can you talk some sense into her and convince her to care about the future of our marriage?*

But he only said: *Will do, thank you. How's your day going?*

Putting in work at the gym with my trainer. My second home. LOL.

Gina sent him a selfie. Posing in front of an elliptical machine, she angled her body and the phone to display her side profile. She wore a lime green sports bra that showed off her narrow waist and washboard abs and skintight green Lululemon leggings that emphasized the curves of her hips and her toned thighs.

Good Lord, he thought. He deliberated how to respond without sounding like a drooling fiend.

Put in that work, girl, he typed. *I need to hit the gym soon, myself.*

Trainer said break's over, she replied. *Talk soon. XOXO.*

He gazed at the photo a little longer, his pulse throbbing. He took a sip from the water bottle on his desk, attempting to slow his racing heartbeat.

But when he checked his email and saw the urgent meeting invite from his manager, his heart rate kicked into overdrive again.

"I won't drag this out, Adrian," Keith said when they gathered in the private conference room. "I made a strong case for keeping you on with a permanent role, but it wasn't enough." He spread his hands. "I'm sorry."

Adrian swallowed, his throat dry. "How long do I have?"

Keith winced as if in pain, and that was when Adrian knew the answer was worse than he expected.

"This Friday will be your last day at FiPro."

5

Despite leaving his job at FiPro for the last time that Friday, Adrian's job as a father didn't come with a termination date: that afternoon, he turned in his company laptop and badge and drove to pick up Harper at school for her scheduled visitation that weekend.

He'd exchanged only terse text messages with Steph since learning of the layoff, but he got little from her in the way of empathy: *What's your next step?* she texted back when he told her. *Let me know if you need anything from me.*

He thought: *I may need to move back into our house*. His unemployment benefits and savings weren't sufficient to cover his expenses. But he didn't dare broach the topic with her yet. Her likely response frightened him.

He received a warmer reception from Gina when he broke the news. She FaceTimed him while at a nail salon pampering herself with a mani-pedi. Gushing apologetically, she suggested they meet for a drink, "sometime very soon when it's convenient for you." He responded that since he was unemployed, he would soon have plenty of free time and would check back with her.

He reminded himself that they were just friends, but his stomach fluttered whenever he thought about Gina. He had ogled that selfie of hers a hundred times since Monday. He needed to brush up on that Bible scripture about coveting your neighbor's wife.

The carpool line at Carver Middle School was always busiest on Fridays, the queue of vehicles stretching out of the parking lot and onto the adjoining road. School dismissed at four fifteen, but because of the plodding line, Adrian didn't reach the crowded front entrance until almost four thirty. A staff member directed him to wait for his child to get in at the curbside.

He didn't see Harper.

Usually, she perched like an eager puppy at the curb, ready to hop inside. He turned in his seat, scrutinizing the hordes of students outside. What was Harper wearing that day? He didn't have a clue—one more consequence of the separation. He didn't see his daughter in the mornings before she left for school like he'd used to when living in their house.

No sign of Harper.

A buzz on his phone drew his attention. It was a text message from a website announcing a sale of men's cologne. His chest constricting with tension, Adrian deleted the message and checked to see if Harper had responded to the text he'd sent her a half hour ago: *On my way, see you soon,* he had written when he left FiPro at four o'clock.

She hadn't replied to that message. It wasn't unusual for her to ignore such texts, but . . .

Adrian got out of the car.

One of the school's faculty stood outdoors conducting traffic. It was a teacher Adrian recognized, Harper's Language Arts instructor from seventh grade last year, but the woman's name eluded him.

"I'm looking for Harper Wall," he said.

"I remember Harper. I saw her today. Does she know you're picking her up?"

He ignored the question. "Did you see her mother drive through here?"

"I've seen a hundred cars come through here today, sorry. We'll announce her name over the intercom and tell her you're waiting." She tapped on her phone.

He thanked her, turned away, and kept looking through the crowd of students, a cacophony of voices inundating him.

"Harper Wall, your ride is here!" a man's voice boomed over the loudspeaker.

Although he hadn't seen her during his search, Adrian hurried back to his SUV, expecting Harper to pop up with an embarrassed laugh. *Sorry, Daddy. I was talking to my friends.*

But she wasn't there.

His palms felt clammy. He rang Steph. He didn't expect her to answer, but she picked up on the second ring.

"I'm showing a house," she said. "Is everything okay?"

"Did you pick up Harper from school today?"

"You're supposed to pick her up. Did you forget?"

"I didn't *forget*." How could Steph's most trivial comments make him want to scream? "She's not here at the pickup, so that's why I'm asking."

"She's not there? Did you tell the teachers?"

"They put her name over the loudspeaker." He swung around in his seat, scanning the students yet again, and still not seeing his daughter. "She hasn't come to the car."

"Did you text her?" Steph asked, her tone sharpening.

Adrian checked again to see if he had received a response from Harper. Nothing. He fired off another message, his fingers trembling, and autocorrect kept mangling his words. Finally, he sent off: *Hey, I'm here at the school to pick you up. Where are you? Come get in the car.*

The ellipses that would have shown she was responding didn't materialize.

"She's not replying," Adrian said.

"Shit," Steph said. "I'll try to call her. Don't you have that app on your phone so you can find her?"

"Right. Let me check that."

"I'll hang up and try to call her," Steph said. "Then I'll call you back, regardless."

As his wife ended the call, Adrian pulled up the FindMyPhone app—buried in the sea of the hundreds of apps cluttering his iPhone—and clicked through it to locate Harper's location.

His stomach plunged. What the hell?

Steph rang him back. "Is she there? She didn't pick up."

"She's on the highway," Adrian said, his head feeling as if it were pinched in a vise. "She's going south on 400."

"What?"

Panic had crept into Steph's tone, which was Adrian's cue to chill and keep a level head. It was a learned response to Steph's elevated moods; when she freaked out, he turned to stone. If he joined her descent into hysteria, the situation could rapidly deteriorate.

He stared at the app as the little blue dot showing Harper's phone inched across the map.

"Now she's getting off the highway," he said. "It looks like she's going to . . . North Point Mall."

"The mall? This is crazy. How the hell is she going to the mall? Who is she with? Did she say anything to you about this?"

Adrian shifted into Drive and pulled away from the curb. "I'm going over there."

"Should we call the police? Do you think she's been—"

He knew what she would say and cut her off, maybe because he didn't want to admit to the possibility.

"Not yet. Let me get over there first. Can you meet me there?"

"Leaving right now," Steph said.

6

Like many shopping malls across the United States, North Point Mall was a shadow of its former self. Adrian remembered visiting as a kid and finding it a lively place full of crowds, amusements, intrigue, and excitement, where everyone assembled on the weekends and especially during the holidays when finding a parking spot was nearly impossible.

But nowadays, many of the flagship stores that had anchored North Point Mall had either fled to trendier locales or gone bankrupt. The parking lot was practically barren when Adrian steered into the section by Macy's.

According to the locator app, Harper was still there.

It seemed unlikely that someone had kidnapped her. Who would kidnap a teenager and take them to a shopping mall?

But Harper had never pulled a stunt like this before. She'd always been obedient and well-behaved, never causing trouble at school or requiring stern discipline from Adrian and Steph—a model teenager.

She had to be there with someone. But who?

Adrian had his suspicions. After he parked, he texted Steph: *I'm here. I'm going inside. Looks like she's still here.*

Three minutes away, Steph replied.

Adrian got out of his Kia and hurried inside the Macy's. He couldn't remember the last time he had entered the store, and the new look disoriented him: a Toys "R" Us section lay just inside the entrance. But he saw employees milling around, checking their phones, and chatting with one another, and he wondered how much longer this store would stay open, too.

The app didn't pinpoint Harper's exact spot inside the mall. It wasn't that precise. They'd have to scour every inch until they found her.

His head swiveling back and forth, he wandered down the aisles. Where would a teenage girl go here? A clothing store? A jewelry shop? Harper loved video games, fast fashion clothes, and sweets.

She could be in any number of places.

As Adrian left Macy's, entering the mall's cavernous atrium, Steph pinged him.

I'm here. Where are you?

Just outside Macy's, near the jewelry repair kiosk.

Wait for me.

He kept his attention fastened on the phone locator app, but his thoughts had turned to his wife. Wouldn't it be ironic if this stressful experience triggered a reconciliation with Steph? One of the happiest periods of their marriage had occurred after his mother had died several years ago. Steph had adored his mom, and their shared grief had fused them more strongly than ever, making them more mindful of each other's emotional states. *How're you doing today? Feeling okay?* They hugged more often than before, and even their sex life had improved as if the jarring realization of how fleeting life could be had stoked their cravings to live to the fullest.

But after about three months, they had relapsed into the bad habits that had ultimately driven them apart. Wrapped up in their routines, cocooned in the minutiae of their individual lives. Arguing about Harper and how best to raise her. Disagreeing on seemingly everything and being vocal about those disagreements. Their paths diverged from the common lane they had once shared until one day, in the heat of another nasty argument, Adrian announced that he wanted a separation. Steph responded: *Finally, we agree on something.*

But he missed his wife. He was no good as a bachelor, and the prospect of dating felt as terrifying as moving to a foreign country where he didn't speak the language. He wanted Steph back and wanted to rekindle their marriage. But it might be too late.

He turned at the staccato click of heels. Steph burst from Macy's into the two-story atrium, purse swinging, phone clutched like a weapon. She wore a pink blouse and black skirt, a killer combo on her svelte figure. But her hair looked like she'd weathered a windstorm.

He wanted to hug her and assure her everything would be okay, but instinct warned him to hold back.

"Do you know where she is?" Steph asked.

"I only know that she's here somewhere." He showed her his phone.

She didn't look at the screen. "I'm going to throttle her."

She charged forward. He had to race to keep up with her.

"Ten minutes ago, you asked me if we should call the police," he said.

"Right, then it hit me," she said through gritted teeth. "This new friend of hers she's always talking about and texting. I *know* she's got something to do with this. Mother's instinct."

"Yeah," he said because he had thought the same thing.

"I bet I know where she is, too. She's like me. She's quiet, but she's headstrong. I did stupid shit like this when I was a teenager, sneaking out of the house to be with my boyfriend."

Adrian followed Steph onto the escalator, ascending to the second level. He couldn't help but notice her sensational legs in that skirt—he'd always thought them her best asset—and her alluring scent swirled around him. He recognized the perfume he'd gifted her years ago for her birthday, and oddly, that made him proud, as if he still had some claim on her.

"You're looking good today, babe," he said. "Smell lovely, too."

"I can't believe I had to skip out of a showing for *this*." She ignored his compliments.

At the next floor, Steph swiveled to the right, and he hurried to match her urgent strides.

"Watch, I'm going to be right," Steph said. "I *know* where she is."

"Today was my last day at my job," he said.

"Right, it's been a helluva day all around. I'm sorry. Let's get through this first."

Steph headed toward the food court, which had lost its luster like the rest of the mall. In its heyday, every storefront had been occupied by a different type of restaurant, an array of cuisines, the area brimming with delicious smells. But over half of the sections were dark now, and the signboards were empty. A worker at a Chinese restaurant tried in vain to divvy out samples to the trickle of browsers passing by.

Steph pointed. "*There*."

Adrian followed her finger. He saw several teenage girls clustered at a round table, chatting and eating ice cream.

It was the same group that Adrian had seen at the party on Saturday. Harper sat next to Scarlett, giggling at something on her phone. Scarlett raised her own phone and took a selfie with Harper.

Adrian's galloping heart slowed seeing his daughter here, unharmed.

"*Harper!*" Steph screamed.

Now the fun part begins, Adrian thought.

7

Harper had never been so embarrassed in her life.

She was having the best day ever, hanging out with Scarlett, Ava, Chloe, and Emily at the old shopping mall, unwinding from a long week at school (two summative tests, *three* class projects), sipping a chocolate milkshake, everyone having fun and looking forward to the weekend when her parents showed up. Her mother screamed from fifty feet away like Harper was a criminal.

Harper wanted to crawl under the table.

But Scarlett had warned her that this might happen. Her new friend was so smart about things like this, with so much experience in literally every kind of situation, that it stunned Harper. She was the wisest kid she had ever met, even if her grades didn't necessarily show it.

They're probably tracking your phone, Harp, Scarlett had said. *They might show up to ruin things and ground you afterward like regular, boring parents do. But don't worry. I've got you.*

Scarlett had opened her designer purse. Harper spotted a pink-handled thing in there that looked like a weapon, and Scarlett winked at Harper and whispered: *Yeah, it's a pocketknife, sis. I keep it on me, always; you wanna know why?*

Why?

Sparks danced in her eyes as she said, *'Cause snitches get stitches and wind up in ditches.*

Oh, okay.

Don't worry about it, sis. You'll never snitch, will you?

Harper shook her head.

Scarlett had pulled something else out of her bag and given it to Harper, something amazing, and made her promise to keep it secret. Harper readily agreed and buried the item in the depths of her backpack, somewhere her parents would never bother to check.

Scarlett was the best friend she'd ever had, and they had known each other for barely a couple of weeks. She said they were sisters.

No one else had ever said that to Harper; it made her feel accepted. Harper didn't have a biological sister, and neither did Scarlett.

Sisters stick together, Scarlett said. *Trust me.*

When Mom appeared shrieking like a crazy woman, Daddy trailing behind her, looking upset but keeping control of himself, Harper got up from the table. She lifted her backpack off the floor. Fun time was over.

Scarlett got up, too.

"Sisters, remember?" Scarlett whispered. "Let me handle this, sis."

8

"Get your ass up and come with us *now*," Steph demanded.

To Adrian's surprise, Harper *and* Scarlett rose from the table as if they were conjoined twins. Although Scarlett stood nearly as tall as Adrian, about five-nine and four inches taller than Harper, the girls were dressed almost like twins, too: crop tops and high-cut shorts.

Had Steph allowed their daughter to go to school dressed like that? he wondered. What was going on?

Pouting, Harper pulled her backpack over her shoulder and shuffled toward them, her gaze downcast. Scarlett strode past her and approached Adrian and Steph.

When he first met her at the party, the girl struck him with her self-possession. It was almost eerie how she met their gazes, even in a tense situation, showing no apprehension. Was it the confidence of a rich kid, perhaps, accustomed to getting whatever she wanted?

He noticed that Steph, too, seemed taken aback, her eyes widening. He supposed this was her first time meeting the new girl.

"Hello, Mr. and Mrs. Wall," Scarlett said in an even tone. "I'm

Scarlett; nice to meet you, Mrs. Wall." She tilted her head at Adrian. "It's good to see you again, sir."

"Hey, Scarlett," Adrian said. "What happened here?"

"I take full responsibility for this situation. I hired the Uber and invited Harper to come with me."

"You got an Uber?" Steph gawked at the girl. "By yourself?"

"I take Ubers all the time." Scarlett shrugged like this was yesterday's news. "We like to have an ice cream social on Fridays after school's out. I invited Harp to come. She was worried you guys wouldn't let her."

"Do your parents know you're here?" Adrian asked.

"My parents trust me to take care of myself." Raising her chin, Scarlett flicked her long hair over her shoulder and stared at him.

Is this kid for real? Adrian wondered. Because that look was plain to him: it was a *you-can-kiss-my-ass* gaze if there ever was one.

"I can't speak for your parents, but this isn't happening for our daughter." Steph shook her head. "We don't roll like this. Nope, no, not happening, never. Harper, let's go."

Head down, Harper started toward them. Scarlett touched her shoulder, and she turned. The girls exchanged pinkie handshakes, and Scarlett bent and whispered in Harper's ear. Harper's lips curved in a conspiratorial smile.

Adrian felt as if a stone had shifted in his stomach. What were these girls plotting now?

"*Now*," Steph said. Stepping forward, Steph seized Harper's hand as if she were three years old, not thirteen.

Harper snatched her hand away. "I'm *coming*, Mom. Shit. Chill out."

"Harper, language!" Adrian said.

Steph reached for Harper again, and Adrian could tell by the look on his wife's face that she was about to lose her composure in a public place, in front of an audience—an audience that was taking video. One of the girls from the group had angled her phone toward them. If Steph lost it . . .

"Steph." Adrian put his hand on his wife's shoulder. "Not here."

Steph swung to him, nostrils flaring.

"People are watching," he whispered.

She blinked, and he saw the realization click on her face. Stepping back, she dropped her hand and clutched her purse. He noticed her knuckles were white as milk.

"Come on, then," Steph said to Harper in a lowered tone. "We'll discuss this in private."

Harper mumbled something under her breath but trudged forward as if walking to her doom. Adrian cast one last look at Scarlett.

The girl smiled at him.

Steph could not *believe* her daughter had done something like this.

When Adrian had called her, she had been showing a hot property to a qualified lead, and it was only by sheer luck that she'd noticed her phone vibrating. He called her so rarely—typically, they communicated via text—that she knew it had to be important.

Her first thought was that he had forgotten to pick up their daughter. She didn't know why she thought he would have done something like that because he usually wasn't absent-minded. Her opinion of him had dropped so low that these days she believed he could screw up anything.

Like their marriage, for starters.

She walked on Harper's left, and Adrian kept pace on Harper's right as they escorted her out of the shopping mall, like correctional officers transporting an inmate to a jail cell. If Steph got her way—and she would—Harper's next couple of weeks would be like a prisoner's. She deserved severe discipline for what she had done.

And what the hell was she wearing? She wasn't wearing those clothes when she left the house this morning for the bus stop. Steph knew she owned such clothing, but she never would have consented to her wearing those pieces to school.

This child, I swear.

"You're going to be under punishment; I hope you know that," Steph said as Adrian opened the doors for them to exit the mall via the Macy's entrance. "Kiss that iPhone and your iPad goodbye for a while."

Harper didn't react, only shuffled forward, head lowered. The kid was damned lucky that Adrian had checked her back there in the food court because Steph had literally felt on the verge of strangling her.

She'd meant what she said when she told Adrian their child had her ways. When Steph was a teenager, she had entered a seriously rebellious phase that had vexed her parents. She had been a quiet child, like Harper, but stubborn.

Steph had rebelled over her boyfriend. Harper didn't have a boyfriend—to Steph's knowledge anyway—but she had evidently picked up a relationship that could be just as troublesome: this Scarlett kid.

The girl had strolled right to them as if she were their equal, talking like a lawyer. Getting her own Uber? If her parents allowed her to have a teen account, that was their business. But they weren't raising Harper like that.

Adrian guided them to his SUV and unlocked the doors.

"Get in the damn car," Steph said to Harper.

Letting out a dramatic sigh, Harper slid inside onto the back seat. She slammed the door hard enough for the sound to ricochet like a gunshot across the empty parking lot.

Steph squeezed her hands into fists.

Lord, give me the strength to keep my hands off this child, she prayed.

Adrian turned to her, leaning against the vehicle. He pinched the bridge of his nose.

"That was an adventure, huh?" he said. "At least she's safe, Steph."

"You might need to call the police to keep me off her narrow ass."

"Let's calm down and try to handle this rationally." He touched her shoulder.

She brushed off his hand. "Do *not* tell me to calm down. Why aren't you upset? Our daughter took off in an Uber with some kid we barely know; we had no idea where she was, and you aren't furious?"

"It's unacceptable. I'm still shocked that she did it."

Steph moved several feet from the car; she didn't want Harper eavesdropping on every word they exchanged. She beckoned Adrian toward her, and he seemed to get her intent and followed her.

"It's that new friend of hers," Steph said in a lowered voice. "Scarlett. She's a bad influence. Did you see how she walked up on us? Like she's a grown-ass woman."

"She's different. I noticed that when I took Harper to her party last week. Fearless."

"What kind of parents let their thirteen—maybe she's fourteen, I don't know—but what parents are okay with their kid at that age taking Ubers all over the place in this day and age? Here in Atlanta? The freakin' human trafficking hub of the Southeast?"

"I know." He pulled his hand down his face.

"She's a bad influence, Adrian. Mark my words. This is a red flag. We'd be crazy to ignore it."

"What are we supposed to do, Steph?" He stared at her, and she saw the irritation tightening his eyes. "She goes to school with this girl."

"Harper needs to cut her off."

"Harper doesn't *want* to cut her off. She's gaga over this girl."

"Then we make her cut it off with her. We start off by grounding her. I meant what I said about taking her iPhone and her iPad. This toxic friendship ends if they can't chat outside of school."

Adrian was shaking his head. For a moment, Steph wanted to

shake him, too. Why couldn't he see what was so apparent to her? These differences in perception had been a blessing at one point in their marriage, early on, because it helped them consider multiple solutions to a problem. But now, their viewpoints were so wildly divergent that finding common ground often seemed impossible. The topic of child-rearing was a frequent battleground.

She was old-school, like her parents, and she didn't apologize; those rigid rules kept her out of trouble (despite her rebellious phase), ensuring she graduated from high school and then college. But Adrian's upbringing had been far more liberal. His father hadn't been around much after his parents had divorced, and his mother had coddled him and attended to his every whim. When she and Adrian started dating, even though Adrian had his own apartment, his mom would still visit, do his laundry, and change his bedsheets as if he were a child and not a grown man. He brought that same accommodating mindset into his parental approach with Harper.

"If we let things stand, what's next?" Steph asked. "Sleepovers at this kid's house that are actually teenage drug and sex parties? You know they do that these days, don't you? Even at her age, kids are having orgies right under their parents' noses."

"Harper is going to have to learn how to choose her friends," Adrian said. "We can't control everyone she lets into her life, Steph."

"Yes, we can. That's our job. To keep her out of trouble."

He crossed his arms, his lips drawn into a firm line. Someone parked in a spot near them and got out of their car, gaze trained on them, and it reminded Steph that although they had left the food court, they were still in a public place, maybe making a spectacle of themselves.

"You like me to be the bad guy," she said, "while you get to keep your hands clean and play nice with her."

He winced, and she enjoyed the effect her words had on him. As the old saying went, *a hit dog will holler.*

"Look, how about we chat with Scarlett's parents?" he said. "We share our concerns."

"No iPhone or iPad this weekend while she's at your place," Steph said. "But fine, if you want to talk to this brat's parents, we can do that. I need to be part of that discussion."

"Of course," he said, but he didn't meet her gaze, and she wondered about that. He looked back at her. "No iPhone or iPad, I agree."

"I mean it, Adrian. Don't give in to her when she starts whining and crying. You're always so soft on her."

"Because you're always so hard on her."

She thought: *Someone has to be tough on her. The world is hard and unforgiving, and it will chew you up and spit you out. How else can we prepare her for it? Our job is to prepare her.*

But Steph stopped herself. This argument was going in circles, like most of their fights now. They rarely agreed on anything.

"I need to get back to work." She glanced at the SUV and saw Harper watching them sullenly. "Take good care of our child. Keep her out of trouble."

"You know I will."

You'd better, she thought.

9

After the shopping mall fiasco, Adrian had low expectations for the remainder of his weekend with Harper. Friday evening, at his apartment, he confiscated her iPhone and iPad, as he'd promised Steph.

He expected Harper to be sullen, but she seemed oddly low-key about giving up her devices. Had she expected this punishment all along and resigned herself to this outcome?

For dinner, he ordered a pizza—cheese and pepperoni, her favorite—and while waiting for the food to arrive, she shuttered herself in the unit's second bedroom, a room he had designated hers for whenever she visited. When the delivery driver dropped off the order, Adrian called out for her, but she didn't respond, and when he knocked on the bedroom door, she didn't answer.

"Harp, the pizza is here!" he said again.

He was about to turn the knob when Harper snatched the door open. Redness touched her cheeks; she looked like she struggled to hold back a giggle.

"What are you doing?" he asked. "What's so funny?"

"I was reading a book." She ran her fingers through her hair.

Why didn't he believe her? But what else could she have been doing in her room? She had no electronics in there: no phone, tablet, computer, or television. It was like a holding cell, missing only a toilet.

"Okay," he said. "Well, dinner is here. Wash up and come eat."

"All right, Daddy. Be right there."

A few minutes later, they settled at the small dinette table in the apartment's minuscule kitchen and started eating pizza and sipping soda. He and Steph didn't usually provide soda to Harper, but Adrian stocked up on her favorites (Sprite and Hawaiian Punch) so that she could indulge in some forbidden treats when she visited. It was one of the secrets they shared.

Adrian decided to bring up the big topic of the day, which hung like static electricity in the air between them.

"Your mother doesn't want you hanging out with Scarlett anymore," he said.

"What?" Her eyes ballooned as big as the pizza on the table between them.

"She's worried the girl is a bad influence. I have those same concerns, too, to be honest. This mall incident scared us to death, Harp."

"But she's the best friend I've ever had!"

"You've only known her for what? Two weeks or so? You've had other friends since grade school."

"I'm going to be sick." She put her hand to her chest.

"Don't be so dramatic. I said we're *thinking* about it. It's not been decided yet. We'll need to chat with Scarlett's parents."

"I'm going to say it, Daddy: I'll never forgive you and Mom if you make me stop talking to my sister."

Adrian put down his pizza slice. "Your sister?"

She bobbed her head. "Obviously, we're not like blood sisters. But we're really close. Like sisters. That's what we call each other."

Adrian felt as if he had stumbled into foreign territory. He understood that friendships were important for a teenage girl, probably more critical than they were for adolescent boys if he thought back on his concerns at that age (sports and video games, in that order). Still, he didn't understand the sudden bond that Harper had formed with Scarlett. The two girls seemed to have little in common except that they attended the same school. What was it between them, anyway?

Also, her comment that *I'll never forgive you* jarred him. He didn't need his daughter to resent him more than she already did these days. He believed that, unfairly or not, she blamed him mainly for their family's separation and upending. With further slipups, he could dig himself a hole with her that might take years to repair.

"Nothing's final yet," he said, but he saw the warning flash in Harper's gaze.

After dinner, she hurried back to her bedroom to "finish reading a book," as she said. He eased onto the sofa in the family room, and on his iPhone, he reviewed his thread of texts from Gina.

That memorable selfie from her was one of the last messages she had sent him. He lingered on the photo for a beat, tongue dry, then scrolled past it.

We need to talk about our girls, he typed.

Based on his prior experience, he expected a fast response. Gina was one of those people who was perpetually tethered to her phone, but she didn't write back.

Several hours later, around eleven, he and Harper were streaming a movie (he had to coax her out of the room with the promise of popcorn) when a FaceTime ping arrived from Gina.

"Who's FaceTiming *you*?" Harper asked, glancing away from the TV screen.

"I'll be right back." He got up from the sofa and rushed to the master bedroom.

"Hey, boo," Gina said. "I saw your text. I was gonna ping you. My baby told me what happened."

Adrian didn't hear a word she said. It looked as if Gina had settled down for a romantic evening: she wore a black lace negligee with a plunging neckline, her luxurious hair cascading to her shoulders.

He swallowed. Where was her husband? Could the man possibly be comfortable with her calling another guy, dressed to kill, at eleven o'clock at night?

"Come again?" he said. "Sorry, I thought I heard Harper asking me for something . . ."

Gina smiled knowingly, obviously aware of her effect on him.

"My daughter told me about the thing at the mall," Gina said. "I wanted to chat about that, too."

"My wife wants to take some extreme measures. She doesn't want Harper and Scarlett hanging out anymore."

"She's a scorched earth mama, huh?" Gina made a tsk-tsk sound. "I can't do that, boo. That's way too stressful for me."

"I told her we need to chat with Scarlett's parents."

"Can we meet tomorrow? You and I can grab that drink we talked about."

"I've got Harper this weekend," he said.

"Bring her with you! That'll be perfect. I'll bring my baby, and the girls can hang out. We'll have a good time and clear the air on this itty-bitty thing."

It sounded as if Gina had no intention of inviting her as-yet-unseen husband to this meeting; it also sounded as though she didn't want Steph included, either. *You and I can grab that drink . . .*

Adrian knew his wife: allowing Harper to spend time with Scarlett while she was on punishment was more egregious than allowing her to keep her iPhone and iPad. If Steph found out, she would be livid.

"That sounds like a plan," Adrian said, his brain thinking one thing but his lips voicing something different.

They agreed on a place and a time, and Gina blew him a kiss and ended the call.

Adrian returned to the family room and found Harper munching on the last of the microwave popcorn.

When he told her tomorrow's plan, she cried, "Daddy, that's perfect!" She bounced off the sofa and hugged him.

He imagined Steph's sour rebuke: *Always wanting to play the good guy, aren't you, Adrian? You're way too soft on her.*

"Under no circumstances can you ever tell your mother about this," he said. "If you let it slip, we'll both face her wrath. Understood?"

Harper gave him a thumbs-up.

I hope I don't regret this.

10

On that balmy Saturday afternoon, Adrian and Harper arrived at Avalon. Avalon was a massive mixed-use development in Alpharetta that featured dozens of high-end shops, a plentitude of restaurants, a cinema, and pricey condos and townhomes. Outdoor live-work-play centers such as this one had essentially replaced the traditional indoor shopping mall; Adrian had visited before and noticed that several retail spots that had once been in North Point Mall had relocated there.

He had suggested to Gina that they meet at the fountain near the movie theater, a notable landmark. As he strolled down the wide sidewalk with Harper at his side, he saw Gina and her daughter were already there, taking playful selfies in front of the fountain, the wind whipping their hair in their faces.

Scarlett wore her usual excessively skimpy clothing, which only made Adrian wonder about her parents' standards. He had required Harper to wear modest, age-appropriate clothes, and she had reluctantly tossed on a T-shirt and jeans on the threat of leaving her behind.

"Hey, guys!" Gina beamed. She wore a figure-flattering yellow sundress and open-toe sandals with chunky heels. As she stepped toward Adrian, he thought for a fleeting moment that she might try to kiss him (wishful thinking?), but she only gave him a friendly hug.

The girls were thrilled to see each other. Adrian looked around the area, worried that Steph might suddenly appear and unleash her fury at their clandestine gathering.

"How about you girls meet us back at this spot in, let's say, three hours?" Gina said and looked at Adrian for confirmation.

"That would be about five o'clock," Adrian said.

"I don't have my phone," Harper said, lips downturned.

"I do." Scarlett wiggled her smartphone at them. "We'll be back here at five o'clock on the dot."

"And be *good*," Adrian said, directing his statement to Harper. "Remember what we talked about."

On the drive there, he had warned her to stay out of trouble, advising that if Scarlett wanted her to do anything uncomfortable or wrong, she should refuse. He hoped he wasn't trusting his child's judgment too much.

"Yeah, Daddy, I know." She rolled her eyes.

"You've got sixty dollars on your debit card," Adrian said. "I checked. That should be plenty for you two to grab lunch somewhere or whatever."

"I've got my own money," Scarlett said.

Of course you do, Adrian thought. The kid probably had more money in her bank account than he did.

"Can we go now?" Harper asked, bouncing from foot to foot.

"Have fun," Gina said with a wave.

The girls took their leave, giggling and ambling along the sidewalk. Gina turned to Adrian.

"So," she said. "We're right here in front of the theater—and this one serves drinks. We can catch that sci-fi movie you wanted to see, too."

"Kill two birds with one stone, huh?"

"I already bought us tickets. It starts in about forty-five minutes. We can get our drink on first."

She had already bought the movie tickets? That was presumptuous of her, but considering that he was officially unemployed and needed to conserve his limited funds, how could he refuse?

"I won't be drinking, but sure," he said.

At that afternoon hour, the small bar located inside the movie theater lobby was vacant except for a bored-looking bartender skimming her smartphone. Gina perched onto a barstool, crossing her legs, and Adrian took the seat on her left.

Sitting so close to Gina, Adrian was acutely aware of her fragrance, the curves of her legs, her impeccably styled hair, her perfectly manicured nails, her expertly applied makeup, her expensive jewelry, and her overall superb fitness level. This woman invested a tremendous amount of time, energy, and money into her appearance, and she was breathtaking.

There's no way she's interested in me, he thought. *Number one, she's married. Number two, she's way out of my league anyway. Number three—related to number one—I'm married.*

Indeed, today, she wore her wedding band, the big diamond catching the light and reflecting it back at him in a blinding ray. By comparison, the modest wedding ring he had given Stephanie looked like a cheap trinket from a vending machine.

Gina ordered an Old-Fashioned. Adrian asked for a club soda with lime.

"You and these club sodas, honey, I swear." Gina stirred the amber cocktail with a straw. "Before I'm done with you today, you'll have to take a shot of something."

"I'll do another shot of club soda. No liquor for me."

"Are you a recovering alcoholic?" Her gaze was direct.

"I don't like how alcohol makes me feel."

"Hmm." She took a delicate sip of her drink. "How does it make you feel?"

"Like I'm out of control."

She smirked, displaying adorable dimples. "Isn't that the point?"

"I may take a sip on New Year's Eve or a special occasion like my wedding anniversary or birthday, but that's it for me. But I don't judge anyone else who likes to indulge. Do your thing, girl."

"I most definitely will." She took another leisurely sip as she held his gaze.

He drank his soda. "I need to ask you about what happened Friday. Your daughter ordering an Uber and taking Harper to the mall. It sounds like Scarlett does that sort of thing all the time?"

"Her dad and I have taught her to be independent. She just turned fourteen, you know."

"She's fourteen already?"

"We redshirted her because her birthday was close to the kindergarten cutoff—we didn't want her to be the youngest kid in her class. We were thinking about sports, too." Gina's gaze darkened. "Now that she's no longer at Queen's Academy on the lacrosse team, it doesn't make a hell of a lot of difference."

He was still taken aback by the girl's age. Harper had turned thirteen this past May, only three months ago. For teenagers, such an age difference felt huge.

"Why did you guys take her out of Queen's Academy?"

"We didn't have a choice." She brushed a lock of hair away from her forehead. "It was that or get expelled."

"Expelled? What happened?"

"My baby likes to test boundaries. We've taught her to do that. Don't accept the limitations that society places on you. Especially for a young Black girl—hell, a young woman, period—it's all too easy to accept the tiny box the world has in mind for you. We've raised her to be fearless."

"I can see that."

"She likes to push. Sometimes, she pushes too hard."

"Exactly what did she do for the school to want to expel her?" he asked.

"Does it matter now? That's the past. Honestly, Harper is good for her. She's a breath of fresh air, a positive influence."

How ironic: my wife thinks your daughter is a negative *influence,* Adrian thought.

"As long as Harper stays out of trouble, we'll be good," he said. "My wife is very strict. That's how her parents raised her, and she has the same standards for Harper."

"You're not strict?" Gina asked with a giggle. She bumped against him playfully. "Mr. Flexible, huh?"

"My wife and I don't agree on everything," he said. "As I mentioned last night, she wants Harper to cut things off with Scarlett."

"That's sort of extreme." Gina puckered her lips as if her drink had turned sour. "They're only kids, for God's sake."

"I'm trying to talk her out of it."

"Is your wife this paranoid about everything?"

Adrian sipped his soda. Despite his difficulties with Steph, he felt obligated to defend her. "I wouldn't call it paranoid. She has her concerns, though. The whole episode scared her."

"Fair enough." Gina turned her hot gaze on him again. "Tell me: Why are you guys separated? 'Cause I've got a few ideas at this point on what sista girl is doing wrong."

Although he thought about the topic daily, he struggled to form an answer that Gina would understand.

"We've grown apart," he said. "It's like we're incompatible now on almost everything. Small things explode into major things. We could have an argument about something as trivial as who used the last of the coffee creamer and didn't buy a new bottle."

Gina was nodding. "I've been married sixteen years. I totally understand. Marriage can be tough, especially once you have children."

"Preach." He raised his glass.

She clinked her cocktail tumbler against his glass and shifted on the stool to face him. As she swiveled, one of her knees brushed against his thigh.

"How was your sex life?" she asked.

He almost spat out his soda. "What?"

"We're friends now, boo. Don't be such a Puritan. How's the sex?"

He drained the rest of his drink down to the ice cubes. "About as empty as this glass."

"That's a damn shame." Gina clucked her tongue. "About five years ago, my husband and I found the secret to keeping the flame alive."

"I'm all ears."

"Polyamory."

"An open marriage?"

"It's a game changer, boo. He does his thing; I do my thing. It's totally revamped our relationship."

She gulped the rest of her cocktail, checked the time on her phone, and ordered another round.

He still struggled to grasp what she had shared with him. He had heard about couples who practiced open marriages, obviously, but he had never known anyone personally who admitted to the lifestyle.

"You haven't said anything since I dropped that on you." She grinned. "You think I'm a freak, hmm?"

"Well—"

"It's written all over your face, boo." She gave his arm a playful swat. "It's only fun and sex, baby, and a lot of scheduling to make sure everyone gets what they need. What's not to like?"

"I'm not judging you, but Steph is a traditional woman. She would never go for something like that."

"But you would?"

"I'm not sure I could handle it, either. I'd be too jealous. The other day, I heard that Steph was going on a date, and I couldn't stop thinking about it. It felt like a betrayal."

"But you're open to having sex with other women if your wife didn't mind."

"I didn't say that."

"Uh-huh. Right. Have you ever cheated on her?"

"Never."

"What if I wanted you to be my new boyfriend?" She fluttered her eyelashes coquettishly.

The room's temperature seemed to spike forty degrees. The icy soda wasn't enough to quell Adrian's rising heat.

"You're teasing me," he said.

Her smile deepened, showing off her dimples. She checked her phone.

"We should get some popcorn and grab our seats," she said. "The movie's starting soon."

Gina had purchased seats located in the theater's final row, flush against the wall and centered in the aisle. As they headed to the chairs, Adrian, carrying a bag of popcorn, noticed that the auditorium was empty, too.

"Doesn't look like a sold-out show," he said.

"We can have it all to ourselves." She reclined into the plush chair, her bucket of popcorn perched on her lap. Slipping off her sandals, she elevated her legs onto the back of the seat ahead of her.

Out of the corner of his eye, he admired her shapely calves.

What if I wanted you to be my new boyfriend?

He couldn't purge those words from his mind. Surely, she was kidding. She couldn't really be interested in him. They just happened to be the parents of children who were friends, tossed together by circumstances.

He does his thing; I do my thing.

Did that mean this meeting of theirs was sanctioned by her husband? Was this actually a date?

The movie trailers began. Gina reached into her purse and pulled out a couple of airplane-bottle-sized shots of liquor. She passed one to him.

"Gina—" he started.

"Don't be such a prude. Do one shot with me. Please?"

"You don't quit, do you?"

"I can be persistent when I want something." She dropped the bottle into his lap.

Against his better judgment, Adrian took it. In the flickering light from the big screen, he saw it was a famous brand of bourbon that he used to drink back when he would drown his sorrows in booze.

This is a bad idea, he thought. *But I'll do this one drink so she'll stop bugging me.*

He twisted off the cap; Gina cracked hers open, too.

They clinked their bottles together, and she knocked back the shot in one gulp. He took a deep breath—and drank. It was like acid searing his throat.

He coughed. "Damn. It's been too long."

"I'm proud of you." She thumped his back. "Did you finish it?"

He showed her that it was empty.

"Good boy." Beaming, she leaned back in her chair. "Now we can chill."

He didn't feel chill; he felt dizzy, as if the liquor had shot straight to his head.

The theater darkened, and the feature film started. He scanned the rows ahead and saw that only one other audience member had slipped inside, sitting about six rows ahead of them.

It was a Japanese monster movie, subtitled. It had earned fantastic reviews, and Adrian wanted to give the film his full attention, but Gina's presence distracted him.

He shouldn't have been there with her. He loved his wife and wanted to reconcile with her and restore their family. What the hell was he doing on a date?

But Steph is going on dates, too, isn't she? It's not like she cares about what I think of it.

What would Harper think if she happened to come in? Their daughter wanted him and Steph to reconcile more than anything.

I'm not doing anything wrong by sitting here. I haven't touched this woman at all.

His mouth felt grainy, his head throbbing. He shouldn't have drunk that bourbon.

About halfway through the film, Gina got up. She bent down and whispered: "Be right back. Ladies' room break."

She squeezed his hand as she slid past him, her luxurious fragrance leaving him dizzy. He watched her gracefully descend the auditorium steps. Her hips swayed in the sundress, the outfit designed to display a vast expanse of her glorious, toned back.

He forced his gaze back to the screen, but his groin had tightened, a dangerous feeling that he didn't trust under the circumstances. Drawing deep breaths, he tried to calm down.

But when Gina returned a few minutes later, edging past him through the narrow aisle, he reached for her hand and pulled her toward him.

Her mouth opened into an expression of delighted astonishment. She sank onto his lap, straddling him in the chair, and wrapped her hands behind his head.

He hadn't been physically intimate with another woman in over fifteen years. He knew Steph's curves as well as his own, but at some point, possibly due to his own laziness, familiarity had devolved into boredom.

With Gina, he felt like a teenager again, high on lust and low on experience. Hands trembling, he traced his fingers along her firm thighs to her slender waist. He leaned forward to kiss her, and she kissed him back hungrily. Her lips tasted like sweet, fiery bourbon.

He slid his hands up to her breasts and cupped them through the sundress's thin fabric. He realized she wasn't wearing a bra, and he wondered if she had taken it off when she visited the ladies' room, knowing that he was going to make a move on her or planning to make one on him.

She pulled his groping fingers away and clasped his hands in hers, their faces so close their noses touched, her sweet breath warm against his cheeks.

"I want this, but are you ready for it?" she whispered. "Or is this the booze at work?"

The question gave him pause, and he felt a raw pulsing in his head that was a giveaway. Still, he lifted his pelvis a couple of inches, grinding his hardness against her: "Don't I *feel* ready?"

She studied him, her eyes like fathomless pools in the darkened theater.

"Hmm, I don't think so, boo." She kissed him once more, allowing her soft lips to linger. "But you might be soon. I promise I'm worth the wait."

She tapped his nose playfully with her manicured finger, climbed off his lap, and settled back into her chair.

Frustrated, slightly embarrassed, but mostly relieved, Adrian resumed watching the film. When it concluded, he checked his phone out of habit.

Steph had sent him a text message: *Call me. We need to talk.*

11

With three hours to spend at Avalon with her best friend, Harper was overwhelmed by all the possibilities.

Should they go get ice cream? Stop in a restaurant and grab a cheeseburger? Go shopping? All of the above?

"This is perfect, Harp," Scarlett said as they ambled along the wide sidewalk, looking at the glittering storefronts and the bubbling crowd streaming past in colorful waves. "I wasn't sure we'd ever get to hang out again after how your parents flipped the fuck out yesterday."

Scarlett dropped f-bombs in casual conversation all the time. It had taken some getting used to for Harper because she usually felt guilty when she used swear words, even when her parents were nowhere in sight. Yesterday, she had shouted "shit!" when Mom had tried to grab her at the mall, and the word had slipped out of her, past her usual filter. She could tell it had shocked both her parents, and she regretted that but chalked it up to the time she spent with Scarlett.

"Yeah, this is perfect," Harper said. "That was my mom going batshit crazy, mostly. My dad doesn't get mad very often."

"Yeah, your dad is nice. Gina likes him *a lot*."

Scarlett was allowed to call her parents by their first names, which always sounded weird to Harper. But it was part of how her folks let her live without silly rules.

"Gina said she's gonna make your dad her new boyfriend," Scarlett said. "She said he wants to be her side piece."

"What?" Harper halted in the middle of the walkway. "My parents are married, Scar. Aren't yours married, too?"

Shrugging, Scarlett kept walking; Harper resumed her pace, but her mind spun. Was Scarlett playing games with her?

"Gina gets new boyfriends all the time," Scarlett said. "My parents have an open marriage. They do whatever they want."

"My parents aren't like that."

"But I bet your dad wants Gina. It's so obvious. They're on a *date* right now, didn't you know that, Harp? They're back there watching a movie together."

Harper didn't like the shift in the conversation. Scarlett knew her parents were separated and that Harper's mom was going out with other guys, but still, her parents were supposed to be working things out so they could all live in their house again together. She didn't like any of the news that Scarlett had revealed.

Is Daddy really dating Scarlett's mother?

She had to change the subject, or she would be sick.

"What do you wanna do first?" Harper asked.

"We need to get you out of that ugly-ass T-shirt." Hands on her hips, Scarlett looked her up and down. "You need to show off some skin—you've got beautiful skin, sis. Show that shit off. That T-shirt makes you look like a boy."

"It's my dad's fault, sorry."

"Come on."

Taking her by the hand as if she were her mother, Scarlett veered off the sidewalk and into the street, barely bothering to look to ensure it was safe to cross. Someone driving a big SUV hit the brakes and honked at them.

Scarlett flipped the driver a middle finger and stuck out her tongue.

God, she's crazy, Harper thought. Like certifiably insane. But in a fun, exciting way.

Shrieking with glee, Scarlett dashed down the sidewalk, her long legs taking giant strides, and Harper struggled to keep up with her. After sprinting for about half a block, Scarlett swung left, shoving open the door of a women's clothing boutique. Harper followed her into the brightly lit, air-conditioned space, where electronic dance music played on the speakers.

"Damn, that was so much fun." Scarlett grinned. "I love flipping people off 'cause they never expect a kid to do it. How many friends do you have who would do that?"

"Only you."

"Exactly, sis." Scarlett straightened, spread her arms, and twirled in a circle. "Now, this, sis, is one of my favorite boutiques. I shop here *all* the time."

Harper looked around. She had never ventured into the store, but the clothes looked trendy—and expensive. Stepping to a nearby clothes rack, she checked the price tag on a cute-looking blouse. Her mouth dropped open.

"This place is super expensive, Scar," she said. "I can't buy anything here."

"Sis, sis, sis. Do you think I'd bring you here if I wasn't gonna make sure you get something? I've got you."

Another thing Harper wasn't accustomed to about Scarlett was that her family was wealthy. Not like Elon Musk rich with helicopters and jets and billions, but much more affluent than anyone Harper or her parents knew. Scarlett's family lived in a mansion, and a housekeeper lived there with them.

Nevertheless, she didn't want Scarlett to buy clothes for her like she was a charity case.

"I don't need you to buy anything for me," Harper said.

"Who said I was gonna *buy* something?" Scarlett's eyes gleamed with mischief, a look Harper recognized well. "Come on, sis, let's shop."

They browsed the aisles. A sales clerk, a young woman probably not much older than Scarlett, approached them with a smile, and she and Scarlett chatted like they were old friends. Scarlett seemed so comfortable with people that being around her was almost a magical experience. Harper hoped that some of that self-confidence would rub off on her if they spent enough time together. She felt mortified whenever she had to speak to strangers, shied away from looking people in the eye, and was constantly being advised to "speak up, 'cause I can't hear you." It drove her crazy, but she couldn't help how she was.

"See anything you like?" Scarlett said. "Pick out something cute."

A midriff-baring blouse in the Petite section had caught Harper's eye. She showed it to Scarlett.

"Oh, yeah, this is definitely you." Scarlett lifted the piece off the rack and held it against Harper's torso, scrutinizing her with a practiced gaze. "Do you want it?"

Harper glanced at the price tag. "Whoa, that's out of my budget."

"I told you we aren't buying it, sis."

"Okay." Harper went to put the blouse back on the rack, but Scarlett stopped her.

"Give it to me." Scarlett took it from her and draped it casually over her arm, along with some other pieces she had picked out for herself.

"But you said you're not buying it," Harper said.

"I've got you. Don't worry about it. See anything else you want?"

"Are you putting it on layaway?" Harper asked.

"What the hell is layaway?"

"My mom told me about it. It's like when you put a deposit on something, and the store keeps it for you. You keep paying on it until you've paid it off, and then they let you have it."

Scarlett laughed. "Wow. No. Just. No."

Harper felt embarrassed for bringing it up. Sometimes, she said or did something that made it painfully clear that she and Scarlett came from different worlds.

"Look, sis, wait for me outside," Scarlett said. "You're going to bring heat on me. I'll finish up here in a few."

Harper waited outside on a bench, watching people stroll past, hoping none of them happened to be her mother. What would Mom do if she saw Harper sitting there? What lie could Harper fabricate to explain her presence at Avalon?

She fidgeted with her purse. What was Scarlett doing in the store? What did she mean by saying, "You're gonna bring heat on me"?

You know what she means, Harper. Don't be stupid.

Harper was too nervous to stay seated on the bench, and without her iPhone, she had nothing to keep her occupied while she waited. She got up and twirled around, watching people pass by and studying their faces, praying that none looked like her mother.

After about ten minutes, Scarlett popped out of the store. She didn't carry a shopping bag.

Relief washed over Harper.

"Did you decide not to get anything?" Harper asked.

"Follow me."

She walked so swiftly that Harper had to jog to keep up. Scarlett led Harper off the main shopping concourse into a covered area that housed the public restrooms. Scarlett darted into the ladies' room and rushed into a toilet stall.

Harper waited outside near the sink.

"Harp, get in *here*," Scarlett said.

Harper joined her in the stall. Scarlett bolted the door shut. It was barely large enough for them to stand inside without bumping against each other.

Scarlett started to take off her blouse.

"What're you doing?" Harper asked.

Scarlett wore a different top *underneath* the one she had been wearing. It was the cute piece that Harper had wanted.

Scarlett peeled that one off and slipped on her own clothing again. Then, she used her pocketknife to slice off the price tag on the new blouse.

"Here you go, sis." Scarlett handed her the shirt. "I've got you like I promised."

Harper hesitated to accept it, but Scarlett thrust it into her hands.

"Did you steal this?" Harper whispered, though she believed they were the only ones in the restroom.

"I spend a lot of money at that store. Sometimes, they owe me a little bonus gift."

Harper's hands trembled. "I can't take this, Scar. It's not right."

"I put my neck out for you. You'd better take it. We're sisters, aren't we?"

"Yeah."

"Sisters look out for each other. That freakin' store has been ripping off people, Harp, making everything so goddamn expensive. They're not gonna miss one itty-bitty blouse."

The clothing felt hot in Harper's trembling fingers.

This is wrong, she thought. *I can't wear stolen stuff. Scarlett is so wrong for this.*

But she didn't want to upset her friend by turning down the gift. She had seen flashes of Scarlett's anger before, at school. Scarlett could be downright scary when she got mad.

Harper accepted the piece. She started to cram it into her purse.

"Put it on!" Scarlett said. "I didn't lift it, so you can stuff it in your bag. I'll wait for you."

Scarlett stepped outside the stall, leaving Harper behind to change. Tears hung in her eyes, and she chided herself for feeling like she needed to cry. She wasn't a baby anymore. Scarlett was fourteen, and if Harper wanted to hang with her, she needed to grow up fast.

She took off her T-shirt and slid on the blouse. After adjusting it on her frame as best she could, she stepped outside the stall.

"That's what I'm talking about, sis." Scarlett beamed. "Come here, and let me get a better look at you."

Harper approached her. Scarlett smoothed the front of the shirt with her fingers.

"Yep, you look hot now, sis." Scarlett put her long arm around Harper's shoulder so they could face their reflections in the large mirror above the sink.

Harper put on her best smile.

"Do you really believe I lifted this, sis?" Scarlett asked as they looked at each other in the mirror. "You know I'm rich, right? Why would I need to steal anything when I can buy whatever I want?"

Harper didn't know what to say. Had Scarlett stolen the blouse? She wanted to believe she had not, but Scarlett loved playing around so much that you could never tell when she was serious.

"Look, they gave it to me for free 'cause I'm such a good customer," Scarlett said. "I wore it under mine just to mess with you. You're so *gullible* sometimes, Harp, but I love you anyway."

"Oh, okay. Well, thank you."

"And *now*, we're ready to hang out," Scarlett said.

12

Call me. We need to talk.

Adrian's stomach had churned with worry when he read Steph's text message while watching the movie with Gina. But he need not have fretted: Steph invited him to stay over for dinner at the end of his scheduled visitation time with Harper on Sunday afternoon.

The invitation jolted him. He hadn't enjoyed a meal in the company of his wife and daughter in a couple of months, and the prospect of ever having one again had seemed slim. However, as Steph explained on the phone when he called her, this family time was crucial.

"Harper's showing out because of us," Steph said. "It's our fault, Adrian. We need to try to pull things together for her sake."

He couldn't believe it. Steph was admitting she wanted to try to reconcile. He had felt like the only one who cared about repairing their marriage for so long, but clearly the mall incident had rattled Steph so severely that she was willing to do anything to put their relationship back on track.

Around four o'clock that Sunday, he parked in the driveway of their house, Harper sitting in the passenger seat.

"Remember what we talked about," he said to her.

"Daddy, you've told me a million times. I'm not gonna say anything about yesterday."

"Sorry, peanut. I know." He gazed at the front door of their house. "I want this to work out with your mom."

He had told her what Steph had said about making a new effort at reconciliation, with this dinner being the first tentative step.

"What about Scarlett's mom?" Harper asked.

Adrian felt as if a chicken bone had lodged in his throat. "What about her?"

"Scar said you and her mom went on a date yesterday."

"It was *not* a date."

"But you guys went to the movies. Scar said you and her mom were kissing."

Jesus Christ, did these kids talk about everything? Why had Gina shared that with her daughter?

Also, when did Gina disclose that information to her daughter, and when had Scarlett told Harper? Harper didn't have her iPhone all weekend. The sequence of events didn't add up.

Did it matter now? That Harper knew these things at all was bad enough.

"Let's be clear: we weren't kissing," he said. "Scarlett is making that up to play with you."

Harper raised her eyebrows in a skeptical expression.

"She said her parents have an open marriage," Harper said. "I Googled it. So that means her mom can date you, and her husband doesn't care."

"That's their business. It has nothing to do with me and your mother. We don't have an open marriage and don't want one."

"But do you like Scarlett's mom?" Harper asked. "She's super pretty."

Adrian couldn't meet her gaze. Although she was only thirteen, she could read his face as if it were a teleprompter.

"Peanut, let's go inside," he said. "Your mother's waiting for us."

"Whatever." Mumbling, Harper opened her door and got out.

I've got to address this situation with Gina, he thought. *She needs to keep her damn mouth shut.*

The fact was, he and Gina hadn't talked about their brief kissing episode at all. When the movie ended, they left the theater as if nothing had happened. Adrian had appreciated her discretion and hoped she would forget about the entire thing and not share the details with her daughter. Why did she do that?

Steph answered the door as soon as they arrived on the doorstep.

"Hey, guys," Steph said. She hugged Harper and kissed her on the forehead, and when Adrian stepped inside, they embraced, too, a natural, full-body hug.

He missed the feeling of his wife in his arms. It was as if they were two interlocking puzzle pieces that fit together perfectly.

"Thanks for inviting me over, Steph," he said. "Hmm, something smells amazing. Is that lasagna?"

"It is."

"My favorite."

"Mine, too," Harper said. "Do you have the garlic bread, too, Mom?"

"Of course, honey."

Adrian's chest felt tight with emotion. For that moment, everything was perfect between them again—the way it used to be before their marriage had tumbled downhill and dropped into a chasm. If he could have frozen that instant and kept it close to his heart forever, it would have given him hope that they could return to how things used to be.

In addition to the lasagna and garlic bread, Steph prepared a Caesar salad and bought a dessert, key lime pie.

When they sat around the dinette table, sitting in their usual spaces, Steph picked up her glass of Cabernet, looked from Adrian to Harper, and asked, "What did you guys do this weekend?"

I apparently went on a date, Steph, with the mother of the child that you distrust and want to keep away from our daughter. I made a move on her in the theater, and we would have gone all the way if it had been up to me, and now I feel like shit when I think about it.

But Adrian said nothing and gestured to Harper with his fork.

"We went to Avalon yesterday," she said. "It was fun. Then we went to visit Grandma's grave this morning. That wasn't fun, but I'm glad we went. I miss her."

"I miss her, too, sweetie," Steph said. She reached for Adrian's hand and squeezed it.

Adrian squeezed her hand back, grateful for the contact. Steph knew how close he had been to his mother; his mom's death had nearly destroyed him, and Steph's unwavering love had pulled him back from the brink. Grief could wound, but also bond.

After dinner, Harper asked if she could be dismissed from the table to finish a homework assignment due tomorrow. With their child upstairs in her room and out of earshot, Steph directed her full attention to Adrian.

"How did the weekend go with no iPhone, no iPad?" she asked.

"I kept her busy with other things." *Did he ever.* "She didn't miss them at all."

"I hope I don't regret this, but since I want to start fresh, what do you think about giving the devices back to her this evening?"

"I think she's learned her lesson." *I hope.* "We can talk to her again before we hand them over."

Nodding, Steph swirled her wine in the glass. "Thanks again for coming. It's nice having you here like this."

"Like old times." He paused, added: "The good ones."

"But I have a confession to make."

He hesitated, his glass of club soda near his lips.

"The other week, when you thought I was going on a date?" she said. "I wasn't. I was only meeting up with an old coworker, Brian. You remember Brian?"

He remembered Brian. A very nice guy he had met before, who also happened to be gay and married to his husband.

I was sitting here all this time thinking she was on the market again.

"Brian, wow." He laughed, relief rushing through him. "That's a blast from the past. How's he doing?"

"He was laid off recently. He wanted to chat about his resume and job opportunities in real estate." She sipped the wine and lowered her gaze. "But when you came, I decided I sort of wanted to make you jealous."

"Mission accomplished, babe."

She wrinkled her nose. "Sorry. I shouldn't have done that. It was silly game playing."

"If you want to see other people, it's not against the rules, Steph. We're still married, but I won't make an issue of it anymore."

"Are you seeing other people?" she asked in a softer tone. "It's fine if you are, but I need to know if we will make this work."

Does kissing and dry humping in a darkened theater count?

"My focus right now is finding a job," he said. "I could probably use your help with my resume, too, as a matter of fact."

The deflection worked. She speared a slice of pie with her fork and chewed.

"One other thing: we need to chat about this new friend of Harper's," she said. "Did you connect with her mom?"

"I did." *In more ways than you can imagine.* "She invited us to dinner at their house next Saturday. They live in St. Martin's."

"St. Martin's? These folks have got money, it sounds like."

"Are you interested?"

"If we're going to allow Harper to stay friends with this girl, we need to know her people, like my grandma used to say. I'm in."

13

Next Saturday.

Adrian welcomed the weekend. He had spent the entire week in a fruitless hunt for a new job. Although he was due a final paycheck from FiPro, once that deposit arrived, his only source of income would be unemployment checks—and not only were those insufficient to cover his monthly expenses, but they would also last only a few months.

His temp agency didn't have any promising leads. Trevor (who kept his position at FiPro, the lucky bastard) had sent Adrian a handful of newly posted openings. Adrian was infuriated to find that one of the postings was the same job from which he had been laid off. Why hadn't they hired him as a full-time employee to fill the role?

No one higher up had advocated for him; that was why. Trevor had shelter from a VP, while Adrian had been cast out in the cold with a thin sweater.

Gina had requested that they arrive at their home at five o'clock. Adrian picked up Steph (Harper was already spending the weekend with him), and they drove to the immense, gated golf club enclave, which, despite its short distance from their neighborhood, might as well have been in a different universe.

"Wow," Harper said from the back seat as Adrian steered his SUV toward the community's ornate gates. "How rich do you have to be to live here?"

"Richer than we'll ever be," Steph said. "But money's not everything, sweetie. I guarantee you, some of the folks who live here are miserable."

"I'd rather be miserable and rich than miserable and broke," Adrian said.

Steph frowned. The topic of money—precisely, how much they needed and how it should be spent—had long been a significant source of friction in their marriage. He had a background in finance and still believed one should accumulate as much wealth as possible and be liberal about spending it after you cover your basic needs. After all, you couldn't take it with you when you passed on. But Steph had a more traditional attitude, valued earning only as much as you needed and living beneath your means. She distrusted the pursuit of material things. On that point, they had to agree to disagree.

But Steph looked good today. Her hair was newly done, and her summer casual outfit flattered her figure. For his part, he had gotten a fresh haircut and wore some of his finer casual clothes.

How would he feel when he saw Gina? He could still remember the sensation of her soft lips touching his, the firmness of her lithe body.

Stay focused. That's your job today.

Adrian arrived at the guard booth. He entered the guest pass code Gina gave him into the keypad next to the station. The gate arm lifted, and the guard waved him through.

"This place is amazing," Adrian said as he navigated the broad, gently curving roads, heading deeper into the community.

Palatial homes sat on vast, meticulously landscaped lots. Adrian had Googled the place earlier but couldn't stop gawking and pointing.

"It's like something from a TV show," Harper said. She was grinning, too. "I'm so glad you guys are doing this. Scarlett's been *begging* me to come over after school sometimes."

"Slow your roll," Steph said. "We need to meet her family first."

"It'll be fine," Adrian said, but Steph gave him a hooded look.

Following the Google Maps app, he made the final turn. Their destination stood at the end of the lane, in a cul-de-sac.

They live here? he thought.

The photo he had seen on the real estate website didn't do the home justice. It was an immense, brick French Provincial–style residence sitting on two or three acres, with Instagram-worthy views of the golf course.

"A different world," Steph said, shaking her head.

Adrian pulled into the wide driveway and parked behind a black Mercedes G-class SUV with a vanity plate that declared: HOTMOM. Déjà vu tickled his spine. Hadn't he seen this vehicle before?

The driveway ended at a four-car garage, one of the doors hanging open and revealing a sleek blue Porsche 911 Carrera. A white panel van also occupied the driveway, its rear facing the house, and a business name printed on the side in a fancy font read: *First Class Catering.*

"Hurry up!" Harper said. She rushed out of the car.

"I hope we don't live to regret this," Steph said.

"Keep an open mind," he whispered. He got out, and hand in hand, he and Steph walked to the elegant front entrance.

Harper awaited them, literally bouncing on the balls of her feet. As soon as they approached, she rang the doorbell. A series of melodious chimes echoed from within.

Scarlett opened the door. This time, the girl was modestly dressed, for which Adrian was grateful, since inappropriate clothing would have given Steph one more reason to dislike these people.

"Hey, sis!" Scarlett squealed. She and Harper collided into each other's arms as if they hadn't seen each other in weeks.

Gina stepped forward and beckoned them inside. Wearing a sleeveless blue dress that showed off her toned arms, she looked as attractive as ever.

Gina hugged Adrian—a friendly hug with minimal body contact—and embraced Steph.

"It's so nice of you all to make it," Gina said. "I'm excited that you're here. Come on in and make yourself comfortable."

"Thanks for having us," Steph said. "Your home is gorgeous."

"Thanks so much, girl," Gina said. "Come, I'd like you all to meet my husband."

The entry hall reminded Adrian of a castle: soaring ceilings, rich hardwood floors, and a crystal chandelier that probably cost more than he earned in a year.

He and Steph followed Gina down the hallway, passing arched doorways that led into vast, sumptuously decorated rooms.

At the end of the hall, he saw a very tall, slender Black man standing in the kitchen. He wore a blue polo shirt and gray slacks. The man turned at their approach.

Lamont Washington III, the chief executive officer of FiPro, stepped forward to shake Adrian's hand.

14

Gina was married to Lamont Washington III.

His daughter's best friend, Scarlett, was the daughter of Lamont Washington III.

This can't be happening, Adrian thought. A jarring sense of the surreal had taken hold of him as he stood in the immense kitchen and this imposing man, this Rick Fox look-alike, extended his racquet-sized hand toward him.

Acting on autopilot, Adrian offered his hand, and they shook. Lamont's grip was surprisingly weak, considering his size and stature. Adrian had expected a bone-crushing handshake.

"It's a pleasure to meet you, Adrian," Lamont said, chuckling. "Finally, I have the honor of meeting the father of my daughter's favorite new friend."

"You work at FiPro," Adrian said. As soon as the words escaped his mouth, he realized how dumb he sounded. *No shit, he's the freakin' CEO, dude.*

"Indeed, since day one." Lamont smiled, showing a cosmetically enhanced grin. "You must have done a background check on us, eh, brother?"

"I worked at FiPro, too," he rambled, but he couldn't stop himself. "I worked there for six months as a contractor and was let go last week, even though I had a great performance review. I wanted to stay on. I loved that job."

He could sense Steph's disapproving glare in the corner of his eye. Knowing her, she found his unfiltered comments embarrassing.

"Is that so?" Lamont clicked his tongue. "I don't like hearing about that at all, brother. We'll revisit this topic later this evening, in private."

Adrian stepped aside so Lamont could greet Steph and Harper. Adrian glanced at Gina, who was smiling at him.

He smiled back automatically, but he wanted to yell at her. She had set him up. Hadn't he told her where he worked when he was laid off? She knew all along that her husband ran the damn company, and she hadn't said a word. What sort of game was this woman playing with him? This revelation complicated things so much, on every level, that he felt his head might implode.

Other people clustered in the kitchen. He had been only peripherally aware of them at first, as Lamont's unexpected presence had stunned him. Wearing black uniforms, they bustled about, and he remembered the catering company van he had seen parked in the driveway.

One of the workers, a waifish young woman, caught his eye and approached him, balancing a drink on a tray.

"Would you like a club soda, sir?" she asked.

Dimly, he realized that Gina must have told the catering staff that he preferred soda to alcoholic beverages. He would have been impressed if he weren't so annoyed with her.

Adrian accepted the beverage with a mumbled thanks and slurped half in a couple of gulps.

"Where's the restroom?" he asked no one in particular.

"I'll show you, dear." Gina stepped forward and took his hand.

She squeezed his fingers as she led him down the hallway.

"I'm so happy to see you, honey," she said in a lowered tone.

Adrian pulled his hand away from her. In a whisper, he said, "You knew I worked for FiPro, Gina."

She strolled like a lazy cat, hips swaying. "So?"

"So your husband is the CEO. Why didn't you tell me?"

She waved her bejeweled fingers dismissively. "I knew you boys would meet eventually. I don't get involved in work stuff with my husband or boyfriends."

She gave him a meaningful look, lips curved to show off her dimples to maximum effect.

"I'm not your boyfriend," he said. "I'm never going to be."

"You're only a little upset right now, boo." Stopping in an alcove, she gestured to an ornate door. "Here we are. Bathroom number one of seven in our humble little home. Don't be too long. We've got a lot of fun for you guys tonight."

As she passed him, she patted his butt. He watched her go, shaking his head.

Was this woman out of her mind?

But she was married to the man who might be able to salvage his career.

15

After exchanging a greeting with Scarlett's dad, Mr. Washington—probably the tallest man Harper had ever seen up close—she and Scarlett broke off from their parents. Her friend took her on a tour of their house.

Harper wondered if it could really be called a house. It was more like a mansion. There was enough space for ten or twenty people to live and hardly ever run into one another.

"This place is amazing, Scar," Harper said. "Seriously."

"It's all right." Scarlett shrugged as if living in an estate was no big deal. "I want to show you my swimming pool."

Harper followed her to a pair of enormous glass doors. Scarlett opened the doors and led Harper outside into the late afternoon sunshine.

It was an enormous backyard that looked more like a high-end resort space than someone's house. There were lounge chairs, a hot tub, an area with a kitchen, a gazebo, and, most amazing of all, a swimming pool nearly as big as the one Harper used to swim in at the local YMCA when she was younger and taking swimming lessons.

"Wow, Scar."

Scarlett grinned. "I hope you brought your swimsuit, Harp. We're gonna go for a dip after dinner."

"It's in my bag." Harper approached the perimeter of the pool. "How deep is it?"

"Eight feet at the deepest part." Scarlett removed one of her sandals and slid her foot into the water. In a hushed tone, she said, "My cousin died over in this part."

Harper thought she had misheard. "Your cousin what?"

"She wasn't a good swimmer. I told her to stay out of the deep end. She didn't. She drowned." Scarlett made a *whatever* gesture with her hands. "Everyone was so sad."

Harper felt a chill as she gazed at the water.

"You're joking with me, right?" Harper asked.

Sometimes, Scar played mind games with her, got her to believe something outrageous, then revealed that she was kidding and teased Harper for being gullible.

But Scarlett didn't smile.

"If you're not a good swimmer, you should stay out of the deep end, Harp," Scarlett said. "Are you a good swimmer? Or are you scared of water?"

"I took swimming lessons." Harper lifted her chin.

She wouldn't reveal that those lessons had occurred six years ago. She had never swum in water more than four feet deep and hadn't gotten into a pool in a couple of years since their last family vacation to Florida. She didn't want Scar to look at her as if she were unworthy of being her friend.

Still, she had no intention of swimming in the deep end, whether a kid had drowned in it or not, which she wasn't sure she believed—or wanted to believe.

"That's good, 'cause I'm like a dolphin in the water," Scarlett said. "That's what Gina says. I would have been on the swim team if I hadn't played lacrosse. I've got the talent and body for it."

"Did your cousin really drown in the pool, Scar? Be serious."

"You can ask Gina about it if you want. It was a long time ago."

Scarlett tossed her hair over her shoulder. "Don't ask Lamont. It'll upset him. It was his brother's kid."

But that was your cousin, Harper thought. Scarlett talked about the child as if they weren't related.

Harper decided that she didn't want to know any more about it.

"No more depressing talk," Scarlett said. "Let me show you the rest of the house. Well, the fun parts, anyway. Not the boring adult shit."

Scarlett guided her back inside through a warren of rooms. The house was like a maze; Harper would need a map to navigate it.

Scarlett showed her a game room full of video games like one would find at Main Event, and their home theater. The movie room actually had its own popcorn machine.

"Finally, my bedroom," Scarlett said with a sweeping gesture.

Harper stepped inside, her mouth hanging open. Scarlett's bedroom was as big as the entire first floor of her parents' house. It was painted blue and had glass display cases full of shoes, purses, and dolls—hundreds and hundreds of dolls.

"I thought I had a doll collection—wow," Harper said. "This is amazing, Scar."

"I've never played with any of those things. We bought them for fun. Whatever. Gina says they're worth a lot of money now."

Harper pointed at one of the toys, still encased in the original packaging. "This doll is super rare, Scar. It's the one I've wanted to get for my collection."

"You still play with dolls, Harp? You've gotta be kidding me, sis."

"I mean, I don't play with them anymore, but I sort of collect them sometimes when I get money from my parents."

"You want that one?" Scarlett stepped closer, opened the case, and took out the box. "Maybe I'll let you have it. But you've gotta earn it, sis. I can't just give it to you, even though we're sisters."

"What do you mean, earn it?"

"You've got to do something for me. Let me think about what that's going to be." Scarlett put the box back inside the display case and shut the door. "All right, let's get outta here and get some drinks."

Frowning, still wondering what sort of task she would have to do to "earn" the doll, Harper trailed Scarlett out of the bedroom and back into the hallway. As they strolled along the corridor, Harper saw a middle-aged Hispanic lady up ahead, carrying a duster and brushing off a painting.

The woman turned as they drew near.

"Hey, this is Rosita," Scarlett said by way of introduction. "She cleans the house. Whatever. Rosita, meet Harper. Harp is my new best friend. You'll be seeing a lot of her around here."

"Nice to meet you, ma'am," Harper said. She focused on meeting the woman's gaze like Scar did whenever she talked to new people, and she offered a smile, too.

"Hello," Rosita said.

The woman smiled back, but it looked like a nervous expression to Harper, and her gaze darted to Scarlett for a beat, the skin around her eyes tightening.

She looks scared, Harper thought.

But why would this woman fear Scarlett?

16

Gina took Steph on a tour of the house. At the same time, Adrian stayed behind talking to Lamont, who had begun chatting about golf and wanted to show Adrian the indoor putting green he had recently installed.

Lamont seemed like a nice enough guy to Steph, well-grounded and friendly. The fact that he was the CEO of the company where Adrian had worked was an interesting turn of events, and she suspected Adrian was eager to find a way to capitalize on that discovery.

But Gina was something else.

When she had taken Adrian to show him the location of the restroom, she had been holding his hand, sashaying like a runway model. The casual way she held Adrian's hand in hers seemed so familiar that Steph felt a twist in her stomach. Exactly how well did Gina and Adrian know each other? She knew they had met at the daughter's party, but had they talked outside of that?

Maybe I'm only jealous, Steph thought. It was hard not to be because Gina was gorgeous. She was one of those self-assured, enviable women who could bend the wills of men to her whims with only a bat of her eyelashes. Steph got her share of attention but felt positively homely next to Gina.

Despite her beauty, Gina had an air of excess and decadence that put Steph on guard. It was as if she understood she had money, looks, and status—and she enjoyed flaunting them. She reminded Steph of someone from the cast of a reality show like *Real Housewives of Atlanta* or *NBA Wives*. A woman like her might try anything because she could probably get away with it.

Gina sauntered through the house, talking nonstop, her abundant platinum and gold jewelry glittering. She held a tumbler full of brown liquor, and from the whiff that reached her, Steph figured it was cognac. For herself, she had accepted a glass of Chardonnay from the server, and she intended to limit herself to one glass during their visit.

Despite her cool feelings so far toward the woman, Steph had to admit that Gina knew how to host a dinner party. In addition to a plentitude of alcoholic and nonalcoholic beverages, including Moët champagne, the catering crew had provided a slew of appetizers: a charcuterie tray, shrimp cocktail, raw and cooked oysters, smoked salmon, tomato bruschetta, sushi, spinach and artichoke dip, and more.

For the main course, a hibachi chef was setting up a grill outdoors in the spacious entertainment area. Steph had never seen anything like it in her life.

It gave her another perspective on their bratty kid, Scarlett. No wonder the girl behaved like she had the world on a leash. Too much money could do that to people, in Steph's opinion. Wealth could rot your soul if you didn't know how to put it in perspective.

"And this, girlfriend, is where the magic happens," Gina announced. She flung open the doors to a gargantuan master bedroom that looked like the penthouse suite in a five-star hotel.

"Oh, all right." Steph felt heat flush her face.

"I don't mean in *here*, girl," Gina said, giggled, and sauntered to another set of doors. "I mean in here... *Voilà*."

It was a walk-in closet, but it was unlike any Steph had ever seen. Easily larger than the master bedroom at Steph and Adrian's house, it featured multiple glass-fronted display cases full of purses, shoes, and clothes, plush leather seats, plenty of floor-to-ceiling mirrors, silk wallpaper, two sparkling chandeliers, and a small bar. It was like a private boutique one might have found in a shop in Beverly Hills.

"It's incredible," Steph said and meant it.

"Not too shabby for a former stripper, huh?" Gina gulped down her liquor.

Steph almost spat out her wine. "Excuse me?"

"That was a long time ago, girl." Gina cackled. "But back in the day, when I was working the pole at Magic City . . ." Holding her drink aloft, she made a quick, nimble twerking motion. "They called me Honey Cat."

Nothing about this woman could surprise Steph anymore.

"Where did you meet your husband?" Steph asked. Because how did a former exotic dancer hook up with the CEO of a financial services company?

"We met at a private party in Buckhead full of high-roller athletes, music moguls, and hotshot execs. Lamont was married at the time. He divorced that ho three months later." Gina's eyes twinkled. "But let's talk about *you*, girl. Do you want another drink?" She strolled to the bar, uncapped a bottle of cognac, and topped off her glass.

"I'm good," Steph said. "There's not much to tell about me. I was born and raised in Atlanta and work as a realtor now, after spending a decade in corporate America. Adrian and I have been married for fifteen years."

"But you guys are separated. Why is that? He seems like such a great guy and a wonderful dad."

Steph was not prepared to explain the innermost details of her marriage to this woman she had just met.

"We're working things out," she said. "Every marriage has ups and downs."

"Don't give up, girl. That's my advice. Be willing to try *new* things, too. You gotta step outside your comfort zone to keep that sizzle."

Gina sipped her drink and smiled as if she was making a joke, but Steph wasn't in on it.

"We're in counseling," Steph said. "We're going to make it work for the sake of our daughter. She's our top priority."

"And she's so adorable, by the way. So smart and well-behaved. My baby loves her some Harper."

"They've been fast friends for sure." Steph pursed her lips, picking her following statement carefully. "But you know, we raise our daughter under a different set of rules than you and your husband might have for your Scarlett."

"Oh, you mean the Uber and the shopping mall thing? I talked to Scarlett about it, and I let her know that she can't assume you guys are cool with stuff like that. The message has been delivered, girlfriend. It won't happen again." She smiled brightly.

It sounded like a rehearsed response to Steph, but she saw no way to pursue it without coming off like a rude guest. She didn't want to spoil the rest of the evening for Adrian and especially Harper.

"Thank you," Steph said.

"Hold up."

Something at the big, curtained window had attracted Gina's attention. She hurried to the glass and snatched away the silk curtains.

"Was that car parked outside when you guys got here?" Gina asked.

Steph moved to stand beside her and looked outside. "Which car?"

"That blue Honda Accord in the cul-de-sac." Scowling, Gina tapped her acrylic fingernail against the glass. "Do you remember?"

"Sorry, I don't. Why?"

Cursing under her breath, Gina hustled past Steph, heels clicking like gunfire against the floor.

Steph followed her, and Gina didn't slow down to wait for her to catch up. What was going on?

"Is everything okay?" Steph asked.

Gina ignored her, arms swinging as she marched, clutching her drink.

Steph trailed the woman all the way to the front entrance. Gina flung the door open and pounded down the brick staircase, her hair blowing in the brisk breeze.

"Get the fuck outta here!" Gina shrieked. She pointed at the Honda, finger shaking. "I will call the motherfuckin' police and report you for harassment, goddammit!"

Steph froze at the front door, wary of getting pulled into this further, but she couldn't look away.

With a squeal of tires, the Honda veered away from the house. Gina charged across the walkway and flung her cocktail glass toward the vehicle. The glass struck the Honda's rear windshield and exploded, but the fleeing driver didn't slow. The car sped off and soon disappeared.

"Shit." Running her hands over the front of her dress and fussing with her hair, Gina spun back toward the house. Redness flushed her cheeks. She saw Steph gawking at her and offered a weak smile that didn't reach her eyes.

"What was that all about?" Steph asked.

"I'm sorry you had to see that, girl." She tossed her hair over her shoulder. "There are a lot of haters out there. It comes with the territory when you're living this life."

"But who was that, Gina?"

Gina ascended the staircase. Steph stepped aside to allow her back inside her house.

"Are you ready to eat, girl? I am. Let's go see if that little hibachi man is ready. I need another drink, too. Do you want one?"

Whatever the drama was about, Gina obviously wasn't going to share it with her.

"I think I need one now," Steph said.

17

For Adrian, the dinner at the Washington family's residence was easily the most memorable meal he'd ever enjoyed at anyone's house, bar none. From the varied assortment of appetizers to the drinks (he allowed himself a nonalcoholic beer) to the private hibachi chef's entertaining cooking presentation to the delicious food, this evening would stand in Adrian's memory as a life-changing event.

The most noteworthy aspect of all, of course: hanging out with Lamont, Mr. CEO, one-on-one.

During one of his restroom visits, he had texted Trevor with a clickbait-worthy message: *Man, you won't believe who I'm rolling with this evening.*

To which Trevor had responded: *Well, who? Don't keep a brother on standby.*

Adrian didn't write back. But when Lamont had taken him to his putting green before dinner, Adrian asked for a selfie with him, and Lamont graciously agreed. Adrian sent the picture to Trevor. His friend responded: *WTF! The CEO???*

Details soon, Adrian wrote back.

But frustratingly, Lamont avoided the subject of FiPro. During their putting-green exercise, he rambled endlessly about golf. Adrian was grateful he knew enough about the sport to add intelligent commentary and tap some golf balls into the hole.

During dinner, Lamont chatted with their wives and daughters. He was a good conversationalist, but he seemed to defer to Gina on most matters regarding their family. It was clear to Adrian: Lamont made money and played his golf, traveling the world to tour renowned courses; Gina spent the money, doted on their daughter, and in general, did whatever she damn well pleased.

Adrian didn't care how they ran their marriage, whether they genuinely practiced polyamory or not. Before the evening ended, he had to get Lamont to hook him up with his old job.

When they finished dessert, Lamont said, "What do you say we retire to the lounge for cigars and cognac?"

"Sounds like a plan."

"I've got club soda, too." Lamont clicked his tongue.

Adrian couldn't wrap his mind around the idea that this multi-millionaire cared enough about him, a rank-and-file former employee, to remember that he didn't drink alcohol.

"Thanks, but I'll take you up on that cognac."

"My man."

Adrian felt Gina watching him as he got up from the table while Steph chatted with Harper and Scarlett. Gina set down her drink (he lost count of how many cocktails she had consumed) and put her hand to one of her breasts, her boozy gaze riveted on him. She puckered her lips in a kiss.

Adrian swiveled away. What was the matter with her? Was this woman *trying* to get him in trouble with Steph?

He followed Lamont inside, down a winding set of stairs, and into a basement that was less of a man cave and more of a men's club. The only thing missing was a live pianist playing jazz standards.

They sat side by side on a pair of leather club chairs, snifters with cognac in one hand and cigars in the other. Lamont stretched his immensely long legs in front of him. Ahead of them, a gigantic flat-screen television played an old Herbie Hancock video, music pumping from speakers at a muted volume.

"Now that our bellies are full, we can have a substantive conversation, brother," Lamont said.

"I've been looking forward to that," Adrian said. "Not that I haven't enjoyed our chat so far."

"I got it." Lamont chuckled. "I hear you're considering taking on the role of my wife's new boyfriend."

The cigar tasted like a severed finger in Adrian's mouth. He swallowed a gulp of cognac and stammered. His head spun.

Lamont's lips crinkled in a gentle grin.

"She genuinely likes you, Adrian," Lamont said, taking a small sip of his drink. "She's quite a woman. You might want to seriously ponder her offer."

"I'm sorry, Lamont, but I'm not comfortable having this conversation with you."

"She explained our arrangement, did she not? Our marriage is *very* open, brother." He puffed on his cigar and exhaled a ring of fragrant smoke. "You could have your own bedroom here if you'd like. We've got seven, and a few are usually vacant."

"My own *bedroom*?" Adrian gaped at him.

"Gina likes having her boyfriends close at hand. Easy access, she says."

"Are you serious? This feels like a joke, man. Straight up."

"Ponder my wife's offer, Adrian. That's all I suggest."

"I'm married, Lamont. There's nothing to ponder."

"You're separated from what I hear. Gina says the two of you had a brief episode last weekend at the theater?"

"That was a mistake—it won't happen again." Adrian shifted in the chair. "Can we change the subject, please? I'd like to get your thoughts on my situation at FiPro."

"What situation, brother?" Lamont asked.

Did this guy have a memory lapse issue? Hadn't Adrian told him what had happened?

"I was laid off recently. I was only a contractor, but I was doing a good job until you all cut me loose along with the other folks who got riffed."

Lamont puffed on his cigar, exhaled another column of smoke, and sipped his cognac.

"Do you know what's more important to me than anything in this world, Adrian?" Lamont asked.

"Your family?" Adrian asked.

Lamont snapped his long fingers. "Exactly. Not money, not another acquisition, not opening a new office in Singapore, not material possessions. Family. My child."

"Scarlett," Adrian said.

"She's my only child. Her happiness and well-being matter more to me than anything. Do you know what makes her happy?"

"New clothes and shoes?" Adrian smiled.

Lamont grinned. "That would be second. First: friendships. You have a teenage daughter. Their lives revolve around friendships to the exclusion of all else, yes?"

"No truer words."

"We arrive at my request of you: Let your daughter remain friends with Scarlett. Allow their friendship to *thrive*, brother." He jabbed his glowing cigar like a teacher tapping a ruler against a blackboard, driving home his emphasis. "Nurture their friendship. Protect it. These adolescent years are important in their lives, and friendships are integral to their overall health."

"I get that," Adrian said.

Lamont sipped his cognac. "We've had our concerns over the years with our daughter, I won't lie to you. We've encountered some severe challenges I won't elaborate on. She can be a handful."

A cloud passed over his face. He took another pull on his cigar, and his next exhalation of smoke seemed to clear away whatever troubling thoughts he'd been mulling on.

Adrian was tempted to ask, *What severe challenges?* But the moment had passed. Gina had mentioned the threat of expulsion hanging over the girl at her old school, so Adrian surmised that Lamont's comment was related—though he still wondered what the girl had done to get in trouble in the first place.

"From your brief time here this evening, it's evident that Harper is a good influence on our girl, a great influence, I'd say," Lamont said.

"Gina said the same thing," Adrian said. "Harper takes after her mother."

"If you promise to do whatever you can to keep their friendship intact, the sky's the limit for you at FiPro. You have my word, brother."

Lamont set down his snifter and extended his big hand across the space between them.

This had to be the most bizarre proposal Adrian had ever heard. A career lifeline in exchange for letting their kids be friends?

Rich people and their weird ways, Adrian thought. This "deal" was a total no-brainer.

"I'll do what I can," Adrian said.

"Can you finesse this with your wife? She seems like a tough nut to crack."

"Steph will be fine if Harper doesn't get into trouble."

"Of course, brother. That goes without saying, naturally. Neither of us wants any trouble for our precious daughters."

"Then we're good," Adrian said.

They shook hands.

"Welcome back to FiPro," Lamont said.

18

Later that evening, after dinner, when their parents had gone inside the big house, Scarlett took Harper back to the swimming pool.

The multi-colored lights twinkling outside made the pool look like a party spot to Harper, but they had the space all to themselves. Hip-hop music played from a set of outdoor speakers, too, from a Spotify playlist Scarlett had created. The bass boomed like an earthquake.

For Harper, the entire experience was like something out of a dream.

Or a nightmare, she thought. She couldn't get Scarlett's earlier joke (was it really a joke?) about her cousin drowning in the deep end out of her mind. It pulsed in the back of her brain like an oozing paper cut.

Before their mothers had retired inside the house, Harper's mom had pulled Harper aside.

I expect you to behave out here, Mom said. *Keep that swim vest on and stay out of the deepest part of the pool. Got it?*

Yes, Mom. Harper had to fight to keep from rolling her eyes.

Mom had fixed her with that stare that said more than words ever could: *Don't disappoint me, child*, that look said.

After she and Scarlett changed into their swimsuits—they had a little building outdoors with a bathroom and a shower—and put on their hair caps, Scarlett raced to the water and dove in, headfirst, right into the fearsome deep end. With her goggles, she looked like an Olympic swimmer barreling into the pool.

Harper hung back and turned around, looking for the life vest.

Scarlett bobbed to the surface. "Sis, get in the water!"

Harper spotted a small stand on the other side of the outdoor area at the pool's edge. Various inflatable toys—including a life vest—lay on a table. Harper hurried over there and picked up the vest.

"Oh, hell no!" Scarlett shrieked, her piercing voice audible despite the music. "You're not a baby!"

Harper put down the flotation device, her face burning. She reminded herself that she had taken swimming lessons at the YMCA. She knew how to float and how to paddle. Why couldn't she be confident in her abilities, like Scarlett?

Now was the time to stop acting like a baby and be confident in herself.

Harper stepped to the edge of the pool, the shallow end. She tested the water with her foot. It was delightfully cool, a welcome respite from the humid evening.

"Why are you down there on the baby's side?" Scarlett asked. "Jesus, sis. Get over here!"

Harper tightened the cap on her skull and climbed into the water. It rose to just beneath her armpits. She sank her arms and wriggled them around in the blue, chlorinated coolness.

Scarlett dipped underneath and darted toward her, smooth as a barracuda. She popped up a few feet away from Harper, water streaming down her cap.

"You said you could swim," Scarlett said.

"I'm warming up," Harper said.

Scarlett lifted her goggles and smirked at Harper.

"You're scared, Harp. I see it all over your face."

She flicked water toward Harper. Harper flinched.

"Knock it off," Harper said. "I'm not scared."

Scarlett grinned.

"Come to the deep end, and I'll let you have the doll," Scarlett said.

"I don't want the doll."

"Liar, you want it *so* bad. All you have to do is follow me to the grown-ups' side."

Harper looked past Scarlett toward the deep end. The black marking on the side of the pool glowed in the soft light like a warning: *8 Ft.*

Her heart throbbed.

Be confident, Harp. Stop acting like a baby, being scared of everything. It's only water.

"I won't let you drown," Scarlett said.

"Did you see your cousin drown?" Harper asked.

"That was a made-up story." Scarlett scowled. "Why are you still thinking about that?"

"I guess I'm gullible, like you always say."

"I'm getting cold standing here, sis. Come on." Spinning around with a flourish, Scarlett swam toward the deepest region of the water, reached the wall, and turned back to Harper. "Swim to me, sis. Trust me, I got lifeguard training.

"The doll is yours if you can do it."

Harper wasn't thinking so much about the stupid doll—well, it would be great to add it to her collection—she was thinking about Scarlett's challenge. What would Scar feel about her if she failed to try? Would they have more fun nights like this one, one of the best days of Harper's life? Or would Scarlett look down on her, say she was a baby, and return to her old friends, casting Harper back into her dull, predictable world?

I can do this, Harper thought. *I've had swimming lessons.*

She sucked in a deep breath and pushed forward, paddling her arms and legs. At first, it didn't feel so scary because her toes brushed against the bottom of the pool, a reassuring feeling.

But soon, her feet no longer touched the bottom.

Her heart plunged.

Now I'm in the deeper side; if I stop swimming, the water's gonna be above my head.

Scarlett's story about the cousin, the little girl who drowned, flashed through Harper's mind. Scar said it was a made-up story, but whether fictionalized or not, an image had appeared in Harper's imagination: a little brown-skinned girl like her, arms waving, a scream bursting from her lips, the howl of terror soon cut off as she plummeted underneath the surface...

I can't do it, I can't swim, I'm going to drown...

Harper flailed, water splashing. Water invaded her mouth as if it were a malevolent entity intent on her death. The world got blurry, but she saw or thought she saw Scarlett still poised against the wall, laughing, doing nothing to help her.

I'm gonna die...

She sank into the water. It filled her nostrils, the pressure making it feel like her head would rupture like a balloon.

A little girl lay at the bottom of the pool—

—no, that's not real, it can't be—

—and Harper believed she would join the child there, forever. She would drown in this water, and no one would ever find her body until the next kid came along who believed they could swim, and they would try and see two dead girls lying at the bottom of the pool.

Oh, God. No.

Darkness flickered at the edges of her vision like a growing shadow. She fought against it, batted at it blindly, but it grew. She knew this was how it would end for her, swallowed by darkness, swallowed by the gaping maw of water sucking her down into eternity.

I'm sorry, Mom. I'm sorry, Daddy...

She had only wanted to be strong, like her friend.

Hands hooked underneath her armpits and tugged her upward. She gasped. Warm, sweet air rushed into Harper's mouth.

"I've got you, sis."

It was Scarlett, her voice in Harper's ear. Harper coughed, water spraying from her lips. Her chest ached as if she'd swallowed a mouthful of razors, but it felt wonderful to breathe again.

Scarlett tugged her to the shallow side of the swimming pool. Harper coughed hoarsely. Scarlett thumped her back with the flat of her palm. Water spluttered from Harper's mouth.

"I saved your life, sis. I could have let you die. Now you owe me, big-time."

"Thank you," Harper said. It took her a lot of effort to get the words out. Her throat hurt, and water trickled from her ears.

"But you don't get the doll, Harp. Sorry. You didn't make it. Lamont says there's no trophies for losers."

Harper couldn't meet her friend's gaze.

"But you had fun?" Scarlett asked. She touched Harper's chin, raised her head, and gazed at her as if trying to read her thoughts. "Wasn't it fun to almost die like that?"

"It was scary."

"But now, you know what it feels like to live on the edge, sis, and that's a great thing."

"I guess so." Harper coughed once more. The music was so loud it made her head hurt. "Can we go back inside and play games or something?"

Without responding to her request, Scarlett climbed out of the pool. Taking long strides, she went to the big doors leading inside the house and didn't look back at Harper or speak another word.

Had she angered Scarlett? The girl had a strange way of shutting down sometimes; she would just walk off and not respond, even when you called after her.

Harper waited, wondering if Scarlett would return, but after a couple of minutes, the girl hadn't returned. She climbed out of the pool, found a towel, and dried off.

Scarlett was the weirdest friend she had ever had in her life.

A text message chimed on Harper's phone. She checked and saw it was from Scarlett.

What are you doing, sis? You said you wanted to play a game. So come inside and try to find me.

Harper laughed to herself.

Scarlett was also the most exciting friend she had ever had, too.

19

They finally left the Washingtons' home around ten o'clock that night, which for Steph was about two hours too late. After dinner, Gina had dragged her back inside the house, into her glorious closet / ladies' lounge with the plush seating and the bar, cranked up the music on the sound system to raunchy hip-hop and old-school ATL snap music, and proceeded to get absolutely smashed.

The woman was undoubtedly animated, a character, but she talked incessantly, her words growing more slurred as she drank. The encounter wore on Steph's patience. She was more of an introvert, and social outings such as this one took a toll on her inner reserves. Gina talked so much that Steph imagined that she would hear the woman's voice ringing like discordant music from a nightclub when she went to bed later that night.

Despite all the blather, Gina said nothing about her glass-throwing incident at the alleged stalker. Steph wasn't inclined to ask. The woman had a temper, and Steph saw no reason to antagonize her.

As they parted ways, Gina promised to give her a tour of their

Buckhead penthouse they were considering putting on the market. *I wanna hook you up with a nice fat commission, girl,* she said. Steph wasn't sure if the woman was sober enough to remember the conversation later, but Gina told Steph to get her number from Adrian and to call her early next week.

She didn't like the idea of getting another woman's number from Adrian—exactly how much had they been communicating? she kept wondering—but she said she would do so.

Naturally, Adrian had loved every minute of their visit. As he drove them out of the neighborhood, he raved about every minute detail of their outing, but most of all, Lamont.

"He's giving me my job back, Steph!" Adrian said. "Can you believe it?"

"He *is* the CEO," Steph said. "If anyone can rehire you, it would be him."

"He's a solid brother, too. So down to earth, real people." Adrian glanced in the rearview mirror at their daughter. "Harp, I need to thank you for making friends with Scarlett. This might be the best professional contact I've ever had. The CEO!"

"Sure, Daddy." Harper beamed.

Steph turned and glanced at Harper in the back seat. "Did you have a good time with Scarlett, sweetie?"

"It was fun, Mom." Harper was busy swiping and tapping her phone and didn't look up at Steph.

Steph felt a tightening in her gut: maternal instinct.

"Are you sure?" Steph asked. "Did something bad happen?"

"No." Harper glanced up from the glowing screen and smiled at Steph, but it looked forced. "I'm tired."

Steph decided to let it go.

"I'm wiped out, too," Steph said. "It was an interesting evening, but it was exhausting. Gina is something else."

"What do you mean?" Adrian's head swiveled toward her.

"I'll tell you later," Steph said.

Adrian drove to their house and continued to chatter about

Lamont, who had told him to report to FiPro's office on Tuesday morning after the Labor Day weekend. Steph was happy for her husband, but something about the situation and the Washingtons felt off to her. It was hard for her to pinpoint it exactly, but a feeling lingered with her, like an undigested meal that soured in your stomach.

Was it the great divide in their social and economic standing? These people were millionaires, and Steph had long harbored a distrust of the wealthy despite always striving to improve her own financial stability. Lamont earned more in a year than she and Adrian would earn collectively in their lifetimes. Why did he want to reach down from his lofty throne and help Adrian? Why did Gina want to "hook her up" with the commission on a luxury condo? Was it only because their daughters were friends? How could two children from such different socioeconomic backgrounds be friends, anyway?

Adrian pulled his SUV into their driveway but didn't cut off the engine.

"Why don't you come in?" Steph asked.

His eyebrows arched. "I thought you were tired."

"You can spend the night."

He switched off the SUV. "Don't have to tell me twice."

"We're all staying here?" Harper asked. "I'm not going back to Daddy's place?"

"We're all staying here like a family," Steph said.

That pulled a genuine smile out of her daughter.

Inside, Harper said she was going to bed and went upstairs. Steph kicked off her shoes and settled onto the couch in the family room. Adrian sat with her, picked up the remote control, and switched on the television, but he muted the volume.

"You were going to tell me something?" he asked.

Steph explained what Gina had done when she spotted the Honda parked outside their house.

"How did I miss all that?" Adrian asked.

"You were schmoozing with the CEO all night. Anyway, I don't know why Gina flipped out like that. Who would be stalking them?"

"Haters, like she said. Maybe some disgruntled employee from FiPro. Remember that Lamont just announced those layoffs."

"I got the feeling that this was personal."

"It has nothing to do with us, Steph," Adrian said. "Rich people problems."

"If we allow Harper to spend more time at these people's house, and something crazy with a stalker goes down while she's there, it becomes *our* problem."

"If?" Adrian said in a lowered voice. He glanced at the ceiling as if worried Harper would overhear in her room. "Baby, we need these girls to stay friends as long as they aren't getting into trouble."

"Why do we *need* them to stay friends?" Steph asked.

"It makes them happy, that's what I meant. It's good for them. We shouldn't meddle."

"As long as they aren't in trouble."

"That's what I said."

"But this alleged stalker could be trouble."

"We don't know anything about the situation. Don't jump to conclusions, Steph. You're always second-guessing everything, and it drives me nuts."

Steph opened her mouth, about to fire back an insult of her own . . . but she let it go. She wasn't in the mood to fight with him, to try to "win" the conversation. It was a bad habit the two of them had acquired at some point in their marriage, going tit-for-tat until someone stormed out of the room or otherwise refused to engage further, and that type of "winning," even when making certain points was justified, always felt like losing in the end.

"You're right. I shouldn't second-guess, but I don't want to keep blinders on, either."

"Right." Adrian pulled his hand down his face. "Sorry. It's been a good day. I don't want to ruin it with a fight, babe."

The admission surprised her and sparked a flare of hope in her chest.

"Me neither," she said.

"Do you still want me to spend the night?" he asked. "We haven't done this in a while. I can sleep down here on the couch."

Steph lifted her legs off the carpet and swung them around toward him, allowing her feet to settle in his lap. He laid one of his hands on her calf and slowly massaged her.

Did she feel the need to reclaim him because of Gina's obvious affection for him? Perhaps she did. So be it. Gina might have lived in a mansion and owned a closetful of pricey things that Steph would never own, but this was *her* husband, dammit, and she wasn't allowing that woman an inch.

"I want you in our bed tonight," she said.

20

On Tuesday, Adrian arrived at FiPro at quarter to eight o'clock. Lamont had directed him to be there at eight, and to Adrian, that meant getting there fifteen minutes early. As one of his uncles, a former Army sergeant, used to say: *If you're on time, you're late.*

In the company parking lot, he parked next to a blue Honda with a damaged rear window, checked his appearance in the sun visor mirror, and headed inside the building.

He gave his name to the receptionist, an older Black woman. He stated that he had an appointment with Lamont Washington III, which raised the woman's eyebrows.

"The CEO?" she said, her voice dripping with skepticism.

"That's right." He had worn his best suit, the navy blue one he pulled out for interviews.

"Please have a seat, Mr. Wall," she said.

A tremor passed through his knees as he walked to the waiting area. What if Lamont failed to keep his word? What if he had changed his mind? What if he hadn't told his staff that Adrian should be rehired?

He didn't have Lamont's phone number. If he wanted to contact Lamont, he would have to go through Gina, and that prospect felt like navigating a thorny forest. Things had taken a turn for the better with Steph, and he needed to limit his interactions with the woman, who had become more brazen in her flirtations.

He sat in a leather chair. Across from him, a young woman in a business suit sat; she was obviously there for a job interview. She gave him a nervous smile. He should have been able to smile back confidently, but he felt as if he were about to vomit.

His phone rang. It was a local number that he didn't recognize. However, under the circumstances, with him still technically out of a job, he answered. It could be a recruiter.

"Good morning, brother." It was Lamont.

This is when he tells me it was only a joke.

But Adrian said, "Good morning, sir." Calling the man by his first name while sitting in his office felt like a breach of etiquette.

"Sir?" Lamont chuckled. "Lamont will do fine, brother. My assistant pinged me that you've arrived. I'm traveling to Chicago to speak at a conference, but Maya will come right down and help you get settled in. Is that okay?"

"That sounds great, sir—sorry, Lamont."

"We're reinstating your contract, effective today. I understand you prefer a permanent position, and that will certainly happen, but our HR staff is overwhelmed with processing severance packages. It's more efficient for us to get you back on board this way for now."

Continuing in a contractor role wasn't what Adrian had hoped for, but he didn't dare complain. Besides, Lamont's call to him personally was proof that he intended to deliver on his promise.

"I'm eager to get back to work," Adrian said.

"Excellent. How's the family doing?"

"We're good. We had a fantastic time on Saturday; thanks again for having us."

"My wife and daughter had good things to say as well." Lamont clicked his tongue. "We'll have to hit the links soon, Adrian."

I need to brush up on my game before we do that.

"I look forward to it," Adrian said.

"This is my personal number. Put me in your phone, hit me up if you need anything. Are we good?"

Adrian saw Trevor enter the lobby. Grinning, Trevor opened his arms and mouthed: *What the hell are you doing here?*

"Oh, yeah," Adrian said. "We're good."

21

Steph arrived at the Buckhead high-rise luxury condominium, imaginatively called "The Pines at Buckhead," shortly before eleven on Wednesday morning.

Yesterday, she texted Gina to follow up on their conversation on Saturday night about the condo tour in preparation for a potential listing with Steph's brokerage. Steph hadn't expected the woman to remember since she had been three sheets to the wind, but Gina responded and proposed a meeting for the next day. *Let's do business, girl*, Gina typed, followed by a money bag emoji.

I hope she's serious, Steph thought as she stared at the glittering, thirty-six-story high-rise ahead. The towering structure was impressive even in a posh district of Atlanta full of jaw-dropping properties. A mid-tier unit in the building fetched half a million dollars—and Gina said they owned a penthouse suite. If she were telling the truth, the prospect of snagging the commission on such a lucrative sale made Steph dizzy.

She turned onto the access road. Gina had directed her to use the underground parking garage, available only to residents and approved visitors. At the gate's passcode box, she punched in the temporary access PIN Gina had given her—the moneyed class loved gated access—and the arm lifted.

She cruised into the building's shadowed bowels. The visitors' parking section lay ahead, with several vacant slots.

She parked and texted Gina: *I'm here.*

Meet me in the lobby, Gina replied.

Steph climbed out of her sedan and gathered her satchel containing her company papers and other materials. If Gina was ready to make a move, she wanted to be prepared to get the woman to sign on the dotted line today.

As she walked to the elevators, she saw a blue Honda Accord with a damaged windshield parked at the end of the visitors' section.

Steph halted.

Is that the same car that Gina flipped out over?

Gut instinct said, yes. But she wanted to verify.

If it is the same car, what will you do about it, Steph?

She wasn't sure about that, but the knowing and confirmation felt important to her. She approached the Honda and looked around to see if anyone was following her.

A web of cracks marked the center of the rear windshield. Although she wasn't an expert on such matters, the damage looked fresh.

She edged closer to the driver's side. The vehicle was unoccupied, and glancing at the interior offered no hints about the owner's identity.

But if it was Gina's alleged stalker, why was the person there? Were they following Gina again and doing surveillance?

I'm here, Gina texted.

Looking around again, feeling like an amateur sleuth in a dime novel, Steph took a picture on her phone of the Honda's cracked windshield; she took it from an angle to ensure the Georgia license tag was visible, too.

What was she going to do with this evidence? She wasn't sure, but again, her instinct quivered like a needle on a pressure gauge at maximum capacity.

She headed inside the building to meet Gina.

~

"Welcome to our humble abode," Gina said, beckoning Steph inside the penthouse unit.

Already, everything about the condominium had blown Steph away. When Gina pressed the elevator button to travel to the top floor, she knew she was in for another stunner. The unit didn't disappoint.

"This is spectacular," Steph said.

The penthouse was furnished like a demo unit intended to show a potential buyer the possibilities of owning such an exclusive property. Everything, from the furniture to the painting to the lighting, looked as if it had been selected by an interior designer with a limitless budget.

Steph didn't see any photos of the Washington family. The unit was spotless and had an air of emptiness, too.

"We're rarely here," Gina said, anticipating Steph's question about the lack of personal touches. "Sometimes, if we do something in the city, like go to a show, we'll hang out here overnight. I mostly bought it as an investment property, girl."

Steph approached one of the floor-to-ceiling windows. It offered a stunning view of the hazy Atlanta skyline.

Not many buyers would be able to afford such a view, but if she could locate one who could close a deal, Steph would pocket a handsome commission that would boost her earnings well beyond those in any year since she had been agenting.

Despite the exciting possibilities, she ached to ask Gina about a different topic: the Honda in the garage. The alleged stalker. Gina was in a sunny mood, and Steph suspected she had no idea that someone might be tracking her movements.

Don't let her know, Steph thought. *If I tell her, she'll lose her temper and probably won't tell me anything.*

Steph turned from the window to face Gina.

"Well?" Gina asked. "What do you think we could sell this bitch for?"

Inwardly, Steph winced at her coarse language.

"One point two, at least," Steph said. "I'll have to run the comps to give you a more specific figure, but that's my initial assessment. Do you want to move forward?"

Gina pursed her lips. "I was hoping for one point seven."

"It may be possible, Gina. I'll have to do some research."

"How's your husband doing? Lamont told me how much he liked spending time with him the other night."

The abrupt shift in the conversation unsettled Steph. "He's back at FiPro, which for him means he's happy."

"Uh-huh. Are you keeping him happy, girl? You remember what I said about these men, meeting those needs."

"We're moving into a good place if that's what you mean."

Steph noticed a slight downturn in Gina's lips, as though this news disappointed her. She had the impression that it would have pleased her if she had told Gina they were in a rough patch.

Why did she care? She was married to an attractive, wealthy, seemingly lovely man. Was she one of those insatiable women who had to own *everything* she saw—including another woman's husband?

Good luck, girl, because you're not getting him.

"We can move forward with putting together a package," Steph said, bringing their discussion back to the point of the visit. She reached for her satchel. "Do you want to do this?"

"Oh, shit, I need to get going, girl." Gina glanced at her phone. "I've got my medical spa appointment."

"Medical spa?"

"I get IV therapy every week for hydration and vitamins. It's way better than guzzling water or taking supplements, girlfriend." She glanced at Steph with fresh interest. "Are you doing anything else today? I'm sure they could squeeze you in, too."

Steph had never heard of IV therapy—the last time she'd had an IV, it had been for an actual medical procedure at a hospital, not an elective treatment for vitamins or hydration.

"Thanks, but I need to get back to the office," Steph said.

"Maybe we could do lunch sometime when you aren't working."

"I'd like that. Please let me know what you want to do with this property."

But Gina was already rushing toward the door.

She's not serious about selling, Steph thought. *She's only playing around with me, keeping me in her orbit so that she can use me later, like a toy.*

And she's much too interested in Adrian for comfort.

In the lobby, they parted ways. As Steph entered the parking garage, she glanced toward where the Honda had been parked.

The taillights glowed. The vehicle began to inch out of the parking spot.

Her heart leaping, Steph hurried to her car.

What are you doing, Steph? she thought as she slammed into Reverse.

But she already knew the answer to that question.

She was going to follow the Honda.

Everything Steph had learned about tailing another vehicle, she had picked up from watching movies—which meant she had no real training, no idea what she was doing.

Stay close, but don't get too close and make it obvious you're following them. Don't let the car out of your sight.

If she could manage those two things, she could gain insight into this situation with Gina.

She hung back about two car lengths as the Honda exited the parking garage. The vehicle turned left onto the adjacent road.

Steph made a left, too.

Lunchtime traffic in Buckhead was congested, as usual, and in a matter of a minute, multiple vehicles jammed her field of vision, including another blue Honda. But the cracks on her target's rear windshield made it easier for her to follow, the fractured glass glinting in the sunshine.

The driver merged onto Georgia 400 North.

Exactly where I'm going anyway, Steph thought.

Driving on the broad highway simplified tailing the Honda. Fortunately, the driver wasn't a speed demon but went about ten miles per hour above the speed limit—which any ATL resident knew was the minimum speed on their autobahn-like highways. She maintained a distance of a few car lengths as they ventured deeper into the northwest Atlanta suburbs.

At Mansell Road, the Honda veered to the exit lane on the right, and Steph followed. At the end of the ramp, the driver made a left.

Traffic thickened on Mansell, but she didn't have to follow much longer. Just past a car dealership, the Honda got into the left turning lane and swerved into one of the many strip malls along the busy thoroughfare.

Steph also sat in the middle of the turning lane, watching as the Honda parked in front of a storefront.

The sign read: *Barnes Investigations.*

"A detective agency?" Steph said aloud.

A Black man climbed out of the car, a messenger bag slung over his shoulder. He strode to the front door and disappeared inside.

Someone behind Steph honked, snapping her out of her reverie. Instead of turning left, she rejoined the traffic flow, but her mind was whirling.

Why was a detective following Gina?

22

On Friday afternoon, Adrian got a surprise when he went to pick up Harper from school for his usual scheduled visitation weekend.

He'd enjoyed a whirlwind week back at FiPro. Keith, his former supervisor, was flabbergasted upon Adrian's return that Tuesday. *I don't know what you did, dude, but HR told me you were coming back onto the team. Someone here's looking out for you.*

Adrian had only shrugged and behaved as if he were happily baffled by his stroke of good fortune. He didn't dare confide that the "someone" was the CEO. It was better for a sense of mystery to surround his return and for colleagues to wonder who might be pulling strings on his behalf. Trevor was the only one there who knew the truth. Adrian had sworn him to secrecy, a promise Trevor was willing to keep—someday, he might need Adrian to call on Lamont to save his own ass.

He was looking forward to a fun-filled weekend with Harper. That evening, they were going to dinner; tomorrow, they planned to visit an amusement park, Six Flags Over Georgia, with her cousin. To ensure things were on track for a good weekend, he'd checked in several times that week with his daughter via text, casually inquiring about school and "friends"—of which he meant Scarlett. Harper gave no indication that anything was wrong or unusual, which was why Adrian was shocked when he pulled into the carpool line and saw both Harper *and* Scarlett waiting to get in.

What is this?

The girls piled into the back seat.

"Hey, Daddy!" Harper said.

"Hey, Daddy!" Scarlett repeated and giggled. She slammed the door behind her.

"Uh, hi." Adrian inched away from the curb. He glanced at the girls in the rearview mirror. Both of them grinned as if they were about to explode from excitement. "I wasn't expecting you, Scarlett. Do I need to drop you off at home?"

"I'm hanging out with you guys," Scarlett said.

"Oh." He felt as if he'd been slapped, but he didn't dare express any frustration. Lamont had advised nurturing their friendship.

"Can you take us to get ice cream, Daddy?" Harper asked. "Please?"

"Where do you want to go? Dairy Queen?"

"Take us to the mall, Adrian," Scarlett said. "That's my favorite spot to get ice cream on Fridays."

Had this kid called him Adrian?

"Mine, too," Harper said. "Please?"

"All right. I'll take you guys to the mall to get ice cream, then drop Scarlett off at home. Does Gina know you're with me, Scarlett?"

"Gina doesn't care," Scarlett said. "I told you guys, my parents trust me to take care of myself. I'm independent."

"I'll text Gina and let her know," Adrian said.

"You do that," Scarlett said.

This kid's condescending tone worked his nerves; he gritted his teeth. What had happened to the respectful manner when he'd first met her? What had happened to the "Mr. Wall" and formal etiquette?

It was about a five-minute drive to North Point Mall. When he parked his SUV, the girls left and took off across the parking lot without waiting for him.

Reluctantly, he sent Gina a text message. He had been striving to avoid the woman, still annoyed at her behavior the prior weekend. At one point during the week, Gina had texted him and asked: *Are you still mad at me?* He hadn't responded.

The girls are with me getting ice cream, he typed. *I'll be dropping off Scarlett afterward.*

She responded, *See you soon*, and ended with a kiss emoji.

Inside the mall, he found Scarlett sitting at a table in the food court, gaze fixed on her phone.

"Where's Harper?" he asked.

"She went to the restroom." Scarlett looked up from her screen. "How's everything going at my dad's company, Adrian?"

Adrian hesitated. How much did this girl know about his work situation?

"It's going well," he said.

"It was nice of Lamont to bring you back after they fired you."

"They didn't *fire* me. It was a layoff."

"*Terminated*." She made a slitting motion across her throat. She grinned, showing her flawless teeth, which made her look predatory. Was that only in his imagination?

He looked over his shoulder, hoping his daughter was returning soon.

"It's interesting, though," she said. "It's sort of like you work for me, Adrian."

He pivoted back to the table. "Excuse me?"

"Lamont owns FiPro. I'm his only child, his heir. The company will be mine one day."

Adrian stared at her, words trapped in his chest.

"You promised Lamont you would make sure Harper and I stay friends, too," she said. "I know all about the deal you guys made."

"I'm not discussing this with a kid, for God's sake." He started to walk away.

"Get back over here. Or I'll say bad things to Lamont about you." Her brown eyes gleamed. "Nasty things that could get you in a *lot* of trouble."

A chill traced down his spine like an icicle.

He turned back to the table.

"You're way out of line," he said.

She giggled, and again, she sounded like a typical teenager, not some calculating sociopath. Still, the cold shine remained in her gaze.

"What the hell do you want?" he asked.

"Whatever I want. Whenever I want it. That's what I want."

"You're just a kid," he said, trying to laugh, but the sound came out like a strangled gasp.

"I'm fourteen with an IQ of 135," she sneered. "I qualify for Mensa. Do you?"

He said nothing because he didn't know—but he knew a score of 135 was high—awfully high. Mensa was an exclusive organization that required high IQs for admittance, a club for geniuses and the gifted.

She's probably lying, he thought. *If she's so bright, why was she going to be expelled from school?*

"Stay out of my way with Harp, and we'll be good," she said. "Get that bitchy mother of hers under control, too. She's annoying as fuck."

"Little girl, you need to watch your mouth."

She flipped him the middle finger and laughed. He couldn't believe it. What the hell was the matter with her?

When he finally found his voice again, he said, "I'm going to tell your mother about this, Scarlett, and your father, too."

"Go ahead and tell them." Scarlett smirked. "They won't care."

"We'll see about that."

Harper returned at last. "Hey, sorry it took me so long. Ready for ice cream, Scar?"

"Yup." Scarlett bobbed her head. "I was sitting here chatting with your dad, Harp. He says it's okay for you to spend the night at my house tonight."

Harper screeched with glee. "Thank you, Daddy!"

Adrian glowered at Scarlett. The kid grinned.

Together, the girls strolled to the ice cream shop. Adrian sat there, heart thudding, wondering if all that had happened.

23

As Adrian drove, the teenage girls chatting and giggling in the back seat, he struggled to put his disturbing conversation with Scarlett in perspective.

He concluded that she was only a kid. She may have been brilliant, but she was fourteen, not an adult. Her parents allowed her far too much freedom and had taught her zero respect for adults, and thanks to her wealthy family, she believed she could manipulate everyone in her orbit.

Despite her high-handed talk and evident intelligence, she was only a child. She didn't wield any power over him, like some adolescent queen or something.

Then why are you taking your daughter to spend the night at her house, Adrian? Why are you doing exactly what she wants you to do?

He told himself that he didn't mind if Harper spent the night, that it was the sort of friendship nurturing Lamont would have appreciated. He needed to choose his battles, and this wasn't a battle worth fighting. Harper would have been heartbroken if he'd told her she couldn't stay over.

But there was a truth that he was loath to admit to himself: he was nervous about risking anything that might screw up his position at FiPro. He had only gotten his foot back in the door that week and was earning a regular paycheck again. Lamont had promised him "the sky's the limit" and was willing to mentor him. When would an opportunity like that ever come his way again? To be mentored by the CEO of a significant corporation? He'd been waiting his entire career for a chance like this to finally snag the brass ring.

He could suffer Scarlett's bratty remarks and dubious threats. So long as Harper didn't get into trouble with the girl—that was what he kept telling himself—then it was all good. Let the child flap her gums.

She's only a kid. She's harmless.

Their first stop was his apartment since Harper needed to pack clothes for her overnight stay with Scarlett. Scarlett accompanied Adrian and Harper inside his unit.

"You have a lovely residence, Mr. Wall," Scarlett said.

She spoke with such exaggerated civility that he sensed she was mocking him. The apartment was like an outhouse compared to where she lived.

"It'll do," he said and ushered them out.

Ten minutes later, they arrived at St. Martin's Country Club. Scarlett had given him the access code to pass through the community's gated entrance. He pulled into the driveway behind Gina's Mercedes.

"Here we are," he said.

"Thank you, Mr. Wall," Scarlett said. "You're such a wonderful guy."

Shut up and get out of my damn car.

He hadn't planned on going inside, but he worried that Gina might know nothing about this impromptu sleepover. It wasn't as though Scarlett was inclined to tell her parents anything.

Scarlett unlocked the front door with her own key, and the girls hurried inside, dashing away down the wide corridor before Adrian could close the door behind him.

He heard Gina before he saw her. It sounded as if she were arguing on the phone with someone.

"Handle these motherfuckers," she said. "I mean it."

He followed her voice and found her in a large, high-ceilinged library. Floor-to-ceiling built-in oak bookcases lined a couple of the walls. A big window provided a panoramic view of the golf course, and a fireplace spacious enough to roast a rhinoceros dominated one wall.

Standing at the window, Gina spun at Adrian's entrance.

"I'll call you later," she told the person on the line. She brightened as abruptly as if she'd flicked a switch and sauntered toward him.

"Hey, you," she said. "Are you still mad at me? You never wrote back to me."

"I'm over that. Scarlett wants Harper to spend the night. Is that okay?"

"Of course it is. Mi casa su casa, boo." She lifted a glass off a table and found it empty. "I need another drink. Do you want one?"

"A club soda, please."

"You and those sodas. Come on."

He trailed her down the hallway into the kitchen. "Is everything okay, Gina? When I walked in, it sounded like you were upset with someone."

"Dealing with haters, honey. It's part of the glamorous life."

Hadn't Steph said Gina had given her a similar response when Steph witnessed her throwing a glass at a car parked across the street?

"Go on and look in the fridge for your little soda," Gina said with a wave. "You're family now. I'm not waiting on you."

He found a can of soda in the gargantuan refrigerator and popped the tab. Gina mixed a cocktail and took a long sip.

"I had a chat with Scarlett," he said.

She sighed. "Oh, Lord, what did my baby say now?"

Adrian detailed his discussion with the teenager. Gina laughed, but it was the dispirited laugh of a long-suffering parent.

"She's only a baby," Gina said. "You know how kids are, eavesdropping and trying to get attention. Don't worry about it."

"She flipped me off, Gina. To my face."

"She does that for shock value. You can't pay her any mind."

"Right. She said if I told you what she did, you wouldn't care."

"You don't think I care? You have no damn idea the sacrifices we've made for that child." She set her glass down hard on the quartzite countertop, rattling the ice cubes.

He clutched the cold soda can and waited for her to say more, but she only picked up the glass again and drained every ounce of the beverage.

"We'll talk this out right now," Gina said. "I don't want her disrespecting you. You don't deserve that."

"I appreciate it."

Gina picked up her phone and left a message while Adrian sipped his soda. A minute later, the clattering of footsteps signaled their daughters' approach.

"What's up, Gina?" Scarlett strolled into the kitchen, Harper following.

"Mr. Wall here tells me that you made rude comments to him earlier today," Gina said.

Harper's face reddened, a response Adrian would have expected since her friend was getting called out in front of an audience, but Scarlett grinned.

"I was only kidding," Scarlett said.

"You were kidding?" Adrian almost choked on his soda.

"I like to play jokes sometimes, Mr. Wall. I'm sorry if I offended you."

Adrian looked from the girl to her mother. Gina studied her daughter closely, her drink poised at her lips.

"Not everyone appreciates your sense of humor, baby," Gina said. "We've discussed this before."

"I understand, Gina. It won't happen again." Scarlett saluted her mother and Adrian. "Can we go now?"

"Go on."

Harper smiled tentatively at Adrian, but Adrian didn't have any words for what he had just witnessed. He waved her away, and the girls scrambled out of the kitchen.

"See?" Gina said to him. "I told you, she's only a baby trying to get a reaction. You need to lighten up around us—our family doesn't take things so seriously. We live *free*." She spread her arms as if to embrace the whole world.

Is that what you call it? he thought. *I call it gaslighting, and both you and your kid are doing it to me.*

"I'm going to order some dinner," Gina said. "Are you going to stay for a while?"

"I'm going home. It's been a busy week."

"Aww, are you sure?" She pouted.

As Adrian was about to answer, he heard a door open and approaching footsteps. His heart lifted.

Lamont entered the kitchen in a tailored gray suit without a tie, the perfect portrait of an executive who had left the office.

Adrian straightened. He hadn't seen Lamont at the FiPro office that week, and it still felt surreal to encounter the man in his residence.

"Brotherman." Lamont extended his hand.

"It's good to see you, sir . . . sorry, Lamont." Adrian corrected himself.

"Indeed. I'm about to depart for a flight. I've got an eight o'clock tee time tomorrow morning at Seminole."

Adrian wasn't well-versed in every notable golf course in the world, but he vaguely recalled the name of the venue in Florida; it had hosted several high-profile PGA tournaments.

"That sounds great," Adrian said.

"How was your week back at FiPro?" Lamont asked. "Are you getting back into that workingman's groove?"

"It was busy, thanks. My team was glad to have me back on board."

"I'm glad to have you, brother." Lamont put his gigantic hand on Adrian's shoulder. "How are our girls doing?"

"They're having a sleepover tonight."

Lamont made a click with his tongue. "That's what I love to hear. Keep up the good work, brother. I've got big things in store for you." He patted Adrian's shoulder, let him go, and strolled out of the room.

Gina rolled her eyes at Lamont's back. Adrian realized that she and her husband hadn't exchanged so much as a greeting. What was that all about?

"Are you staying for dinner or not?" Gina asked him. "You can keep me company since Tiger Woods there is leaving."

"Sorry, Gina, but I'm going to head out. I need to chat with Harper for a minute before I go."

He didn't know where Harper had gone with her friend, so he texted her to ask her to come back.

When she returned to the kitchen, he pulled her into the hallway.

"Am I in trouble?" she whispered.

Why did she assume she was in trouble? It was an odd question.

"Of course not. I wanted to remind you that we're going to Six Flags tomorrow with your cousin. I'll pick you up in the morning at nine thirty."

"Can Scarlett come with us?" Harper asked.

"This sleepover wasn't part of our original weekend plan, but I'm letting you stay over, Harp. Tomorrow, we go back to our original plan."

"Please?"

"You and Willow will have a great time. You two haven't hung out together since earlier in the summer."

"I'd have more fun if Scar was with us. She has her own flash passes, too, Daddy. We can skip all the lines. Please?"

She watched him, gnawing on her bottom lip. He was going to stand his ground, but his mind flashed back to his chat with Lamont a few minutes ago. *I've got big things in store for you.* Lamont would appreciate their children going to the theme park together. It would be another feather in Adrian's cap. Little things, such as showing his intent to keep up his end of their deal, could ensure that Lamont made good on his promise to boost his prospects at FiPro.

Did it matter that the kid put a sour taste in his mouth? He wouldn't be the first person who agreed to do something objectionable on his climb to the top.

"Okay," Adrian said. "Scarlett can come with us."

"Yes!" Harper did a victory dance. "Thank you, Daddy!"

"Remember, nine thirty," he said as she raced away to tell her friend the news.

Gina insisted on walking Adrian out to his vehicle. As he opened the driver's-side door, she said, "Why don't you take me home with you tonight?"

He paused. "You want to come to my crappy apartment?"

Gina touched his arm. "Have you had a woman there? I bet you haven't, not even sourpuss wifey."

"I was planning to go see my wife tonight, Gina."

"Wow, okay." Gina giggled. "You're something else. Do you know how many men DM me on Facebook and IG? I'm here damn near throwing myself at you, and you're saying no."

"I'm flattered, Gina, but I'm working things out with Steph."

"You go on and do that, boo." She stepped back and sipped her drink. "But I always get what I want, sooner or later. My baby and I are alike that way."

"Have a good evening, Gina. Take care of our girls. I'll see you in the morning."

She wriggled her fingers at him and sauntered back into her house with a dramatic swinging of her hips.

Adrian settled behind the steering wheel. He didn't understand Gina's continued interest in him. This was a woman who had everything at her fingertips. He was only a regular guy, but she couldn't stop coming after him.

That's how rich people are, Steph would have said. *They want everything they lay their eyes on, whether they need it or not. Getting more, more, and more is the thrill for them.*

He wasn't sure he agreed with that perspective. What if he wasn't only a regular Joe anymore? Gina had to see *something* desirable in him, didn't she? Just like Lamont saw his potential. Regardless of their daughters' connection, the great man wouldn't have intervened to rehire a clown.

He felt things opening up for him for the first time, a new world revealing itself. A world where gorgeous women wanted him, yet he could spurn their advances, and a world where captains of industry invited him to enjoy the glorious ride into prosperity.

Yes, big things were coming his way. Finally.

From there, things could only get better.

24

"This is a surprise." Steph opened the door.

Before his arrival, Adrian texted Steph and asked if he could visit. *Of course*, she had responded and, as if due to some motherly sixth sense, asked, *Where's Harper?*

"Thanks for letting me drop in," he said, closing the door behind him. "Things have been a little spontaneous this evening."

He had replied that she was spending the night with Scarlett, but Steph hadn't written back, a sign that more questions awaited him in person.

"It sounds like the sleepover was a last-minute decision," Steph said. "I would have appreciated knowing about that ahead of time."

"Does it bother you?"

"She's there now, isn't she? It's fine, I guess. We've met her family, and they aren't axe murderers."

"But they're different. I see it in your eyes."

"They're rich. We're not. Yeah, they're different than what I'm accustomed to." She glanced at her phone. "I ordered Thai. It should be here in a few minutes."

In the kitchen, Steph poured herself a glass of Chardonnay, and he grabbed a nonalcoholic beer from the refrigerator.

"Is there any other news you have to share?" she asked.

He wasn't going to mention his unsettling conversation with Scarlett. It would give Steph one more reason to dislike the kid and discourage Harper's friendship with her.

"Scarlett is coming with us to Six Flags tomorrow." There, he said it.

"Another unplanned outing." Lips curling, Steph gazed into the depths of her glass. "You understand that this obsessive friendship will probably crash and burn soon."

"That's a cynical way to look at things."

"It's too intense. It's like the infatuation phase of a relationship. It doesn't last."

"They could be best friends for years and years."

She leveled a sharp gaze at him. "You would like that, hmm? Let you stay in Mr. CEO's good graces?"

Adrian hadn't shared anything about his secret arrangement with Lamont, but Steph wasn't a fool.

"Because of Scarlett, Harper is getting exposed to things she never would have experienced before," he said. "That's a good thing."

"All that glitters isn't gold," Steph said.

Her phone chimed.

"Is that the order?" he asked. "I'll go get it."

When he returned with the plastic bag full of hot, fragrant-smelling food, Steph had already set out dishes and silverware at the table. The easy reversion back into familiar, comfortable routines was perhaps one of the things he missed most about living in their house together.

She had ordered pad Thai, their favorite entrée. Adrian forked a portion onto his plate.

"I'm glad you came over," she said as she squeezed lime juice over her chicken. "There's something I wanted to discuss with you."

Adrian chewed and waited.

"Gina's stalker is a private detective."

He swallowed. "You've lost me."

"Do you remember what I said about how she threw the glass at the car parked near their house the other weekend?"

"Right." He tried to hide his annoyance. "But how do you jump from that incident to knowing the person is supposedly a private investigator, Steph?"

"I told you I was meeting up with her this week to tour their condo in Buckhead, which she said she might put on the market—a total waste of time, by the way. She's not serious."

Adrian waited, hoping she would get to the point eventually.

"That *same car*, a blue Honda, was waiting in the parking garage when I was getting ready to leave the condo. The rear windshield was damaged."

She picked up her phone, tapped and swiped it, placed it on the table, and slid it toward him. He saw a photo taken in a parking garage, the Honda of which she spoke maybe twenty feet ahead, with a web of cracks visible across the rear windshield.

Coldness tickled the base of his spine. Had he seen this car before? Why did he feel as though he had?

"You recognize it?" Steph asked.

"I didn't say that."

"But you blinked."

"Blinking is normal for healthy eyes."

"Do you have to be a smart-ass about it?"

He took another bite of his food. "You were going to tell me how you found out this car belongs to a detective."

She leaned back in her chair, folded her arms over her chest, and smiled with self-satisfaction.

"I followed it," she said.

"You followed a stranger?"

"I had to know. I followed him all the way from Buckhead to Mansell Road. He parked in front of Barnes Investigative Services and walked right inside." She tapped and swiped on her phone again. "I looked them up. They have a website. Here."

He barely glanced at the screen. He could have told her about how he'd overheard Gina's conversation earlier—*handle these motherfuckers*—but he didn't want to share that with her. Because he knew his wife, he sensed precisely where she was headed with this, and he didn't want to give her any justification to pursue it further.

"I can't believe you actually tailed someone," he said. "That's another level of nosiness, Steph, even for you."

"Why is a detective following Gina? They could be investigating their entire family. Why? What did they do?"

He put down his fork. "It has nothing to do with us. Let it go. Please."

"Our daughter is spending the night at their house. You *should* be concerned, too."

"Whatever it is, it's probably rich folk problems. People on their level are always getting sued, harassed, whatever. It comes with the territory."

"You sound like Gina." She scowled at him.

"Can we enjoy our evening, please?" He picked up his fork again.

She picked up her fork, too, and she didn't raise the subject again, but Adrian knew his wife. She wasn't going to let this go despite his pleas. She could be like a pit bull when she got hold of something, snagging it in her teeth and clamping down her jaws tight.

For some reason, it scared him.

25

As they hung out in Scarlett's gigantic bedroom, Scarlett shared her newest obsession with Harper.

"This app is *so* amazing, Harp," Scarlett said. "Look."

Legs crossed, they sat side by side on Scarlett's immense bed, bigger than the bed that Harper's parents shared. Scarlett had opened an app on her phone (of course, she had the latest generation iPhone, while Harper's model was three years behind). She rapidly thumbed in text and pushed a button.

A baritone voice that sounded eerily like Scarlett's father issued from the phone:

"This is Mr. Lamont Washington III. I regret to inform you that my dear daughter, Scarlett, will be absent from school today due to an unexpected illness. Her mother and I hope that she will return tomorrow."

"Oh my God," Harper said. "How did you do that?"

"I cloned his voice, Harp," Scarlett said with a smirk. "It's AI tech. Cool shit, huh?"

"Did you actually try it?"

"Twice. Worked perfectly for getting me out of school."

"Wow."

"I've got Gina's voice on here, too." Scarlett thumbed in more text.

A voice that sounded exactly like her mother's said: *"Adrian, you know you want to spend the night with me, boo. Your little girl doesn't have to know."*

Harper made a noise of disgust deep in her throat. Scarlett cackled.

"Let's get your voice in here, Harp," Scarlett said. "It'll be fun."

"Well . . . okay."

Harper recorded a few sentences into Scarlett's phone, Scarlett tapped the screen, and a minute later, Harper heard a cloned voice say: *"Motherfucker, asshole, goddamn, pussy, bitch, dick, shit, shit, shit!"*

"Hey!" Harper said, but she was laughing. "I don't talk like that!"

"It's only for fun, Harp. What other friends do you have who would do something like this?"

"Only you," Harper said, which was the answer Scarlett loved to hear.

Harper rose from the bed. A collection of framed photographs sat atop a dresser. In one of them, a younger-looking Scarlett posed with another girl who appeared to be the same age.

"Who is this?" Harper asked. "I was meaning to ask you about this picture."

"That's Zoey." Scarlett came to stand beside her. She plucked the photograph off the dresser and ran her manicured finger across the surface. "She was my last best friend. She made me mad 'cause she wanted to stop being friends, so I killed her and her family."

Scarlett let the photo drop to the carpet, where it landed with a thud.

Harper gawked, her gaze darting from Scarlett's blank face to the picture on the floor.

"You killed her and her family?" Harper asked. "You're joking again, aren't you?"

"Am I?" Scarlett didn't smile.

Harper's heart knocked. "You killed them because she didn't want to be friends with you anymore?"

"Consider it a warning," Scarlett said. She made a circle symbol with two fingers. "Once I let you inside my circle, the only way out is ... death." She snapped her fingers.

Harper stared at her. Scarlett stared back at her.

Then Scarlett's lips broke into a broad grin. "Jesus, you should see your face. You believe everything I tell you—damn, you're gullible! I'm kidding, Harp."

"Oh." Harper let herself exhale.

"Her family moved away, so we kind of lost touch." Scarlett took the photo off the floor and placed it back on the dresser. She pressed her lips together. "I miss her, but life goes on. Now I've got you. You won't ever leave me, will you, Harp?"

"I'm not going anywhere unless my parents move, too."

"Your parents aren't going anywhere. Lamont won't let your dad leave his job."

Harper didn't necessarily like how her father worked for the company that Mr. Washington owned, but she knew Daddy loved working there. In Harper's mind, it put her family in a weird position, as if they owed something to the Washingtons. Scarlett wasn't shy about bringing it up, either.

"I've got something special planned for tonight, Harp. It's a surprise."

"What is it?"

"If I told you, dummy, it wouldn't be a surprise anymore." Scarlett walked out of the bedroom, and Harper followed.

"Let's go get ice cream now," the older girl said.

That night, Harper had a nightmare about Scarlett. They were at a shopping mall getting ice cream, but when Harper looked inside the glass-fronted freezer case, she saw her own decapitated head standing inside, her dead eyes opened wide with apparent shock, the top of her head scooped out and full of blood-red ice cream. Scarlett said, *I'd like a triple scoop of that in a waffle cone*, finger mashed against the glass to indicate the frozen dessert inside Harper's hollowed-out head. As the server bent inside to scoop out a portion, Scarlett turned to Harper (who was somehow also standing beside her at the counter) and said, *You're not really dead, Harp. Sis, you're so gullible!*

Harper woke with a scream erupting from her lips.

"What the hell, sis? Be *quiet*."

Scarlett gazed down at her. Harper had retired for the night on a sofa standing along the wall of Scarlett's immense bedroom; the couch offered a pull-out bed as comfortable as the mattress in Harper's own room at home.

Harper blinked, her head swimming as the lurid images drained out of her mind. A dim light glowed from a bedside lamp.

"What time is it?" Harper asked.

"Time for your surprise. Come on. And be quiet." Scarlett raised her finger to her lips and stepped away from the bed. She wore a long T-shirt, pajama pants, and white Crocs. "Meet me downstairs."

Harper sat up. She had left her phone charging on a nearby end table. The time read 2:34 a.m.

"Where are we going?" Harper yawned.

"You'll see. Be quiet. Come on."

Scarlett left the room, her soft footsteps retreating down the second-floor hallway. Harper yawned again and climbed off the mattress. She slipped on her Crocs and tucked her phone into the pocket of her pajamas.

As she crossed the room, she realized she needed to pee. A bathroom lay on the other side of the hallway. Quickly, she stepped inside to relieve herself.

She was so tired she could climb back into bed and sleep. She and

Scar had been up watching horror movies until past midnight. Her head felt as if it had been stuffed with cotton balls.

What kind of surprise did Scar have in store? Her stomach fluttered at the thought, a mixture of anxiety and excitement coursing through her.

She left the bathroom and almost ran into Rosita, their housekeeper. The petite older lady put her hand to her chest, clearly as surprised as Harper was to encounter someone wandering the hallway at this late hour.

"Sorry," Harper said.

"It's okay," Rosita said in thickly accented English. "Are you okay, chica? Do you need anything?"

"Estoy bien, gracias." Harper had taken two years of Spanish in middle school, knew the basics, and could speak a few sentences, but she was far from fluent.

"Ah." Rosita's face tightened, and her gaze shifted to a location behind Harper.

Harper turned to look. Rosita had indicated Scarlett's bedroom.

"Ten cuidado, por favor," Rosita said. She made the sign of the cross and whispered, "Pequeno diablo."

Did she tell me to be careful because Scarlett is a little devil?

Harper's phone vibrated. Scarlett had texted her.

Get down here, Harp. Come on!

Rosita scurried away down the corridor, not giving Harper a chance to ask her what she meant by her cryptic comment. Why would she call Scarlett a little devil?

The question lingered as Harper crept down the grand spiral staircase. Scarlett waited for her near the front door.

"I had to use the bathroom," Harper said.

"Whatever. Let's go." Scarlett punched a code into the security system panel near the doorway and opened the front door.

"Where are we going?"

Scarlett dangled a key fob in front of Harper's face like a hypnotist's pendulum.

"We're going for a ride."

~

Dazed, as if she had slipped out of one strange dream and fallen into another, Harper followed Scarlett outside into the humid evening.

"Scar, wait," Harper said. She halted at the bottom of the steps leading to the front door and glanced at the big Mercedes SUV parked in the driveway. "You can't be for real."

"It's your surprise, Harp." Scarlett grinned, her teeth seeming luminescent in the night. "A little nighttime spin for my best friend."

"But you don't have a driver's license or even a permit."

"Are you trying to ruin the surprise? Obviously, I *know* how to drive. Lamont and Gina let me drive all the time."

"Are you serious?"

Instead of answering, Scarlett spun and made a beeline to the SUV. Harper hesitated, unsure what to believe, but she followed her as if she were a pin and Scarlett were the magnet.

Scarlett had climbed into the driver's side. She reached across and popped open the passenger door for Harper. Harper looked around, saw no one watching, and got in.

Scarlett pushed a button, and the engine hummed to life.

"Your mom is really okay with you driving?" Harper asked.

"She's drunk off her ass, Harp. She won't care."

"But your dad—"

"He's in Florida playing golf or whatever."

"Rosita—"

"She's only the help. No one cares what she says."

Scarlett shifted gears and mashed the accelerator. They bolted into Reverse out of the driveway, the sudden motion flinging Harper forward in the seat so suddenly she almost cracked her skull against the dashboard.

Steadying herself, Harper snapped on the seat harness.

"Are you going to put on the seat belt?" Harper asked her friend.

"Boring. But that stupid safety alarm is gonna drive me crazy." Muttering, Scarlett clicked her seat belt into place.

Scarlett shifted into Drive. The SUV surged forward with a roar. Harper braced herself as they zoomed through the neighborhood.

Oh my God, she's driving way too fast, Harper thought. Houses and cars floated past like figments from a sped-up reel in a movie. A cat darted into the road ahead, yellow eyes glowing. Scarlett giggled and increased her speed as if she wanted to mow down the animal.

"Hey!" Harper said.

The cat raced from their path, narrowly avoiding winding up as roadkill.

"I freakin' hate cats," Scarlett said. "That little asshole just spent one of his nine lives."

She's absolutely insane, Harper thought.

Cackling, Scarlett swerved around a corner, taking it so fast it felt as if the SUV would tip over on its side. Harper's stomach did a nauseating somersault.

"Will you slow down, please?" Harper asked.

Scarlett cranked up the volume on the stereo. Thundering bass threatened to rupture Harper's eardrums.

"Look, no hands, Harp!" Scarlett cried above the music. She removed her hands from the steering wheel and raised her iPhone to take video while the SUV rolled down the street.

Harper screamed. Scarlett shrieked with glee.

The SUV slewed to the right, a giant elm tree looming in their path. Scarlett grabbed the steering wheel and wrestled it to the left. They bounced onto the curb. A tree branch skidded across the windshield like a skeletal arm groping for Harper, and she was suddenly convinced this would be the last thing she would ever see in her young life. They were going to smash into this tree at sixty miles an hour, and her life would be over.

Scarlett swung the SUV out of the tree's path, barely avoiding crashing into the massive trunk.

"Oh my God," Harper said. She had been saying the same thing, over and over, in a frenzied prayer. Her chest ached from panting. "Oh my God."

Scarlett stopped the vehicle in the middle of the road and muted the music. She looked at Harper.

"That was intense," Scarlett said.

"I think I peed on myself."

Scarlett giggled. "I wasn't gonna let us die. I had total control the whole time, sis. But it was fun, wasn't it?"

"Can we go back now?"

"First, tell me if you had fun."

"It was terrifying."

"But fun? Right?"

"It was sort of like a roller coaster."

"Next time we go cruising, we'll hit the highway, maybe in Lamont's Porsche. Now *that* will be crazy, sis."

The prospect of a high-speed ride in a sports car on a highway curdled Harper's stomach like a sip of sour juice. Either Scarlett couldn't drive well, or she could, but she took far too many risks for riding anywhere with her to be safe. If she had been a split second slower in turning away from that tree, both of them might be dead right now.

But she could never say such a thing to her friend. Scarlett would never forgive her.

"Can't wait," Harper said.

26

When Adrian picked the girls up on Saturday morning for their outing to Six Flags Over Georgia, they chattered like chickadees.

"Y'all are in a great mood this morning." He glanced at them in the rearview mirror as they hustled into the back seat of his SUV. "What did you guys do last night?"

"We went joyriding in Gina's G Wagon," Scarlett said.

Adrian had been about to back out of the driveway. He tapped the brakes and looked over his shoulder.

Harper wouldn't meet his gaze; she was intent on her phone. But Scarlett looked right back at him.

"Joyriding?" Adrian said. "You're only fourteen, Scarlett. You're too young to have even a learner's permit."

"I'm *kidding*, Mr. Wall. Sheesh." Scarlett grinned. "Now I know where Harp gets it from."

Harper's head snapped up.

"Gets *what* from?" Adrian asked.

"Never mind," Scarlett said, but she wouldn't stop smiling.

"Anyway," he said, "we're going to pick up my niece, and then we'll grab breakfast somewhere before we hit Six Flags. Food in the park is overpriced."

"You're the boss, Mr. Wall," Scarlett said.

Adrian gritted his teeth. That snide tone was coming from her again. How would he endure the next several hours in the company of this child?

Keep your eyes on the prize, Adrian. Think about snagging a full-time spot at FiPro.

His sister-in-law lived in a townhouse in Roswell. Willow, his twelve-year-old niece, and Harper's first cousin, bounced outside when Adrian pulled into their driveway.

Willow approached and opened one of the rear passenger doors. Harper started to scoot over, but much to Adrian's chagrin, Scarlett spoke up.

"There's no room back here for you, little girl," Scarlett said. "Go sit in the front with your uncle."

"Scarlett—" Adrian started.

"We're packed in like sardines back here already," Scarlett said. "Why can't she sit up front with you, Mr. Wall?"

"Fine," Adrian said. "Willow, come sit up front. It's fine."

Willow opened the front passenger door and got in. Twelve years old, Willow was petite and brown-skinned, short for her age. Her dark, curly hair flowed down to her shoulders. She wore a pink T-shirt, shorts, and sneakers.

"Good morning, everyone," Willow said in a hesitant tone.

"Good morning," Adrian said. "I'm glad you could join us. I think you guys will have fun today."

Harper greeted her cousin, but Adrian noticed that Scarlett said nothing. He hoped the entire day wouldn't be like this; if so, he would regret having allowed this child to accompany them.

The children busied themselves on their respective smartphones while he drove to a restaurant for them to grab breakfast. He pulled into the parking lot of a Waffle House.

"You've got to be kidding me," Scarlett said. "Waffle House? This is like gross trucker-fucker food."

Harper and Willow gasped.

"What did you say?" Adrian asked, glaring at Scarlett in the rearview mirror. "Did you just use the f-word, Scarlett?"

"I said gross *trucker* food, Mr. Wall."

"That's not what you said."

"If you know what I said, Mr. Wall, then why are you asking me what I said?"

Willow gawked at both of them, and Harper's mouth had dropped open, too.

Adrian slammed the gears into Park. "We're eating here, kids. Scarlett, if this place offends you, you can eat something when we get to Six Flags. I'm sure you have plenty of money to buy your meal anyway."

"I'll wait in the car, thank you very much." Scarlett smirked. "Watch out for the rats and roaches in there, guys."

This kid is unbelievable.

Adrian was happy to leave her behind.

Adrian, Harper, and Willow found a booth in the corner inside the diner. Willow was typically a shy child, but she voiced the question that had been simmering in Adrian's thoughts.

"How are you friends with that girl, Harp?" Willow asked. "She's so mean."

"She's not mean to me," Harper said, raising her chin in a defensive posture. "She's super nice when we're hanging out."

"I would never talk to an adult like she did to you, Uncle Adrian." Willow's face reddened as if the mere thought embarrassed her.

"Let's not talk about the kid anymore," Adrian said. "Let's check the menu and find something we want to order. I'm starving."

They had ordered beverages—coffee for Adrian, orange juice for the girls—when he looked up and saw Scarlett enter the diner. Inwardly, he groaned.

Scarlett plopped onto the seat on Adrian's side of the booth.

"I thought this low-class establishment was beneath you?" Adrian asked.

"Someone has to be here to call 911 after you guys gag on the food," Scarlett said. "I say that respectfully, Mr. Wall."

Adrian shook his head, but Harper giggled while Willow looked stunned at the exchange.

"Can I see a menu?" Scarlett asked.

"Why do you want to see a menu?" Adrian asked. "If you want to see it so you can criticize every item on it and tell us how disgusting it must be, then *no*, you can't see a one, kid."

Harper passed Scarlett her menu. Adrian frowned at his daughter. Whose side was she on, anyway?

But Scarlett said nothing, only perusing the laminated menu card. When the server arrived at their booth to take their orders, she surprised Adrian by requesting three scrambled eggs, a stack of waffles, hash browns covered with cheese, a side of bacon, a side of sausage, a bowl of grits, toast with butter and jelly, a cup of coffee, and a large orange juice.

"You're going to eat *all* of that?" Adrian asked.

But Scarlett only smiled thinly and busied herself with her phone. Harper's phone chimed, and Adrian realized the girls were texting each other at the table, ignoring him and Willow.

"How is school going, Willow?" Adrian asked his niece.

"You're in kindergarten, right?" Scarlett asked Willow.

Harper giggled.

"I'm in seventh grade!" Willow said. "I'm twelve."

"Sorry, you're so tiny. I thought you were only five or something," Scarlett said.

Harper snickered. Adrian scowled.

"Scarlett," Adrian said. "Please, don't be mean."

"I wasn't trying to be mean, Mr. Wall. She's small, like Oompa

Loompa tiny. Are you tall enough to ride the roller coasters at Six Flags, Willow, or will you stay on the kiddie rides?"

"I can ride a roller coaster!" Willow said. She looked at Adrian. "Uncle Adrian, tell her I can ride the roller coasters!"

"Look, our food is here," Adrian said, relieved to break up the exchange. "Let's eat up and get out of here, okay? Phones down, forks up, kids."

Harper and Willow complied with his request as the server set plates full of hot food on their tables, but Scarlett continued using her phone. The dishes before her offered barely an inch of free space on the table.

Adrian dug into his hash brown bowl, and his niece and daughter began eating. Scarlett ignored her food.

"Are you going to eat?" Adrian asked her.

"Everything looks gross," Scarlett said. "I had to see it for myself."

He set his fork down. "You sat here and ordered all that food, but you're not going to eat any of it?"

She grimaced. "Nah. I'll pass."

A pulse in his temple throbbed. He massaged his sweat-filmed forehead.

Count to ten, man. Don't let this kid rattle you.

"I can reimburse you for my meal if it's a problem, Mr. Wall," Scarlett said. "What's your Cash App name?"

"Don't worry about it," he said. "I've got it."

"Of course, because Lamont—my father—gave you a job because of me. You've got money coming in again. My apologies, Mr. Wall."

He decided to ignore her. He shoveled food into his mouth, and on impulse, he picked up the bacon and sausage sides Scarlett had ordered and shifted those to his side of the table.

"I'm not allowing all of this food to be wasted," he said, scraping some of the grits she had requested into his own bowl.

"You make yourself eat it only because it's there?" Scarlett asked. "That's a fast path to obesity, Mr. Wall."

"Not everyone in this world has the luxury of throwing away food, kid."

"Clearly." Her lips curled as he resumed eating. She muttered: "Like pigs at a trough."

"If you aren't going to eat anything, you can wait outside in the car," he said. "We won't miss your attention-seeking behavior."

"Attention-seeking behavior? Whoa, are you my therapist now, Mr. Wall?"

Responding to her, getting further caught up in this back-and-forth, would be pointless. He drank his coffee, chewed a slice of bacon, and forked hash browns into his mouth, his cheeks bulging. He wanted to finish his meal, get to the theme park, and escape this child's presence.

"Was something wrong with the food?" the server asked when she stopped by their table. She peered at the mostly full plates gathered in front of Scarlett.

"I found snot in the eggs and rat hairs in the hash browns, ma'am," Scarlett said. "I was afraid to eat."

Adrian could have covered his face with his hands. The server's eyes swelled as large as one of the plates on the table.

"Did you, really?" the woman asked.

"She's only joking," Adrian said. "The food is fine, ma'am. The kid's eyes were larger than her stomach, that's all. Can you give me the check, please?"

Adrian promptly paid the bill and ushered the children out of the diner.

Outside in the parking lot, Adrian asked Harper and Willow to get inside the SUV but requested Scarlett to remain outside the vehicle with him.

"Before we go any further," he said, "I need to know you'll

behave yourself. This disruptive behavior must stop if you're going to hang out with us today."

"I'm sorry, Mr. Wall. I don't understand what I did wrong. What did I do that was disruptive?"

He ticked off each point with his fingers. "Criticizing my choice of restaurant. Being mean to Willow. Your snarky remarks about the food in there. Not eating anything after ordering enough for two people. Lying to the server about finding crap in your meal."

"I was only kidding with most of my comments, Mr. Wall, and I'm not hungry right now. I had avocado toast at home for breakfast, sir. I thought I might want to eat something, but my eyes were bigger than my stomach like you said."

Adrian pinched his nose. The headache gathering strength in the diner had expanded into a full-blown migraine.

"Can I get in the car now, please, Mr. Wall?" she asked. "I'm super excited to go to Six Flags. I told Lamont you guys invited me, and he's excited, too."

Scarlett showed him her phone. He skimmed the text message conversation between her and her father; Lamont had responded with a thumbs-up emoji to the news that Scarlett was accompanying them to the theme park.

This kid set me up again.

"Go on and get in," Adrian said. "But remember what I said. Behave."

"Yes, sir!" Scarlett saluted him and, with a smug grin, climbed into the car.

27

They arrived at Six Flags Over Georgia shortly after the park opened at eleven. It was a gorgeous day: cloudless and sunny, with temperatures in the low eighties and a cool breeze to temper the fierce Georgia humidity.

Adrian's simple goal for their visit was to ensure that all the children—including Scarlett—had fun and stayed out of trouble.

Despite Scarlett's behavior thus far, Adrian still believed the teenager was harmless. She thrived on attention; she made remarks designed to trigger shocked gasps and expressions of disbelief, but it was all empty chatter. As he continued to tell himself, she was just a kid. A brainy and smart-mouthed kid, but only a child, all the same.

"Let's take a group picture," he said after they passed through the park's entrance.

He found an employee willing to snap the photo. The four of them posed in front of a big, colorful sign that announced: *Six Flags —Thrill Capital of the South.*

The employee handed back his phone, and he reviewed the picture. Scarlett had poked two fingers behind Willow's head, giving his niece a pair of bunny ears. The kid couldn't resist an opportunity to mock someone.

He opened his text messaging app and sent the photo to Lamont with the comment: *chaperoning kids here makes working at FiPro feel like a vacation.* He closed with a smiley-face emoji.

Was it brown-nosing on his part? Maybe, but if he didn't toot his own horn, who would?

In seconds, Lamont responded with a thumbs-up emoji. *Score.* Adrian smiled to himself.

"What do you all want to do first, kids?" he asked the girls.

"Please tell me you aren't going to follow us around here *everywhere*, Mr. Wall," Scarlett said. "No offense, sir, but you'll embarrass me. I'm fourteen years old, not four, like Willow."

"I'm twelve!" Willow said. "How many times do I have to tell you that?"

"Hey, I like rides, too," Adrian said. "I love roller coasters. I'm a thrill junkie."

"Daddy, please," Harper said with an eye roll. "Can we meet you somewhere later?"

He looked from Scarlett, to Harper, to Willow. They shifted on their feet, eager to be set free.

"What will I do all by myself?" he asked.

"There's plenty of stuff here for old people," Scarlett said.

"I'm not *that* old, kid." He studied their faces again. "Can I trust you all to stay out of trouble?"

"Yes," they answered in unison.

"All right, we'll meet in three hours to touch base," he said. "I'll text you, Harp. And text me if you need anything at all, okay?"

"Aye, aye, sir." Scarlett gave him a mock solute.

He watched the children scatter away from him like leaves in the wind.

I hope I don't regret this later.

Scarlett mostly communicated with Harper via text since they had picked up Willow that morning. It surprised Harper at first, but considering what Scar started saying about her cousin, she was glad that Scar limited her comments to text and didn't say them aloud.

Are you sure this little girl is really your cousin? She's a freak.

Knowing Scar as well as she did, she sent the text not because she was afraid to say these things aloud—Scar wasn't scared to say anything out loud to anyone—but because she wanted to make Willow *wonder* what they were talking about. It was a way to shut her out.

Harper knew in her heart that it was a mean thing to do, but she went along with it. It was hard to avoid going along with anything Scar wanted—being with her was like sprinting down a steep hill at top speed, powerful momentum carrying you forward, with down the only direction you could go.

Pequeno diablo . . .

"I have only two flash passes, guys," Scarlett said as they strolled the blacktopped promenade. She looked down at Willow. "And I'm giving one to my sis, Harp. Sorry, little girl. You'll be waiting in line with the rest of the peasants."

"I have a flash pass, too," Willow said.

"Mines are the platinum ones," Scarlett said. "You probably have just the plain one."

"Mine is platinum, too." Willow raised her phone and showed it to both Scarlett and Harper.

Scarlett's mouth puckered in a scowl. Harper was secretly proud of her cousin right then. Sometimes, she was tired of her friend flaunting her privilege in front of everyone, and it was refreshing to see Willow match her.

"Whatever," Scarlett said. "You're too small to ride the adult coasters anyway."

"I've been on every ride here," Willow said. "Why do you think I have a flash pass, dummy? Right, Harp?" Her cousin looked to her for support.

Harper was about to say something but noticed Scarlett's face twisted when Willow mentioned the word "dummy."

"You little bitch," Scarlett said. "You're only twelve, and you don't know shit."

"You're the only one being a bitch," Willow said.

Oh my God, Harper thought. She knew her cousin had a temper and was often quiet but could "come out her bag," as her mom liked to say, whenever someone pushed her buttons. But she wished she wasn't behaving like this around Scarlett. Scarlett was terrifying when she got angry.

"Hey, why don't we stop arguing and find something to do, guys?" Harper said, trying to play peacekeeper. "We're here to have fun."

Scarlett said nothing but took off ahead of them, taking long strides. Harper had to jog to catch up with her while Willow trailed behind.

Bypassing Scarlett, Harper led them to one of the more miniature roller coasters she had been on before, the Dahlonega Mine Train. The coaster didn't have any loops—it was a kiddie ride, as far as Harper was concerned—but she wanted them to get on something and stop bickering with each other.

Since the park had just opened, they didn't need their flash passes. They went through the regular line and had to wait only about five minutes before the operator invited them to board.

Scarlett had been quiet as they waited, uncharacteristically so, which worried Harper. Then, right before the gate sprang up so they could get on the mine train, Scarlett texted Harper.

I could kill this pint-sized bitch, Harp.

Harper's heart clutched as if squeezed in an iron vice. She thought about herself floundering in the swimming pool at Scarlett's house a couple of weeks ago, convinced she was going to drown and Scarlett would let it happen. Why did that memory flash through her mind just then? She wasn't sure.

They boarded the roller coaster, Harper sitting with Scarlett. Willow rode by herself in the car behind them.

As the ride started up, Scarlett leaned over and whispered to Harper.

"As soon as we can, we're cutting the little bitch loose, sis."

Adrian wandered aimlessly around the park, spending money on worthless amusements, wishing he could have convinced Steph to join them. But his wife didn't like all the walking in the sun and wasn't a fan of large crowds and roller coasters. He would have happily spent time with her in the shade of an overpriced café if it meant he wouldn't be abandoned to entertain himself.

After perhaps an hour, he received a text message. It was from his niece.

Uncle Adrian, they left me!

When the message arrived, he sat under an umbrella, sipping an overpriced club soda. He frowned.

What do you mean, they left you?

We got on a ride, but they got off before I did, or they didn't even get on it. I don't know where they are. I texted Harper, but she didn't write back.

"Shit," Adrian said to himself, setting down his beverage. *Here we go.* He was willing to bet his last paycheck that Scarlett had engineered this incident. She made no effort to disguise her disdain for Willow.

Where are you now? he typed to Willow.

By the Riverview Carousel.

Adrian checked the park map on his phone. He was nowhere near the carousel ride but texted back: *Wait there for me.*

Okay.

As he walked toward the ride, he sent another message, this time to his daughter, his fingers trembling.

Harp, where are you? Willow says you and Scarlett left her.

He expected an immediate reply but received no response. Could she be in the middle of a ride, unable to access her phone, or was she ignoring him?

Or was something wrong?

His heart rate kicked up a few notches. He rushed through the crowd, brushing aside those in his path, cutting through the slow-moving knots of visitors, getting more annoyed and anxious with every yard he traveled. Upon rechecking his phone a few minutes later and still finding no reply from his daughter, he tried to call her.

The call went immediately to voice mail.

Dammit, Harp. What's the matter with you?

He remembered he had the FindMyPhone app installed on Harper's iPhone. He opened it.

His daughter was still at Six Flags but on the western side of the amusement park. He breathed a brief sigh of relief.

A few minutes later, he found Willow. She waited in the shade cast by a refreshments stand umbrella, her brown face flushed red.

"Uncle Adrian!" she said. She rushed toward him, and whatever tears she held back started flowing freely.

This is my damn fault, Adrian thought. *I shouldn't have invited Scarlett to come with us.*

"I'm sorry they left you," he said. "We'll find them and put a stop to this."

"Scarlett hates me! Why is she so mean?"

"I'll talk to them about this behavior, don't worry. I've got some idea of where they are. Come on."

They strode across the park. Part of him thought of suggesting to Willow that they forget about the other two girls and find something else to do on their own. He wasn't in the mood for another confrontation with Scarlett.

Are you scared of her? Afraid of what she might say to Lamont?

But he wouldn't allow this child to dictate their outing like she was trying to do. Harper was going along with this nasty behavior and needed to be chewed out, too. He and Steph hadn't raised her to be the kind of child who ditched her own cousin in favor of a bullying friend.

He spotted Scarlett ahead first—the girl stood out in a crowd, no matter the venue. She and Harper appeared to be leaving a ride called Pandemonium, a giant, pendulum-like swing that tested the stomach of every thrill-seeker who dared to board it. The two girls were looking at their phones, chatting away.

"Harper!" Adrian shouted.

Harper swiveled in his direction, and he could see her mouth form the words "Oh shit."

As Harper had anticipated, her father was furious.

"You *know* better than to leave your cousin," he said. "Why would you do something like that?"

Although her dad wore sunglasses, she could feel his withering gaze. She wanted to shrink to the size of an ant, crawl away, and hide somewhere. Her father rarely got angry with her; whenever he did, she felt like she had failed him.

"I'm sorry," she said because she didn't know what else she could say to placate him. Then she said, "We were going to look for her."

It was something Scarlett might have said. Harper realized that her friend's habits had begun to influence her. Was that a bad thing? It seemed like Scarlett did whatever she wanted and never got into real trouble.

"You were going to look for her?" Her father laughed scornfully. "When were you going to look for her? After you rode every coaster in the park first?"

"It's my fault, Mr. Wall," Scarlett said, suddenly alongside them. "I was behaving selfishly, and I apologize. I wanted Harp and I to hang out on our own. Please don't blame her. I accept full responsibility."

Harper could have hugged Scarlett at that moment. She was such a good friend, stepping forward to take the blame. None of Harper's other friends had ever done such things for her.

"You take responsibility, huh?" Her dad took off his sunglasses and pinched the bridge of his nose, something he always did when he was ready to move on from something. "You guys need to apologize to Willow, not me."

It was painful for Harper to meet her cousin's hurt expression, but Harper said, "I'm sorry, Willow. Will you please forgive me?"

"Okay," Willow said.

All of them shifted to Scarlett.

"Friends?" Scarlett stuck out her hand to Willow.

"Friends." Willow accepted the handshake.

"Why don't we hang out together now, guys?" Scarlett asked. "We can get on that next."

She pointed to a coaster on the park's eastern perimeter that rose like a giant dinosaur skeleton against the clear blue sky.

"The Georgia Twister?" her dad said. "Wow, I love that one. I haven't ridden it in years. Let's do it."

"And to show how sorry I am, Willow, you can ride it with *me*," Scarlett said.

"All right," Willow said, bobbing her head.

Scarlett winked at Harper, and for some reason, that gave Harper a bad feeling in the pit of her stomach, an awful sensation. But she wasn't going to say anything because she and Scar were best friends, like sisters, and sisters always had each other's best interests at heart, didn't they?

Adrian had purchased a flash pass for himself for their visit, but he hadn't found an opportunity to use it until Scarlett suggested they ride the Georgia Twister as a group.

Scarlett's willingness to apologize and make amends shocked

him. He wasn't surprised when the teenager displayed cruel, selfish behavior—he should have anticipated that she would convince Harper to ditch Willow, as that seemed typical for her to do—but a gesture of genuine goodwill took him by surprise.

"You've got potential, kid," he said to Scarlett as they entered the flash pass lane for the ride. "Good call on us riding this together."

Scarlett beamed at him. "Will you tell Lamont I was a good girl today, Mr. Wall?"

"There you go again with the sarcasm," he said, but he chuckled.

She's not so bad once you figure her out, he thought. *I can see why Harp loves spending time with her. She's got a lot of personality, that's for sure.*

He watched the girls as they chatted and laughed ahead of him. Earlier, he had experienced misgivings about inviting Scarlett, but he realized then that having her there benefited him. He had no doubt that the girl would gush about this day to her father, and that would add more points to Adrian's scorecard with Lamont. *Nurture their friendship, brother.*

I'm nurturing it all day long, he thought.

A train whooshed onto the loading platform, and the riders disembarked. Adrian and the girls were next in line to board.

"We're up, kids," Adrian said.

The gate lifted. Scarlett sprinted to the first car, Willow following. The train comprised six cars, and each car held four passengers: two in the front row and two in the rear.

"Come on, Willow," Scarlett said, inviting the girl to the front row.

Adrian and Harper settled into the row behind the two kids. A single lap bar paired with individual seat belts secured riders in their seats. After tucking his sunglasses into his pocket, Adrian snapped his belt in place. When Harper was ready, he pulled down the lap bar, ratcheting it to give his knees a little room but not so much it would put Harper at risk.

Bad Influence

"I'm ready to roll!" Adrian clapped his hands. He grinned at Harper, and his child grinned back at him.

"Are you girls all right up there?" he asked Scarlett and Willow.

Willow twisted around and gave him the thumbs-up.

The ride operator raced by to secure their lap bars and seat belts. Scarlett said something to the operator—he was a pimply-faced teenager with a peach fuzz mustache—and the boy blushed.

Never a dull moment with this kid, Adrian thought.

Once the operator had checked all the passengers, the train jerked forward. Butterflies fluttered in Adrian's stomach.

"And we're off!" he said.

Thirty seconds later, Willow screamed.

Willow wasn't sure she would ever *like* Harper's new friend, Scarlett. Still, after the girl apologized to her and suggested they ride the roller coaster together, she was willing to give her a chance.

They climbed into the first car together, at the front of the train, a spot that Willow found scary but also exciting, even though she had ridden the Georgia Twister a hundred times before.

"I'm going to say something super flirty to that guy," Scarlett whispered to Willow. She cut her gaze at the ride operator, a teenager. "Do you dare me?"

"I dare you," Willow said.

Willow buckled her seat belt and went to pull down the lap bar, but Scarlett said, *Hey, that's too tight*, so they left some wriggle room in it. Besides, Willow was wearing the seat belt and had been on this coaster a million times.

"Here he comes," Scarlett said, nudging Willow's ribs with her elbow. "Watch."

As the operator swung by their car and started to reach for the lap bar, Scarlett said: "Can I suck you off when the ride's over, baby?"

Willow gasped. The teenage boy's face got red as a chili pepper, and he hurried past without checking their belts or the safety bar.

Scarlett cackled. "I told you!"

"You're crazy!" Willow said, shaking her head. It was no wonder Harper liked spending time with this girl—she was a lunatic.

The train jolted forward. Although the recorded safety message warned passengers to put away their phones in a storage locker, Scarlett had slipped hers out of her shorts.

"You're not supposed to have your phone," Willow said.

The train inched upward along the first incline at a steep angle.

"We're taking a pic together at the top of the hill," Scarlett said.

"But you might lose it; someone could get hurt—"

"I've done this before. Relax."

Who was she to tell her what to do? The girl was fourteen, two years older than Willow. If she wanted to take the chance of losing her iPhone, that was her problem. Harper said Scarlett was rich, so maybe she didn't care anyway; if she lost the phone, she would just get another one.

The train neared the top of the incline. Willow knew precisely how this ride would go: they would reach the top of the hill and plunge down suddenly in a drop guaranteed to make your heart pop into your throat, and then the upside-down twists, those inversions, would start, and it was going to feel crazy exciting.

The train crawled to the peak of the hill. Willow held her breath.

"Here we go, girl, hands up!" Scarlett cried. She leaned into Willow, one slender arm in front of her, phone in her hand to snap the top-of-the-hill selfie.

Willow raised her arms in the air and grinned for the pic.

She felt Scarlett's other hand on her belt buckle as she did. Her seat belt popped open.

Oh, no...

The train plummeted.

Willow screamed.

Hearing screams on roller coasters was so common, the sounds might have been part of a background soundtrack, like canned laughter on an old TV sitcom.

But to Adrian, Willow's cry was a bloodcurdling scream of pure terror, not delight.

The train plunged down the first precipitous drop, suspending them in a heart-stopping moment of weightlessness. Adrian strained to see what was happening in the row ahead, praying he was wrong, and that Willow was just screaming with excitement.

But as they crashed to the bottom of the hill and rocketed skyward again, he saw Willow hanging sideways out of the car, her arms flapping violently like flags in a gale.

Oh, Jesus. She's falling out.

Beside him, Harper unleashed a bone-chilling scream.

Adrian lunged forward, thinking he could snatch his niece and somehow get her secured, but the lap bar and seat belt pinned him in place.

The train corkscrewed through an inversion, bashing Adrian's head against the seat with a sickening crack.

Willow's hair lashed wildly in the wind as her arms continued to flail, half her torso dangling out of the car precariously.

She's gonna fall out—oh God, no...

The train blasted out of the inversion, hitting a straight stretch of track . . . and ground to an abrupt halt with a piercing screech of brakes.

Sirens sliced through the sudden stillness.

Willow hung halfway in and out of the car, suspended thirty feet above the unforgiving ground.

Adrian was paralyzed in disbelief but heard himself frantically alternating between praying and pleading for Willow to hang on.

"Help is coming, baby, just hang on. Oh God, please."

Behind them, other passengers' cries, prayers, and desperate pleas rose in a chorus of anguish.

He strained to see Scarlett, terrified of what he might find. One glimpse of her made his blood run as icy as an Alaskan river in the dead of winter.

She was laughing.

28

Adrian met his sister-in-law, Kellie, at the hospital in Austell, the medical center closest to the amusement park. He had been on the phone repeatedly with her after the incident at Six Flags. When she arrived, she rushed immediately to see her daughter in the room on the emergency wing.

Willow had been fortunate; she had suffered only a dislocated shoulder and no other injuries. Park officials safely removed her from the train before she would have plummeted to a certain death, and paramedics rushed her via ambulance to the hospital.

The entire park had been shuttered, and investigators and support staff flooded the scene. "Ride malfunction" was the reason Adrian had heard given for the accident.

He wanted to believe that was the answer. But in his memory, he kept seeing Scarlett laughing, doing nothing to assist Willow, laughing and wiping tears from her eyes, as though she had pulled off a wonderfully humorous prank and was so pleased with her cleverness that she couldn't contain herself.

Was he reading too much into what he had seen? Some people laughed by reflex from anxiety or nervousness. Had Scarlett been so stunned by the terrifying spectacle of Willow flailing that she had been shocked, overcome with nervous giggles and tears?

The park authorities had questioned Scarlett, but only briefly. They appeared more worried about whether she had sustained any injuries, which she had not.

In the commotion that followed the incident, Adrian didn't get to question Scarlett about what had happened.

"I'm going home, guys. I feel sick," she'd said. "Wild day, huh?"

"Don't you want to go to the hospital with us?" Adrian asked.

"I hate hospitals. I'm getting an Uber and going home. Later, Mr. Wall." Scarlett hugged Harper and whispered something to her, a remark that widened Harper's eyes as big as ostrich eggs. Scarlett slipped away like a shadow into the departing crowd.

"What did she say to you?" Adrian asked Harper.

"Nothing." Harper wiped the back of her hand across her face and sniffled.

Adrian let it go. Seeing her cousin nearly die had rattled her, and it had shaken him, too.

As they had driven to the hospital, he noticed Harper texting furiously.

"Who are you talking to?" he'd asked.

"Scar."

"Is she okay?"

"Yeah."

He hesitated. "I saw her laughing."

"Laughing?" Harper's brows knitted, but something shifted in her gaze like a critter racing out of the light to hide in the darkness.

"When Willow was screaming and about to fall, Scarlett was laughing. I *saw* her in that little gap between the seats. She wasn't helping your cousin and was laughing so hard she was crying."

"I guess she was scared, Daddy."

"What did she whisper to you before she left?"

"*Nothing.*"

"Don't tell me she said nothing when she obviously said something. Come on. I'm not an idiot."

"She said she was sorry the day was ruined or something like that. I don't remember, really. My head's all messed up."

"That's all she said? Sorry, the day is ruined now?"

"I have a bad headache, Daddy. Do you have some medicine I can take?"

He looked at her, convinced she was keeping something from him, but whatever it was, she had locked it inside.

"We'll ask for some medicine at the hospital," he said.

You never should have invited your cousin, sis. I didn't want her there. She's lucky she didn't die, huh?

Scarlett had whispered those words to Harper at Six Flags, but Harper would never share that information with her father or anyone else.

Because they might try to blame Scarlett for the accident—

—was it really an accident?—

—and Harper couldn't bear the thought of her best friend getting blamed for such a terrible thing. Daddy could ask her until he was blue in the face, as her grandma liked to say, but she wouldn't share details of her discussions with Scarlett with anyone.

We're sisters, remember? Scarlett typed to Harper via text when Harper and her father traveled to the hospital to see Willow. *No matter what, we'll always be sisters, Harp.*

Daddy says he saw you laughing, Harper wrote.

I wasn't laughing. I was crying. There's a big difference.

Okay, Harper responded.

She had an awful headache. She believed it came from the stress of everything that had happened today.

When they finally got to the hospital, she wanted to get some medicine, find somewhere to lie down, curl up into a ball, shut her eyes, and not wake up until this nightmare ended. But they had to check on her cousin first.

Thank God, Willow was okay, with only an injured shoulder.

Tell me everything they say at the hospital, Scarlett had commanded Harper via one of those text messages. *I need to know if anyone is lying about me.*

Okay, Harper wrote.

We'll always be sisters, Scarlett wrote. *Sisters protect each other.*

"Scarlett undid my seat belt," Willow said.

Adrian, Kellie, and Harper were in the room with Willow when the child uttered the words. Willow lay on the bed swaddled in sheets, her right arm secured in a sling, and her brown eyes half-open. Earlier, a nurse had administered an injection to help blunt the pain, and the medicine likely had sedating effects, too.

But Willow's revelation yanked Adrian out of his chair. Lying on a sofa near the window, Harper snapped to alertness, too.

"Who did what?" Kellie asked. She hunched over the bed, hand resting on her child's head. "Say it again, baby."

"The mean girl . . . Scarlett." Trembling, Willow drew in a long breath and paused as though speaking demanded extreme effort. "On the ride, when she took a picture of us, she undid my seat belt."

"Who the hell is Scarlett?" Kellie ratcheted in Adrian's direction, her face clenched like a fist ready to strike.

"Scarlett is Harper's friend." Adrian approached the bed. "Willow, you're sure about this? Scarlett put her hand on your seat belt and pressed the button to unlatch it?"

Willow scrunched up her face. "I think so."

"That's a serious accusation," he said. "You need to be sure."

"Uh-huh." Glistening tears streamed down Willow's cheeks. "I don't . . . I don't know!"

"Hush now, baby." Kellie stroked Willow's hair. "We'll get to this later. You need to rest."

"Okay, Mommy." Willow closed her eyes and pushed out a breath.

Adrian noticed Harper on her phone again, fingers in a blur. He suspected she was texting Scarlett. His emotions wrenched his stomach into a knot.

"Can we talk?" Kellie asked him. "In private?"

Adrian noted that Harper watched them as they exited the room. Kellie pulled the door shut behind them.

"We need to go to the police," Kellie said in a hushed tone. "If what Willow said is true . . . this girl, this Scarlett, is guilty of *attempted murder*."

Adrian massaged his sweat-streaked forehead as if to quell the storm brewing in his thoughts. Scarlett was a brat—there was no doubt about that. But this was something else entirely. Deliberately unlatching someone's seat belt on a roller coaster was not attention-seeking behavior; it was malicious, criminal behavior, and Scarlett would be charged with a felony.

"Willow didn't seem too sure," he said.

"They have cameras all over the park, Adrian. The cops should be able to see what happened on that damn ride."

"Scarlett is a handful, I will admit. But accusing her of trying to kill Willow? I don't know, Kellie."

"Why are you hedging?"

"Scarlett is the daughter of the CEO of the company I work for."

"Oh, I get it," Kellie said, her gaze darkening. "You're worried about your job." She let out a hollow laugh. "This is bigger than you and your job. We're talking about my baby's life."

"If we bring an accusation like this, we need to be sure, damn sure, one hundred percent sure. We need proof."

"We'll get it, then. I'm gonna tell the people at the park to pull the tape. Whatever this kid did to my daughter, I want her held accountable for it—and I don't give a damn *whose* daughter she is."

Glowering at him, Kellie spun and marched back into the room to be with her child.

Instead of joining them, Adrian wandered the hospital corridors until he found a restroom. He stood at the sink and switched on the tap to let cold water trickle into his hands. He splashed the wetness across his face, washing away the grime that filmed his skin.

He wished he could also wash away his memory of what he'd seen on the roller coaster.

Was Scarlett really a killer? Or had Willow's seat belt malfunctioned?

His phone chimed. It was Gina.

Damage control, he thought, and wondered where the idea came from. Instinct? But he knew: *She knows what happened, and she's gonna try to handle me.*

He let the call go to voice mail.

29

Steph drove to Barnes Investigations late that Monday morning, arriving there shortly before eleven o'clock.

A few days ago, when she discussed the matter with Adrian, he tried to persuade her against following her instinct. But look what happened on Saturday—Willow, injured in a bizarre roller coaster "ride malfunction" at Six Flags, the poor girl confiding that she believed Scarlett undid her seat belt.

Steph believed: *where there's smoke, there's fire*. Had Scarlett deliberately tried to harm Willow? Was there another incident in the child's or her family's past? Why was a private detective tracking Gina's movement? He surely wasn't engaged in these activities out of boredom.

She intended to get answers. She hadn't bothered to call the agency before her visit, worried she wouldn't get any traction with a phone call. An in-person visit was the only way for her to guarantee that someone would talk to her.

She switched off the car's engine. She had parked directly in front of the agency's storefront in the strip mall, but tinted windows prevented her from seeing inside.

But she had parked next to the Honda with the damaged rear windshield. The investigator was there.

You don't know what you're doing, girl. Why don't you go back to work?

But her curiosity, her craving for the truth, was downright insatiable. She had known, from the start, that Scarlett was trouble. Now, she needed to validate her worries.

She climbed out of the car and went inside.

Inside, she expected to find a reception area, perhaps with a receptionist, but the interior of Barnes Investigations was a barebones affair: a brightly lit, mid-sized space with a single, large desk flanked by two wingback chairs, an open laptop sitting on the desk surface; a small stand bearing a printer; a couple of bookcases full of titles related to crime and technology. The walls were painted eggshell white, with gray carpeting. A potted fern thrived in a pot in the corner.

Near the door, a Keurig coffee maker with a stand full of coffee pods stood on a small table. Various framed documents hung on the walls amid a handful of photos. One of the photos showed the agency's owner, Raymond Barnes, wearing a black suit and posing next to former president Obama.

Former Secret Service? Steph felt a cramp in her stomach. Suddenly, her whimsical adventure felt much too real, the consequences too great, and she turned—the office was vacant, anyway—thinking she would return to her car and mull over this a bit longer.

"Leaving already?" a man's baritone voice said from deeper into the office.

Raymond Barnes emerged from the shadowed hallway beyond the central area. He looked exactly like he did in his photograph on his website: he was a dark-skinned Black man, perhaps in his late fifties, who bore a notable resemblance to the late actor Richard

Roundtree. Barnes wore a black polo shirt that displayed well-muscled arms, black jeans, and cowboy boots. He had a neat Afro flecked with gray, his salt-and-pepper goatee so finely trimmed it looked as if it had been etched on his face with a mechanical pencil.

"Oh, hi," she said, her rehearsed introduction escaping her thoughts.

Barnes smiled. "Won't you have a seat, Mrs. Stephanie Wall?"

She stared at him. "How do you know my name?"

"I wouldn't be worth a damn as a private investigator if I didn't know your name by now, ma'am." He gestured to the wingback chairs. "Please, have a seat."

Blood pounding in her ears, she shuffled to one of the seats and lowered onto the cushion. She clutched her purse like a shield.

Barnes sat behind his desk, propped his boots on the surface, and tilted backward.

"You knew I followed you," she blurted.

"Again, I wouldn't be worth much in this field if I couldn't spot a tail, ma'am."

Focus, Steph. Get back on your game.

She pushed out a breath and relaxed her hands in her lap.

"You've been following Gina Washington," she said. "I saw you at their house a couple of weeks ago when she threw the glass at your car. I saw you again at the condo in Buckhead."

"Very good, so far," he said, nodding. "But you're missing another angle."

"I don't know what you mean."

He took his boots off the desk and leaned forward in his chair, his gaze intense.

"How do you know, Mrs. Wall, that I haven't been following *you*, too?"

Steph felt as if someone had tossed cold water in her face.

"Following me?" she asked. "You're kidding."

Barnes didn't smile. "You. And your husband, Adrian Wall."

"But why?"

Barnes shifted in his desk chair to an oak file cabinet behind him. He pulled out a manila folder bulging with documents, set it on the desk, opened it, and slowly paged through it.

Steph tilted forward, trying to see what those pages were about.

"Is there any chance," Barnes said, "that you can contact Mr. Wall and ask him to leave the FiPro office to meet with us here? I realize it's short notice." Barnes chuckled. "But you've forced my hand a bit, ma'am, and I'd rather not rehash this case separately with your husband."

"Can you tell me what this is about first?" she asked. "I haven't done anything wrong, and neither has Adrian."

Barnes pursed his lips. "I suppose I can give you the CliffsNotes." He nodded toward the coffee station in the corner. "Want to grab a beverage first? You may need it."

"Just tell me. Please."

Barnes began to speak.

Steph listened.

Twenty minutes later, she called Adrian.

30

Adrian was deeply immersed in reviewing a quarterly financial report when an unexpected person pinged him on the company's instant messaging platform.

Maya Gaines: *Hi, Adrian. I'm Mr. Washington's admin. Can you please come to his office on the tenth floor for a quick chat?*

He remembered Maya; she had helped him on the day of his return to employment at FiPro. His heart rate suddenly felt as if it had doubled.

Lamont wanted to talk to him. Why?

He hadn't spoken directly to Lamont or Gina since the prior Friday—since before the incident at Six Flags. Gina had tried calling him three times, had texted him, and said, *We need to talk, call me,* but Adrian had avoided her.

The truth: he didn't trust the woman. He suspected she was going to try to spin this situation between Scarlett and Willow, and he didn't want to hear it; he didn't want to be finessed, handled, or gaslighted. It was impossible to avoid her forever, he realized, but he had never been comfortable dealing with conflict. He would rather tuck his head down and hope the issue went away on its own.

He could hear what Gina would say to him in his thoughts: *Scarlett would never try to harm anyone, honey. That little niece of yours must've imagined the whole thing. I'm so relieved the child is okay, aren't you?*

But his sister-in-law, Kellie, was not accepting pat answers. She had promised to retain a lawyer to dig into the matter with the amusement park, and Adrian knew her well. She didn't voice empty threats.

Why was Lamont reaching out to him now? Was it another attempt to finesse him? He didn't dare ignore the summons, not with his job potentially hanging in the balance.

If only I had stuck to my original plan and not brought Scarlett along...

But it was too late for those second thoughts. He had to face the fallout from his flawed decision.

I'll be right there, he responded to Maya.

Take a right when you leave the elevator on ten. I'll buzz you through.

Adrian pushed away from the desk. Before he headed to the elevator, he went to the men's room because he had a sudden urge to vomit. He stood over the toilet bowl, stomach churning, but nothing happened. Soon, the nausea passed.

As he entered the vestibule on the ninth floor that housed the bank of elevators, Trevor entered the area from the glass doors on the opposite side of the space. He approached the elevator button panel, too.

"Yo, bruh," Trevor said, pushing up his spectacles on his nose. "What's going on, man? You look sick."

He hadn't shared anything about what was going on with his friend, and he had no intention of getting into the matter now.

"Been busy grinding is all," Adrian said.

"What're you doing for lunch later on? There's a new Korean barbecue across the way we should check out. Yelp reviews are off the charts."

"I'll let you know."

Trevor's smile faltered. "Are you sure you're all right?"

"I'm good."

Trevor pressed the Down button on the panel; Adrian pressed the Up button.

"You're riding up to the baller suite?" Trevor's lips parted with surprise. "Going to see your homeboy, huh? Can I come with you? I was gonna hit the lobby to get a snack, but maybe you can introduce me to Mr. CEO." He chuckled.

If only you knew, Trevor.

"It's not a good time, man. Sorry."

"For real, you gotta connect me with old boy at some point. I've worked here damn near ten years, and I ain't never met the man. You've been here for six months, and you're hanging out at his crib, kicking back, sipping Hennessy, and puffing on Montecristos."

The elevator chimed, going up.

"Later, I promise," Adrian said as he entered the car.

"I'm gonna hold you to that."

He stepped out of the elevator on the tenth floor and faced the vestibule doors. A badge was required for entry, and his badge flashed red from the door scanner. He worked there, yet even he couldn't access the "baller suite."

He hit the call button, and Maya, the assistant, buzzed him inside.

An antechamber housed a large reception area. Maya sat behind the desk. She resembled a slightly younger version of Gina, and the first time Adrian had seen her, he'd wondered if the woman's similarity to Lamont's wife was a coincidence.

"Hi there, Adrian." Maya smiled. "Mr. Washington is ready for you. Go on inside, please."

"Thank you."

Frosted double doors led into an executive suite that exuded power and sophistication. It was a vast chamber, perhaps a thousand square feet, well-lit, with enormous windows that let in the late morning sunshine. A large conference area featured sleek, minimalist furniture. The desk held only photographs and a potted plant, not even a computer. Abstract art hung on the walls, but Adrian also saw framed snippets from publications such as the *Wall Street Journal*, *Black Enterprise*, and *Fortune*.

He saw Lamont in the corner of the office. Wearing a dress shirt with rolled sleeves and gray slacks, he stood on a miniature putting green, big hands clasping a golf club.

Naturally, the man had installed a putting green in his executive suite. Go figure.

"Adrian!" Lamont said. He waved Adrian over with the club. "Come on over, brother."

Here we go.

Adrian approached. Lamont gently tapped the golf ball; it rolled along the smooth, velvety surface and dropped into the hole.

"How was Seminole?" Adrian asked, remembering the exclusive course Lamont had visited over the weekend.

"I shot an eighty-five." Lamont placed the putter into a rack standing nearby.

"Damn," Adrian said, impressed.

"It was a fine trip," Lamont said, wiping his hands with a towel. "But I know you're a busy man, brother. How are you enjoying your time back at FiPro?"

Where was this headed? Adrian wasn't sure.

"It's been great," Adrian said. "I love the work and love working with the team."

"Would you be interested in a new management-level opportunity? Leading your own team of analysts?"

Is this for real?

"My own team? Absolutely."

"It's a permanent position, of course. The base salary is a hundred and fifty. Maya will get you the details. We'll include a signing bonus of ten grand."

Adrian's head spun. A hundred and fifty thousand dollars? That was *seventy thousand* dollars more than his current income. And a signing bonus, too?

He had never earned so much money in his life.

"That sounds fantastic, sir," Adrian said.

"Brother, please. Lamont."

"Lamont, sorry. Yes, this is outstanding. Thank you."

"All right, then. Maya will send over the formal offer letter by the close of business today, and you'll be good to go. We'll chat soon, brother. Be well."

Lamont turned back to his clubs. Adrian waited for a beat, wondering if there was more and if Lamont would inquire about "their girls." The man only selected a putter and lined up another shot.

Did Lamont know what had happened at the theme park? Did he care? The man seemed utterly disconnected, immersed in his own world. Adrian didn't understand it, and perhaps he never would.

Adrian left the office as if he were walking through a dream. Maya waved at him and promised she would have his offer package by the end of the day.

Instead of returning to his desk, Adrian took the elevator to the lobby and hurried outside to his car. He got inside and pulled up his phone to call Steph and share the fantastic news.

His phone chimed. It was his wife.

"I was about to call you," he said. "Babe, I've got incredible news."

"So do I," she said, her tone grave. "I need you to come see me ASAP."

31

After a brief introduction, Adrian sat beside Steph before the private investigator's desk.

"I hope this isn't wasting my time," Adrian said. "I'm supposed to be at work."

On the phone, Steph refused to explain what this was all about, promising him that it was critical for the safety of their family for him to meet her immediately at the detective's office. He hadn't gotten a chance to share the news with her about the job offer, either —which still felt like a dream to him. He wanted to be back in the office to see that email come in from Lamont's assistant but knew he couldn't put off Steph.

"Keep an open mind, please," Steph said. "And listen."

Raymond Barnes seemed like a serious character to Adrian. He had an air of gravity about him that Adrian found slightly intimidating. He had spotted that Secret Service agent photo hanging in the office and knew this was not a man to be trifled with.

Barnes clasped his thick, muscular hands across his flat stomach and studied them with his dark, alert gaze.

"Two months ago, a gentleman hired me to build a civil case against the Washington family," Barnes said.

"Someone wants to sue the millionaires?" Adrian said in a hushed tone and glanced at Steph.

Steph lip-synched: *Listen.*

"It's regarding what happened to his family two years ago," Barnes said. "His daughter, Zoey, was best friends with Scarlett Washington—they attended the same school, Queen's Academy. He's convinced Scarlett influenced Zoey to attempt to murder him and his wife."

Coldness bolted down Adrian's spine.

"Wait, what?" Adrian asked.

"Zoey poisoned her mother and father with barium acetate, a lethal chemical. She obtained it from the school's chemistry lab. She put the substance in her family's taco dinner one Saturday night. Her mother died of cardiac arrest within twenty-four hours; the medical examiner's office studied the mother's tissue samples and validated the presence of the chemical. Her father experienced a heart attack, but he survived." Barnes added: "Barely. He's never fully recovered."

Adrian looked from Steph to Barnes.

"How does he know Scarlett had anything to do with this?" Adrian asked.

"Zoey left behind a written confession before she overdosed on prescription painkillers." Barnes watched him, his features solemn as a mortician's. "She confessed that Scarlett helped her secure the barium acetate—in fact, she wrote that Scarlett planned the entire thing. It was an act of revenge. You see, he and his wife had banned Zoey from continuing their friendship with the girl. They believed she was toxic. Dangerous, even. Zoey didn't want to go on living without her friend, her so-called sister."

"Jesus," Adrian said.

"Yeah," Steph said.

She reached for his hand and squeezed. He squeezed it back, but the shock still held sway over him.

"The case never went to trial," Barnes said. "Zoey was dead; her mother was dead; my client was incapacitated for months after his cardiac event. The police recovered Zoey's diary and found the confession, but they couldn't substantiate any of the allegations against Scarlett Washington. Her family hired a top—and I do mean *top*—team of defense attorneys. Think O. J. Simpson–caliber legal dream team, folks."

"Rich people," Steph said with disgust. "Evil and rich."

"The child avoided so much as a visit to the police station for questioning," Barnes said, his lips curling. "My client's daughter was painted as hysterical and suicidal and held responsible for the crime. The case was closed." He hesitated. "But . . . my client is also a man of means."

"He's launched a vendetta," Adrian said. "But a lawsuit isn't going to bring back his family."

"He wants *the truth* to come out," Steph said. "That's what he wants."

"He sits on the school board of Queen's Academy," Barnes said. "He pressured the administration to expel Scarlett. Evidently, she'd accumulated a long list of disciplinary infractions—"

"That's why they put her in public school," Adrian said, snapping his fingers. "Her mother hinted at issues but never told me the full story."

"And in public school is where she hooked up with our baby," Steph said, shaking her head. "Lord help us. How did Harper become friends with this evil child?"

"What do you want from us?" Adrian asked Barnes.

"The Washingtons know my client isn't letting this go. Already, they've attempted various legal means to make this go away: attempts at restraining orders, a small payoff. But he wants accountability. A substantial civil settlement would be acceptable. But can I tell you what he wants most?"

"He wants Scarlett to be locked up," Adrian said.

Barnes smiled.

"That's where she needs to be," Steph said.

"You've been in their house more than once," Barnes said. "You've spent time privately with these people. You work at Lamont Washington's firm, Mr. Wall. They trust you; you've entered the inner circle. This presents an opportunity to gather evidence to reopen the case."

"Evidence?" Steph asked.

"Loose lips sink ships," Barnes said. "A recorded conversation, a testimony from one of you if you can seek out more information, an email, documentation . . . these could work magic here."

"I don't know," Adrian said and glanced at Steph, who was also shaking her head.

"I'm very sorry about what happened to your client's family," Steph said softly. "I truly am. But my priority is my own family. I can't get involved in any of this."

"My client is willing to offer compensation for your assistance," Barnes said. "As I said, he's a man of considerable means."

"It's a hard no for us," Steph said, looking at Adrian. "Right, babe?"

He squeezed her hand and nodded.

"I'm sorry," he said to Barnes. "My wife and I stand together on this. Good luck with your case."

"And please, stop following us," Steph added.

32

Adrian was too wound up to return to the FiPro office immediately, and Steph seemed to feel the same way. She suggested they visit a Starbucks to discuss their findings.

They grabbed a table in the corner of the café. Steph ordered a latte; Adrian sipped on a plain black coffee.

"Well," Steph said, sitting across from him. She placed both her hands flat on the table and looked at him. "What are your thoughts? Honestly?"

"I'm processing it. Still trying to understand how Scarlett can be some master criminal when she's only fourteen. She was younger than that when this poisoning incident happened."

"Yet this past weekend, Willow almost died on a roller coaster—and says Scarlett loosened her seat belt. Isn't the pattern obvious?"

Adrian didn't have an answer for her comeback.

"Do you know what I think?" Steph said. "The girl is a psychopath. She's cunning, manipulative—and dangerous. I've had a bad feeling about her from the start, but I let you guys talk me into going along with this friendship with Harper nonsense. It's time to face the truth."

"I never said the girl was an angel."

"She gets away with murder—literally—because people refuse to see what should be as clear as the nose on your face."

"Can I tell you my big news? I never got a chance since you broadsided me with this other stuff."

"Go on." She waved impatiently.

"Lamont offered me a job this morning. It's a permanent position in a management role. I'll get a seventy *thousand*-dollar raise and a ten-grand signing bonus."

"Did you accept it?" She sipped her beverage, her gaze never leaving his face.

He put down his cup. "What do you think, Steph? How is that a question?"

"Hmph." She contemplated the depths of her drink. "Don't you find the timing of this job offer to be a little suspect?"

You could count on Steph to find something negative about the most significant career breakthrough he'd ever experienced in his entire working life. It reminded him of what had driven them apart in the first place: She'd long discouraged his ambitions to rise to the top. She was satisfied settling for crumbs from the table while he craved a seat.

"He didn't say a word about Six Flags or the girls," Adrian said. "Not one word."

"If he had, that would have been too obvious."

"I *earned* this opportunity, Steph. I deserve it." His pulse raced, and the caffeine in the coffee wasn't helping matters. He slid the cup aside, wishing he'd gotten cold water instead.

"That's what these people do," she said. "They manipulate with money, promises of better things ahead. It's only a game for them. You're a pawn on this man's chessboard, Adrian. He gives you a better job and keeps you under his control, but he doesn't give a damn about you or us." She sipped her drink and scowled as if it were too bitter. "He's only protecting his own interests—namely, Scarlett."

"I'm taking the job. End of discussion."

"You're saying that despite everything you heard over there?" She pointed, indicating the detective's office down the road. "You learned that Scarlett most likely planned the poisoning of another child's parents, leading to the girl killing her mother and then the child taking her own life, and Scarlett's rich family gets her off the hook, and you're still fine with working for the man bankrolling this corruption?"

"I didn't say—"

"He's a swell guy in your book, huh? So long as he keeps the fat checks coming."

"I haven't done anything wrong. Why do I feel like you're blaming *me* for something?"

She started to answer him when her phone vibrated on the table. She picked it up and answered.

Adrian rose from his chair to fetch fresh water instead of coffee. Steph touched his arm, stopping him in mid-stride.

"It's the school," Steph said, phone angled to her ear. "Harper's in the principal's office."

33

"You found my daughter cheating?"

Adrian posed the question to the middle school principal, Marlene Barlow. The principal, a hawkish, bespectacled woman, tapped the papers on her desk with a ballpoint pen.

"It's far more common than we'd like to believe, Mr. Wall," she said. "Sometimes, the brightest students fall to the temptation."

"What's your evidence of this?" Steph asked from her seat beside Adrian in the office.

"When students turn in essays, we use software to check whether the student used an AI assistant to generate the work." The principal nudged up the glasses on her beak-like nose and peered at the document on her desk. "Your daughter's Social Studies essay rated a ninety-seven percent possibility that she used an AI tool to create the paper."

Steph cursed under her breath.

"Ninety-seven percent isn't completely conclusive," he said. "There's a three percent chance that she wrote the essay herself."

The principal tilted her head, studying him as if unsure whether he was being serious.

"She's never cheated before," he said. "She's almost a straight-A student."

"I understand your concern, but according to the guidelines stated in our school handbook, this score strongly suggests cheating, Mr. Wall. We're obligated to treat it as such."

"Did she admit to cheating?" Adrian asked.

"Of course, she did not. Students never do."

"She didn't admit to it, and there's a possibility that she wrote the paper, but you want to punish her, anyway. How is that fair?"

"It's our policy, sir. Harper will serve in-school detention for three days. Nothing will be added to her academic record as this is the first occurrence. But if it happens again, the consequences are more severe, including suspension."

"I don't agree with any of this, ma'am," Adrian said. "Can we appeal?"

The woman only frowned at him. He started to say something else, but Steph put her hand on his shoulder and gave him a firm headshake. He saw the thunderstorm simmering in her gaze and knew she was struggling to contain her anger.

"Thank you, Ms. Barlow," Steph said in a restrained voice. "We'll deal with Harper. Can we check her out of school early today?"

34

"I know you cheated, Harper," Steph said. "Better yet, I know *why* you cheated. This is all because of Scarlett."

The three of them, Harper, Steph, and Adrian, had gathered in their house's kitchen. Harper sat at the table, her head down, sniffling and wiping tears from her cheeks with a fistful of tissues. She had spoken fewer than ten words since they had brought her home from school.

Adrian felt sorry for his child. He wanted to believe that she hadn't cheated and that whatever essay she had submitted fell within the three percent margin of error; he hated seeing her suffer for something she might not have done.

But he knew better.

"That evil-assed girl has been a bad influence on you from the start, exactly like I knew she would be," Steph continued. She paced back and forth across the kitchen, gesturing as she spoke. "You've no idea what this girl has done in her life. But I do. She's a plague, and she will destroy you."

"You never cheated before," Adrian said, but his voice sounded weaker than his wife's. "Did Scarlett tell you to use AI to write your paper?"

"I didn't use AI to write my paper," Harper said, but she didn't look up at him.

"Harper, please," he said.

Steph came between them, chopping down her arm like a ref ending a match. "It's over now, Harper. You and this heathen child are done. We're not asking you to cut it off with her. We're cutting it off ourselves."

"What?" Harper's head snapped up, and she turned to her mother.

Adrian shifted to Steph, too. "We're cutting it off?"

"Damn right we are, and you know why." Steph grinned at him, but it was a smile as hard as granite. "It's the best thing for all of us."

"No," Harper said.

"Excuse me?" Steph stopped pacing in mid-step. "No?"

"No, no, no!" Rising from her chair, Harper whipped her head back and forth, tears streaming down her face. "You can't stop us from being friends!"

"I absolutely can, young lady." Jaw clenched, Steph tightened her hands into fists and dug them into her waist. "I can, and I will. Watch me."

Steph snatched her smartphone from her pocket like a gunslinger drawing a pistol, swiped, and tapped the screen.

Adrian stepped toward her. "Wait, who are you calling?"

"Gina."

"Steph . . ." Adrian said, but she had already begun talking.

"Gina, this is Stephanie Wall, Harper's mother. Look: Harper and Scarlett can't be friends anymore. Scarlett is a bad influence on my child, and we're not allowing this friendship to continue. We know this isn't the first time with your kid, either. Tell her to stay the hell away from her. I appreciate your hospitality, but this ends now. And I don't want to hear from you again, either—do me a favor and lose my number *and* my husband's."

Adrian slumped against the counter, limp with disbelief. Steph jabbed the phone with her finger and dropped it onto the table, the phone thunking onto the surface like a brick.

"There," Steph said to Harper. "Did you hear that? I left a message and blocked her. It's done. Is there anything else you think I won't do, young lady?"

"You're a fuckin' bitch!" Harper screamed, saliva projecting from her lips. "I hate you!"

Steph snarled like an enraged tiger, and Adrian sensed what was coming next. He pushed away from the counter, but he was too late, too slow to intervene.

Steph slapped Harper across the face so hard that their daughter whirled around like a top and dropped to the floor. The sound was like a firecracker in the kitchen.

"Don't you dare speak to me like that!" Steph said. "I will whoop your narrow ass from one end of this house to the other."

Adrian felt trapped between wanting to help his child and needing to calm Steph down. How had things come to this between them? Why? Was it all his fault? Why did it feel like he might be responsible for their downward spiral?

Because it all started with you, man. You were never satisfied with anything and convinced you were missing out on the so-called good life. You blew up your family, and now you're facing the wreckage.

Crying, Harper raced out of the kitchen. Steph chased after her, and in her haste, she hooked her foot on a chair leg, stumbled, hit the floor on her knees, and swore.

Adrian moved to help her. She brushed off his hand with a grunt, staggered to her feet, and rushed to the staircase.

Upstairs, a door slammed.

Adrian followed Steph up the stairs. Tears hung in his eyes, and he blinked them back, but his chest felt as if he were hiccupping.

Steph had reached Harper's bedroom door. She hammered her fist against it.

"Open this door, goddammit! I'm not done with you!"

Steph twisted the knob, but the door didn't open. Harper had locked them out.

Steph swung to Adrian. "Get me the key. I'm gonna wear her ass out."

"Steph." He raised his hands in a placating gesture, his voice shaking. "Steph, leave her alone."

"Whose side are you on, anyway? If you're not on mine, then get the hell out of my way!"

He flinched. Glaring at him, Steph charged past, pounding back downstairs, presumably to search for the key to Harper's bedroom door. Adrian knew where the keys were stored—they weren't downstairs.

He decided not to tell her. He hoped that she would run out of gas, sit down somewhere, and cool off.

He stepped to the bedroom door and pressed his ear against it. Inside, he heard his daughter sobbing.

He hesitated with his hand poised to knock. What was he going to tell her? That he was sorry? But what would he apologize for?

He backed away.

He heard, from downstairs, Steph ripping open drawers in the kitchen, slamming them shut, items jangling and tinkling to the floor.

Whose side are you on, anyway?

I'm not on anyone's side, he realized. But he didn't know what he could do about it.

He eased down onto the top step of the carpeted staircase and buried his face in his hands.

After a while, Steph still hadn't returned upstairs, and Harper hadn't emerged from her bedroom. The house had fallen silent.

With a rueful glance toward his daughter's room, Adrian rose from his perch at the peak of the staircase and shuffled downstairs.

Bad Influence

Steph was in the kitchen, seated at the table. A couple of drawers hung open, and various items had spilled onto the floor: batteries, menus from take-out restaurants, USB cables, and a set of playing cards that had slipped out of the case and fanned across the tile.

Steph clutched Harper's iPhone in her hands.

"She's never getting this damn phone back," Steph said, almost to herself. Gnawing her bottom lip, she poked at the screen. "I'll figure out her passcode if it's the last thing I do."

He didn't know what to say to her to help the situation. He didn't know Harper's password, either, and if he did, he wasn't sure he would give it to her right then. When Steph got into these scorched-earth furies, the best thing to do was to stay back and let her eventually wind down.

But her message to Gina concerned him.

Adrian had left his work laptop in a computer briefcase in the hallway. He plucked it off the floor, unzipped it, took out the machine in the dining room, and logged onto the FiPro VPN.

He had received at least a dozen new email messages in the hours since he had abruptly left the office.

But none of the messages were from Maya Gaines, Lamont's assistant.

Lamont and Maya had promised to send him the offer letter by the close of business that day. It was close to four o'clock.

Perspiration coated his palms.

What did this mean? Did it mean anything?

He checked Microsoft Teams and found that Maya Gaines, who had pinged him earlier to ask him to report to Lamont's office, was offline.

Maybe it's only temporary. She could log in later to send me the offer letter.

Steph's words echoed in his ears: *Scarlett is a bad influence on my child, and we're not allowing this friendship to continue.*

Had Gina already told Lamont? Had Lamont directed his assistant to cancel the job offer letter?

He rubbed his sweaty palms together.

Be patient, he told himself.

But he couldn't shake the thought that the best thing that had ever happened in his career had just slipped out of his grasp.

35

Hours later, the silence in their household had thickened until it felt tangible to Adrian, like smog in the air. He spent the time trying to work on his computer in the dining room, but mostly, he could not stop checking his email to see if the offer had arrived—which, of course, it hadn't.

What had his mother used to say? *A watched pot never boils.*

He left the room around six o'clock. Steph still sat at the kitchen table but had traded Harper's phone for her laptop. A glass of white wine, filled to the rim, stood on the table beside her, and an open bottle of Chardonnay was next to the glass.

Redness tinged her eyes, her hair disheveled as a bird's nest.

"Are you okay?" he asked, the first words he had spoken to her in hours.

She glanced at him, took a long swallow of wine, and set the glass down.

"Steph?" he asked.

"She's lucky she locked that door; that's all I can say," Steph said, but her voice was softer than he had expected, which he interpreted as a positive signal that the storm had passed. "I would have killed her."

"I'll go check on her," he said.

Upstairs, he tapped on Harper's door.

"Harp, it's me. Please open the door."

After about a minute, Harper cracked the door open. Her eyes were bloodshot, her hair a mess, and it struck Adrian how much alike his wife and daughter looked.

"Yeah," she said, her voice so low he barely heard her.

"Are you all right, Harp?"

Harper shrugged. He noticed the side of her face was crimson and swollen. Emotion wrenched his chest. He hadn't touched his daughter, but his hands felt heavy as if he had laid hands on her himself.

"Your mother's calmed down a bit," he said, "but keep your distance. She's still very upset about . . ." He couldn't finish the sentence. "Everything."

"Are you guys gonna get divorced 'cause of me?"

The question staggered him.

"What? Sweetheart, none of this is your fault, okay?"

"But I cheated, Daddy." Tears trickled down her cheeks. In a quavering voice, she said, "I'm sorry."

"We'll deal with that topic later."

"Okay."

"Everything is going to be fine."

He kissed her forehead. He stepped back, and she closed the door.

When he returned downstairs, he approached Steph. She had already drained her wineglass and was filling it up again.

"Maybe you should slow down," he said.

"Maybe you should stop trying to be my daddy."

He winced. "She admitted to me that she cheated."

"Well, that's the biggest surprise of the year, isn't it?" She set down the bottle, her gaze hot. "You can't stop acting like the good guy, can you?"

"What are you accusing me of this time? I'm keeping my cool because you lost your mind, and now our daughter's got a bruise on her face thanks to you. Do you want to send her to school looking like that, Steph?"

"I'm not letting my child talk to me like that. Ever."

"This isn't 1950. Schools call police on parents like you."

"Parents like me." Laughing to herself, she sipped her wine. "I'm trying to keep our child on the right path. You're either part of the solution or part of the problem. You need to figure out where you stand."

"It sounds like you want me to leave."

"You said that, not me." She shrugged. "Do whatever you need to do."

Shaking his head, he packed up his laptop.

"Bye," Steph said.

He slammed the door behind him.

36

Adrian swung through a Chick-fil-A drive-thru to grab dinner and drove to his apartment. Sitting at his tiny kitchen table, he chewed a chicken sandwich and booted up his work laptop.

Again, he found no job offer had arrived, and Maya Gaines was still offline.

He pounded his fist against the table, salt-and-pepper shakers trembling on the surface.

"Steph screwed me," he said. "Shit."

But could he really blame his wife? Deep down, he doubted it. Somehow, it all came back to him—though he still didn't know what he could have done to stop it.

He picked up his iPhone. Lamont had given him his direct number, along with permission to use it, but Adrian was reluctant to reach out to the man. If he reached out and Lamont responded with *the offer is off the table, brother, and I think you know why*, it would be like a door slamming shut in Adrian's face. But if he held off contacting him, that meant, maybe, there was still hope everything would work out.

He knew his logic was flawed, but he was so desperate that he was willing to cling to anything, even silly, hopeful notions.

After he shut off the computer and finished his meal, he opened a social media app and spent the time watching ridiculous and comical videos.

After perhaps an hour, he couldn't take it anymore, so he texted Lamont: *Hello, it's Adrian. I hope all is well. I haven't received the offer letter yet from your assistant. Is that still on the way? I want to be sure I didn't dream up that conversation in your office.*

He closed with a smiley face emoji.

Clutching the phone in both hands, he awaited Lamont's reply. Five minutes passed, then ten, with no reply.

"Shit," he said to no one in particular.

He's a CEO, he reminded himself. *He's busy.*

But he was going to be sick. He got up, hurried to the bathroom. His stomach convulsed, but he managed only a dry heave. Afterward, he splashed cold water on his face and dried off his skin with a towel.

He had to control himself. He felt he was coming undone as if he were a spool of thread, and his life was unwinding, inch by inch.

Gina. Call Gina.

He hurried back into the kitchen. Lamont hadn't responded, still. *Shit, shit, shit.*

He called Gina.

Please answer. Please.

On the third ring, she picked up: "Hey, stranger."

"I know Steph left you a message," he said, the words charging out of him like water from a burst dam. "A lot is going on right now; you can ignore everything she said; we're trying to work through some serious drama in our family."

"Your girl is a trip, boo." Gina snickered.

"Is Lamont there?" His heart knocked.

"Why don't you come over, hmm?" she asked. "We can have a chitchat. I'll give you the guest code."

He didn't know what she wanted or why she hadn't told him

about Lamont, but he needed to do whatever was necessary to right this situation.

"I'll be there in half an hour," he said.

37

Around eight o'clock that evening, Adrian parked his SUV in the Washingtons' driveway.

I'm here to save my job, he thought. *That's the only reason why I'm here.*

But he worried Gina had a different agenda in mind. The fact that he was aware of such a possibility and had driven to their house despite his misgivings made him feel uneasy about his intentions. What would Steph say if she knew he was there?

Focus on saving your job. Somehow.

Lamont hadn't responded to his text message. Before departing his apartment, Adrian had called him, too, and the CEO hadn't picked up. Adrian hung up without leaving a voice mail, at a loss for what to say without sounding embarrassingly desperate.

Scarlett answered the front door. He hadn't expected to see the kid, and her appearance caught him off balance: she wore a long white T-shirt with a big-eyed anime character on the front, plaid pajama pants, and scuffed white Crocs.

Was this child a cold-blooded, manipulative killing machine? It was impossible to match her ordinary, All-American teenager appearance to the allegations circling her.

"Good evening, Mr. Wall." Amusement sparkled in her eyes as though he were the subject of a joke she had just overheard. "I hear Mrs. Wall doesn't want Harper and me to be friends anymore. Is your wife always so hysterical?"

"This is grown folks' business," he said.

"Lamont's not too thrilled about it."

His stomach felt as though it had dropped to the floor.

"Is your dad here?" Adrian asked.

"I don't keep track of Lamont." She touched her chin, her eyes slit like a reptile's. "Someone ought to straighten out your wife."

The iciness of her tone gave him pause. Something slithered in that narrowed gaze of hers that made it easy to imagine, if only for a heartbeat, that all the frightening things said about this child were true. The unbuttoning of Willow's seat belt—

—*I saw her laughing*—

—but worse, the tale of her influencing a girl to poison her own parents. *She planned the whole thing.*

Adrian shivered.

Scarlett beamed at him, teeth glistening, and that sense of certainty passed. He was once more looking at a kid, a smart-mouthed brat for sure, but in the end, a child that, for all appearances, might only be misunderstood.

"Like I said, grown folks' business." He started to move past her in the entry hall, hesitated, and studied her. "Did you show Harper how to use AI to write essays?"

"AI? What's AI?"

"Don't play stupid. If you have an IQ of 135 like you've claimed, you know what AI is and how people can use it to write papers."

"I don't know anything about that, Mr. Wall. Sorry. Why are you asking me about it?"

"Harper got in trouble at school for cheating. She admitted to me that she did it. But did you show her how to do it?"

"I can't believe Harp would be found guilty of cheating." Scarlett touched her chest and waved her fingers as if experiencing a hot flash. "That's unbelievable, Mr. Wall. My gosh."

"I know you've got something to do with this, Scarlett."

"Why would I need to ever cheat with my supposed high IQ? School is *easy* for me, Mr. Wall. I could score straight A's in my sleep."

Scarlett turned away from him and strode along the hallway.

"Where are you going?" he asked.

"Aren't you here to see Gina?" She looked over her shoulder. "I'll take you to her lair."

"Her lair?"

"She's gonna gobble you up like a big, bad, sexy dragon."

"What the hell are you talking about?"

Scarlett giggled and continued walking. She led him through the house. Adrian looked around for Lamont, but he neither saw nor heard any sign of the man. Perhaps he was out of town, airborne on a transatlantic business flight, and that was why he'd not yet responded to Adrian's inquiry.

Lamont's not too thrilled about it . . .

The kid could be lying; lying seemed to come as naturally to her as breathing. Until he spoke to Lamont, he would keep up his hopes.

"Here we are." Scarlett shoved open the big double doors leading into the master bedroom suite. "The dragon awaits."

"Please stop. I'm here only to chat."

She giggled again and slipped away down the hallway.

Dimly lit with a chandelier, the bedroom was enormous, as expected, easily as spacious as the entire first floor of his house. A king-size Chinese sleigh bed served as a focal point, but there was a lounge area with upholstered chairs and plenty of floor-to-ceiling windows, the curtains drawn shut against the darkening evening. The scent of lavender laced the air.

As he entered, his shoes whispered across plush carpeting deep enough to sink in.

"Gina?" he said.

"In here," she said from somewhere deeper inside.

He found Gina at the entrance to a walk-in closet that looked like a high-end boutique. She wore a luxurious green kimono robe, and beckoned him inside with a curled, manicured finger.

"Welcome to my little slice of heaven," she said. "Want a drink?"

38

"Sure," Adrian said. "I'll have a drink."

"You must be desperate, Mr. Club Soda, to drink with lil' old Gina."

With a blur of colorful motion, she strolled to a bar—*who kept a bar inside a closet?*—and with the practiced efficiency of a professional bartender, she mixed a beverage containing cognac, champagne, orange liqueur, and lemon juice, pouring it into a cocktail glass. She offered it to him.

"Thanks," he said.

"Cheers." She raised her own full glass, clinked it against his, and enjoyed a prolonged sip from hers.

Adrian restricted himself to a tiny sip, enough to taste a heavy-handed pour of cognac that almost made him swoon.

"Quite a spot you have in here," he said.

"I was putting away some stuff I picked up over the weekend." She indicated a collection of open bags on the floor and a couple of tables. He recognized the names of several designer stores printed on the bags: Dior, Hermès, and Jimmy Choo. "I hit Phipps and tore down the mall with my black card."

"Retail therapy?" he asked.

"You got no idea, boo." Shaking her head, she sat on a lounge chair, crossing her bare legs. She patted the chair next to her. "Come. Join me."

"Is Lamont here?" he asked.

"He's either working or on the golf course. I don't keep tabs on that man. You have his number."

"I texted him earlier, but he hasn't responded. I'd like to talk to him in person."

"You're worried about your little job, huh?" She smirked and sipped her cocktail.

He squeezed the glass. "It's not a *little job* for me, Gina. It's a great career opportunity. I don't want to screw it up over some crap between our kids."

"Sit, baby." She tapped the chair again.

He dropped onto the chair and balanced the cocktail glass on his knee.

"Now," she said, rapping her fingers against his knee. "We need to chat about this Six Flags thing. That's why I kept calling you. Why were you ignoring me?"

"I've had a lot going on," he said.

"Hmph." Her booze-tinged gaze lacerated him. "Your little niece says my baby undid her seat belt on a roller coaster. What would make her say some foolishness like that?"

"Willow says that's what happened."

"Did you see it?"

She watched him, leaning forward in her chair. He could smell the liquor on her breath.

"I was sitting behind them," he said.

"Then no one else saw it. Then your little niece is making up stories for what was only a bad accident and no one's fault."

He thought there might be video footage, but he didn't want to raise the point. He sensed that she was trying to handle him, muddle his thoughts, and ultimately create a self-serving narrative of what had happened. The private detective, Barnes, had advised them of this family's history, of their willingness to leave no stone unturned when it came to protecting themselves. He understood their motivation; he would have done the same for his family.

But all he wanted then was to keep his job.

"I can't have folks out there spreading lies about my child," Gina continued. "I'm not having that. Listen, I play rough when people do that, and in case I never told you, I grew up in Zone Six, boo." Her accent had thickened to a syrupy stew that was straight hood. "Born and raised, bitch."

As a native Atlantan, he was familiar with the area; it was a crime-ridden section of the city, marked with poverty and folks trying to make a way out of no way.

"You've moved up in the world," he said.

"Lamont isn't from the streets—his bougie ass grew up in Dunwoody. Who do you think protects our family? *Him?*" She knocked back a slug of her drink. "Don't get me started on him."

"If nothing happened on the roller coaster," he said, "if it was only an accident, then you don't have anything to worry about."

"You keep me posted, understand?" She tapped his knee again. "If folks are spreading more rumors, hiring lawyers, whatever—I want to know about it ASAP. You tell me. You hear?"

"I will," he said, but he had no plans to say anything about Kellie's promise to engage an attorney, a vow he knew his sister-in-law would follow through on. He couldn't get involved any further in this situation; already, it was too messy for comfort.

"Glad that we're clear on that," she said. She flexed her long legs in front of her. "Now, do you want me to talk to Lamont about your job? He does whatever I ask him to do."

"He wants Harper and Scarlett to stay friends. But you heard what Steph said."

"We'll work that out. You shouldn't have to lose this job in the meantime, hmm?"

"You would help me with that?"

"What did I say the first day we met? We're friends, boo." She snapped her fingers. "I've got you."

"I appreciate that, Gina. I really do."

"Uh-huh." She lifted one of her legs, twirled it around in the air in lazy circles like a ballerina, and then laid it across his lap, her pedicured toes brushing against his groin. "But what are you gonna do for me?"

39

But what are you gonna do for me?

Wasn't this the devil's bargain he'd been anticipating? The last time he had seen Gina, hadn't she promised him, *I always get what I want, sooner or later?*

Watching him, a smile on the edge of her lips, she traced her tongue along the rim of her cocktail glass and wriggled her toes against his crotch.

"If you don't want to play along . . ." A husky laugh eased out of her. "Like I said, Lamont does whatever I tell him to do, which could either work for you or against you."

"You're not giving me a choice."

"You've always got a choice, boo." She fished a maraschino cherry out of the depths of her glass, dangled it above her lips, lashed the bulbous fruit with a dramatic flick of her tongue, and dropped the cherry into her mouth, chewed, swallowed. "What'll it be?"

He rested his hand on her calf and slid his fingers to her knee. With her lips pursed, she tucked her hair over her shoulder and watched him.

Am I really doing this? he thought.

His hand reached her thigh.

"This stays between us," he said. "Only for tonight."

She made a tsk-tsk sound.

"I don't think we're on the same page. I'm not looking to add to my body count, boo. I want you to *want* me. Like a drowning man wants air. Over and over."

"Any man would want you. You're gorgeous."

"Do you want to be my boyfriend?"

He stared at her. "You know I'm married. We've talked about this."

"Hmm." She pressed her toes against his crotch again. "I like to have my boyfriends spend the night. You get to pick out a bedroom for yourself. You should find a room, freshen up, make yourself comfortable, and Rosita will fetch you some clothes." She touched his shoulder as if sizing him up. "You're about the same size as my last boo, so we've got plenty for you to wear. I'll call on you in a bit, and we can enjoy each other."

"Gina, be serious."

She smiled. "Or you can take your ass home and hope you still have a job tomorrow."

That was how Adrian found himself standing in a bedroom in their estate that resembled a suite in an upscale hotel: king-size bed, sleek, modern furnishings, expensive-looking prints hanging on the walls. In this luxurious home, even the vacant rooms were nicer than the ones at his house.

What are you doing here, man?

He sat on the edge of the bed and let his head droop as he gazed at the tips of his shoes pressing into the carpet.

This had been an incredible day of exhilarating peaks and terrifying valleys, but this was the steepest dip yet. Every molecule in his body wanted to run out of there. Raw, naked fear glued him in place.

Was this what sleeping your way to the top felt like? Forfeiting every last shred of your integrity for a fleeting opportunity?

I want you to want me.

But he wanted his wife and his family, and he didn't want to sleep over at this woman's house in a spare bedroom like a cheap gigolo.

Someone rapped on the door. With a start, he looked up.

It was Rosita, the housekeeper. She carried a bundle of clothing in her arms.

"I have brought you clothes, Mr. Adrian," she said in Spanish-accented English.

She smiled at him, but it was tough for Adrian to meet the woman's wise, dark-eyed gaze.

"Thank you," he said. "Please put them on the dresser over there."

She crossed the room and placed the folded outfit atop the chest of drawers.

"How many of Gina's boyfriends have you seen?" he asked.

She frowned. "Pardon?"

"I know I'm not the only man who's spent the night. How many others?"

She glanced away from him and clasped her hands in front of her. "*Diez?*"

"*Ten* other guys?"

"Or more?" She laughed and touched her bosom nervously.

"Jesus." He wiped his hand down his face.

Averting her gaze, she ambled to the doorway. "Do you need anything else, Mr. Adrian?"

"Only a time machine so I can go back to the start of my bad choices."

"Pardon?"

"Nothing. Thank you. Have a good night."

She rushed out of the room as if whatever plague of misfortune had consumed him might be contagious. He could only imagine what the woman had seen during her years of service in this den of iniquity.

But you're right here, aren't you, man? Falling right in line with the plan.

He checked the clothing. It was lounging wear: a soft, dark cotton shirt and satiny black pants with a drawstring waist, and they looked as if they would fit him comfortably enough.

You won't need them once you slide under the sheets with Gina, will you?

The room had its own bathroom with a shower stall. A toothbrush was still in its packaging, and a Crest tube lay on the vanity's edge.

Adrian showered, brushed his teeth, and dressed in the clothes supplied to him. As he tightened the pants drawstring, his phone buzzed with a text message. It was from Gina.

Meet me in the theater. We'll pick up where we left off the first time.

She closed with a kiss emoji.

A cramping sensation roiled his stomach. But he responded.

On my way.

Adrian remembered the theater's location from his earlier tour of the house. When he walked into the cavernous, dimly lit chamber, Gina was already there. She sat in the third row of upholstered seats, the aisle farthest away from the immense silver screen.

She had changed into a burgundy lace nightgown that left little to the imagination. He swallowed. How was he going to get through this?

"Where's your drink, boo?" she asked.

He didn't know how much Gina had drunk that evening—a *lot*, was a fair estimation—but she was slurring her words. Next to her, a chalice of orangish-brown liquor stood on the seat's pull-out tray, a cherry bobbing in the depths of the drink.

"I've hit my limit for the evening," he said.

"Damn lightweight." She thrust a remote control toward him. A yawn escaped her. "Have a seat and pick something for us to watch."

The chair was actually a love seat. Accepting the remote, he sat next to her. She cupped her glass and draped her legs across his lap.

He was tempted to slide farther away, to move her legs off him, but he knew that doing so would only irritate her. *I want you to want me.*

She yawned again and slurped her drink like a toddler guzzling grape juice.

It took him a few minutes to figure out how to navigate the projection screen system. After selecting Netflix from the on-screen menu, he found a sci-fi movie.

"Good choice," she said. She had already drunk most of her cocktail—she was on a tear this evening. She thrust the glass toward him and belched softly. "Can you be a sweetie and make me another drink, boo?"

"As you wish."

"Straight Hennessy this time, no ice. Triple shot."

Damn.

But he kept his mouth shut and accepted her glass. Another small bar occupied one cinema wall between a pair of glowing wall sconces. He poured cognac into the glass, not bothering to measure it. Did it matter? He might as well have brought her the entire bottle.

He returned to the love seat. She took the glass, enjoyed another long sip, and sat it on the tray.

As he started the film, Gina suddenly pressed against him. She kissed him sloppily. Her lips tasted of cherries, cognac, and champagne. She dug one hand into his pants, and despite his reservations, he felt himself stiffening.

"You know you want me," she whispered, every word slushy. She squeezed him. "You have been craving me since you laid eyes on me, right?"

She smothered his mouth with a kiss, swallowing the words he was about to say, and then clambered on top of him, straddling him on the love seat. She licked his neck and nibbled on his earlobe. He felt his erection growing.

"There you go." She smiled a lopsided grin.

She plucked her iPhone off the cushions and raised it to snap a selfie, clasping his face next to hers.

"Hey," he said, reaching for the phone. "No social media posts."

"Just for me, boo." She yawned in his face, kissed him, and yawned again. "I'll send . . . to you . . . so you can . . . remember . . . shit . . . I'm tired . . ."

The phone slipped out of her fingers and tumbled onto the cushions. Her head drooping, she yawned as she lay against him, her hair spreading across his cheeks and chest. She exhaled a deep breath, and he felt her body go limp.

Adrian exhaled, too.

Gina had fallen asleep.

But her phone was still unlocked.

Carefully, trying not to awaken Gina as she dozed on top of him, Adrian picked up her phone off the seat cushion. He held it above him in both hands.

His heart thumped so hard he feared the force of it would wake up Gina.

A snippet of their earlier conversation with the detective, Raymond Barnes, looped through his thoughts.

A recorded conversation, a testimony from one of you if you can seek out more information, an email, documentation . . . these could work magic . . . my client is willing to offer compensation for your assistance . . . man of considerable means . . .

He'd fallen low enough to consent to sex with a married woman to secure a job opportunity. Was snooping through her phone any worse? In service of his ambitions, he'd lost whatever moral standing he used to claim.

Maybe he could find something that would make this humiliating episode worthwhile.

His fingers quivered as he swiped through the cluster of apps. If Gina was anything like most people who relied heavily on mobile devices, she stored a treasure trove of information on her phone.

First, he checked text messages. At the top of the list, he found the thread of messages she had exchanged with him. He scrolled past it.

A contact labeled *Hubbie* was next in the series. Adrian tapped it.

Hubbie: *I don't like this news about the girls. This friendship is important to me, and it was going so well.*

Gina: *Steph is a dumb bitch, but I can work it with Adrian. A house divided, boo. I've got it.*

Hubbie: *I'll do whatever you suggest on my end.*

Gina: *Hold for now. More to come. I'm making him spend the night.*

Hubbie closed with a thumbs-up emoji.

Adrian's hands trembled so violently that he almost dropped the phone on Gina's head, which would have awakened her from her boozy slumber. These people disgusted him.

He kept scrolling and read an exchange from that evening with a contact named *Baby Girl*, an individual he assumed was Scarlett.

Baby Girl: *What'd Adrian say about the roller coaster thing?*

Gina: *Same thing you heard from Harp. The little girl says you undid her belt.*

Baby Girl: *So what if I did? She was fucking annoying.*

Gina: *You know you got your mama's temper. (Smiley face) I don't think he's telling me everything, though. I'm working on him. You stay on Harp.*

Baby Girl: *Harp does whatever I tell her to do. No worries.*

Adrian's mouth was dry. Could this text message be evidence admissible in court? Scarlett had admitted that she deliberately unlatched Willow's seat belt on the roller coaster.

He tapped the command to copy the entire dialogue between daughter and mother. He pasted it into a new message sent to himself.

In his pocket, his phone vibrated.

Shit.

Gina stirred and began to lift her head. Holding the phone in one hand, he took his other hand, cupped the back of her head, patted gently, and kissed the top of her forehead.

Murmuring indistinct words, she settled against him again. He breathed.

There were scores of other messages with various parties, but he decided to look for other sources. She had the standard "Files" app buried within a subcategory called "Utilities."

One folder was titled *Legal Misc.*

He opened it and scanned the collected documents.

"Oh my God," he whispered.

Heart pounding, he clicked on the entire folder, selected "Share," and sent it to himself via the text messaging app.

Again, his phone vibrated.

Dammit.

Gina smacked her lips and raised her face to his. Although her eyes remained closed, she kissed him, cooed softly, and gratefully laid her head against him again.

He deleted the text he had sent from her phone to his. He lowered the cell slowly and let it drop back onto the love seat with a soft thud.

A slender shadow flickered on the wall. Alarmed, he turned around.

Scarlett stood in the doorway watching him.

40

How long had Scarlett been watching?

It was too dark in the theater for Adrian to see the girl's face clearly. As the film played on the big screen, undulating waves of brightness and shadow washed over her features.

"Hey there," he said, hoping he sounded chipper and not as anxious as he felt. "How long have you been spying on us, kid?"

"You're the kind of creep who would screw a drunken lady?" she asked, her tone icy. "Real classy, Mr. Wall. What would Harper and your wife think?"

"I didn't do anything," he said. Why did he feel the need to explain himself to this child? "I'm going home. You should come get your mother."

"She can sleep on the floor for all I care. Serves her right. Drunk ass."

"That's cold."

Scarlett flipped him the middle finger, turned on her heel, and left the theater.

The exchange, crude and disturbing as it had been, gave him

hope that she hadn't witnessed anything he'd done with Gina's phone.

Gina had begun snoring, a soft rumble issuing from her. Gently, he untangled himself. He found a pillow stuffed in the corner of the love seat and slid it between her arms as he reclined her across the cushions. Curling up in the fetal position, she squeezed it against her like a teddy bear.

How much of this episode would she remember in the morning? What was she going to say to Lamont? Had it all been worth it?

He slipped his phone out of his pocket, and after verifying that the folder had arrived from her phone, he typed a text message to her.

You got what you wanted, and I enjoyed myself more than I thought I would. Remember our deal about my "little job."

Her phone chimed next to her head, but Gina slept on, undisturbed.

Pleased with himself, he got the hell out of there.

41

Steph strived to behave as a mature woman. A significant aspect of conducting oneself maturely was admitting when you had made a mistake.

Slapping her daughter was a mistake, and she felt guilty about it. It had been a reflex reaction. Harper had called her out of her name, and while she needed to be punished for that, beating her with her bare hands had been inadvisable.

That's what my mama would have done to me, though, if I'd been crazy enough to call her a bitch to her face. I'd have been picking up my teeth off the floor.

When she and Adrian had been dating, they had discussed, at length, the topic of spanking children. He didn't believe in putting hands on your kid under any circumstances, said doing so taught children it was okay to use violence to resolve conflict—but "spare the rod, spoil the child" had been the rule in her family's house. She respected his perspective and agreed to follow his approach, and often, Harper made it easy. Until lately, she had been a well-behaved kid.

But Harper cursing Steph, to her face, had triggered Steph. She'd reverted to her parents' ways, which disturbed her. In a microsecond, she had lost control of her actions.

Troubled by the entire incident, she struggled to sleep. Drinking a whole bottle of Chardonnay didn't help matters.

Lord, I'm a mess. I need to get it together.

At some point during the night, she heard Harper emerge from her bedroom and go downstairs. Steph was tempted to get out of bed, find her daughter, hug her, and apologize, but she couldn't make herself do it; she hadn't seen her since the Big Slap. After a few minutes, she heard Harper return upstairs and shut her bedroom door.

The silence in the house was thick enough to cleave with an axe. Harper was in her room, sullen and alone; Steph was in bed, upset and alone; Adrian was out in his own apartment and surely troubled, too. What had happened to their family?

A few minutes before six the next morning, Steph awoke with a throbbing headache but determined to say something to Harper—she wasn't sure what. After taking ibuprofen to alleviate her headache, she shuffled down the dark hallway to Harper's bedroom door.

The door was unlocked. She pushed it open.

A bluish night-light glowed inside. Harper lay in bed, covers pulled over her head. A bag of Doritos lay on the nightstand. Was that what Harper had eaten for dinner?

Steph's hand that had slapped her child throbbed. Something that stunned her: striking a person with the palm of your hand could hurt you, too.

Although Harper appeared to be sleeping, Steph approached the bed and peeled back the sheets. She needed to see her and make sure she was okay.

Harper's head lay atop the pillow, a silky black hair bonnet protecting her hair. Her hand lay beside her face.

Steph had wanted to get a look at Harper's face, to see how bad of a bruise her slap had caused, but she discovered an unexpected item lying next to her daughter's hand.

A cell phone.

What is this? I took her iPhone yesterday.

Steph picked it up. It was a basic-looking device. She had seen cheap, prepaid models like this on sale at gas stations.

A burner phone, that's what they call them.

Steph felt herself shaking. She drew a deep breath to calm her racing pulse.

Harper's eyelids fluttered as if she sensed her mother nearby. Steph reached for the lamp on the nightstand and switched it on.

Harper sprang upright in bed. She gaped at the phone in Steph's hand.

"We need to talk," Steph said.

In the kitchen downstairs, Steph prepared breakfast: scrambled eggs, bacon, and buttermilk biscuits that had been previously frozen. Harper sat at the table, head lowered, hands pressed to her temples.

The burner phone lay in the island's center like an exhibit in a courtroom trial. Harper had admitted, albeit reluctantly, that Scarlett had given her the phone weeks ago.

Was there no end to that malicious child's scheming? Steph had snapped a pic of the device and texted it to Adrian with the caption: *Harper had this, and I'm sure you know who gave it to her.* Adrian hadn't responded yet, but it was early.

"Come fix your plate," Steph said.

"I'm not hungry," Harper mumbled.

"You need to eat. A bag of Doritos isn't a meal."

Sighing, Harper rose from her chair and, head down, shuffled to the food Steph had prepared. A ghastly dark purple bruise marked one side of her face. When she looked at it, Steph felt like a blade twisted in her heart, and she forced herself to glance away.

Harper tossed a couple of slices of bacon onto her plate, along with a spoonful of eggs and a biscuit. She picked up the jar of jelly Steph had set out on the counter and trudged back to the table. Although she had claimed not to be hungry, she shoveled food into her mouth as if she hadn't eaten in days.

"You're staying home from school today," Steph said.

Harper's fork clattered to the plate. "Why?"

Steph swallowed. "It wouldn't be good for teachers to see how you look."

"Because how I look makes *you* look like a child abuser?" Something hard and spiteful glinted in Harper's gaze.

Had she deserved that comeback? Probably, she did.

"We need to sort through some things," Steph said. "I'll contact the school. I'll let you use your laptop. You can do your assignments online."

"Wow, thanks, Mom." Harper's voice dripped with sarcasm as thick as the grape jelly she slathered on her biscuit.

Steph prepared her own plate. She had a big day ahead and needed food in her stomach.

"I have to go to work today," Steph said. "I've got some showings scheduled. I expect you to stay in the house and do schoolwork. You can watch television on your breaks."

"What if I need to call somebody?" Harper asked. "We don't have a landline anymore. What if there's an emergency?"

"You're not getting your phone back, Harper. Not for a *very* long time. This toxic friendship of yours needs to die out first."

Mumbling under her breath, Harper continued eating.

It's for her own good, Steph thought. *She doesn't see it now, but she will eventually. She'll thank me one day for taking this hard line with her. If it's up to me, she'll never see Scarlett again, and we can get on with our lives.*

But why did she fear that more trouble lay ahead?

42

Early that Tuesday morning, before driving to the FiPro office, Adrian decided to log on to the company VPN and check his email messages. Maybe the promised job offer had arrived in his mailbox overnight.

He couldn't connect to the network.

Authorization failed.

He gritted his teeth as he read the error message flashing on the screen. This was annoying. The network must have been temporarily down; such outages occurred occasionally.

He snapped the laptop shut and got ready for work. When he stepped out of the shower into the bedroom, he saw a text message from Steph had arrived.

After last night's adventure, he had been hoping for a reassuring message from Gina or Lamont, but neither of them had contacted him. Steph's text included a photo of a plain-looking mobile phone lying on their kitchen counter: *Harper had this, and I'm sure you know who gave it to her.*

"Well, damn," Adrian said aloud.

Scarlett had given Harper a burner phone, which explained a few things that had been going on over the past few weeks. Even when they had taken Harp's phone away, she had still been in communication with Scarlett; the girls hadn't missed a beat.

Scarlett was only a kid, yet she consistently seemed to stay one step ahead of them.

It pulled his thoughts back to the folder full of documents he had discovered on Gina's phone and sent to himself. He'd emailed them to his Gmail account and downloaded all the files to a USB flash drive.

However, he had yet to dig through everything and hadn't quite determined what he would *do* with any of it. What he'd skimmed so far painted a portrait of Scarlett at odds with the notion that she was "only a kid."

Shortly before eight thirty, he pulled into the FiPro office parking lot. As he walked toward the gleaming corporate building, he saw Trevor strutting to the entrance.

"Wassup, bruh?" Trevor said.

He and Adrian exchanged a fist bump.

"Another day, another dollar," Adrian said.

They walked into the lobby.

"How did the chitchat with Mr. CEO go yesterday?" Trevor asked. He chuckled. "Is he hiring you as his right-hand man now?"

Adrian remembered seeing Trevor on his way to the executive floor. He wished he could boast about the job offer, but a simmering anxiety held him back.

"It was only a chat," he said. "He loves to talk golf."

"Golf again? You barely play. Shit, I could talk more golf to the man than you."

Adrian shrugged. Trevor scanned his badge at the bank of elevators, and the doors slid open. They got inside, and he hit the button to take them to the ninth floor.

When the car arrived at nine, they got out; Trevor headed to the vestibule doors on the left, and Adrian went to the right. Adrian scanned his badge.

Bad Influence

The reader flashed red and buzzed.

What the hell?

He tried it again with the same result.

"Hey, Trevor," Adrian said. "Something's up with my badge. Let me go in with you."

"Better talk to Mr. CEO about that." Snickering, Trevor let him enter through the glass door on the other side of the vestibule.

At his seat on the eastern wing of the ninth floor, Adrian found a large cardboard box atop his desk. The desk's surface had been cleared of all items except the office telephone. He peeled the box flaps and found his personal effects crammed inside: photos of Steph and Harper and other miscellaneous items he had brought to accent his space.

But he understood the significance of the packed box. Everyone did.

No, Adrian thought. *No, this can't be.*

"Good morning, Adrian."

Adrian turned. It was his supervisor, Keith. A uniformed security guard stood with him. Keith rubbed his hands together vigorously as if trying to kindle a fire, a gesture Adrian recognized as a nervous tic.

"What the hell is going on?" Adrian asked.

"I got a call from HR early this morning, man." More hand rubbing followed, palms scraping together like sandpaper. "I'm sorry. You've been terminated."

"Excuse me?"

"Terminated, Adrian."

"Terminated? What the hell for?"

"I don't know what's going on. I mean, they just rehired you, right? But HR says you need to turn in your laptop and badge and leave the premises."

"But I was promoted! Lamont—Mr. Washington—offered me a new job yesterday!"

The security guard squared his shoulders as if he anticipated

Adrian would be one of those problematic fired employees who needed to be forcefully removed.

"I'm only the messenger," Keith said. "I'm sorry."

"Wait a damn minute." Adrian dug his phone out of his back pocket. "Let me make a call—I'll prove it, all right? This is all a mistake."

Keith glanced at the security officer. "Okay."

Hands shaking, Adrian called Lamont; again, Lamont didn't answer. Cursing, he called Gina. She answered on the fourth ring.

"Hey, you." She yawned, sounding groggy, and he wondered when she had left the theater and staggered to bed.

His phone mashed to his ear, Adrian turned away from his supervisor and the guard and lowered his voice.

"Gina, did you talk to Lamont? I just got into the office, and they said I was terminated."

She smacked her lips. "Did I talk to Lamont about what?"

"My job, dammit!" He couldn't help raising his voice. "That was our agreement!"

"You know I don't get involved in that man's business, boo. That's between you boys."

He ground his teeth. She was gaslighting him again. How had he ever trusted this woman?

"That's what you promised," he said.

"I've gotta go, boo. My hydration tech is here. Hangovers are a bitch."

Click.

The phone sagging in his hand like a heavy dumbbell, he turned back to Keith and the security guard.

"Any luck?" Keith asked.

"This isn't over," Adrian said.

"It's over today, buddy." The guard stepped forward. "Grab the box, and let's go."

Feeling numb, head hanging down, Adrian picked up the box and shuffled out of the office.

43

Adrian dumped the cardboard box into his SUV's trunk, and then he settled behind the steering wheel and gazed out the window at the parking lot.

His heart rumbled like distant thunder. Although parked vehicles filled his range of vision, he saw only the faces of Gina, Lamont, and Scarlett, spinning in front of him like a carousel, grinning at him, mocking him.

"Goddammit!" he shouted.

He hammered the steering wheel with his fist once, twice, three times. On the third punch, he hit the horn, and the vehicle squawked like a kicked cow.

They wouldn't get away with this; he wouldn't allow it. Maybe these people shifted others around like pawns on a chessboard, but they wouldn't do this to him. He hadn't come this far to be swiped aside so easily.

He shouted again, his chest heaving. Catching a glimpse of his face in the rearview mirror, he almost thought he was looking at someone else: the sweaty-faced Black man with the wild, dilated eyes couldn't possibly be him.

He slugged the wheel again.

He'd been so close to reaching the next level that he could taste it. Now, the opportunity was gone as if it had been only a figment of his imagination. Was there any tangible evidence that Lamont had offered him a job in the first place? He felt as if he might have dreamed up the whole episode.

His phone chimed. It was Steph.

He accepted the call, but he didn't offer a greeting. He didn't trust himself to speak without erupting into another scream.

"Adrian?" she asked. "Are you there?"

He licked his dry lips.

"Can you hear me?" she asked.

"Yeah." His voice was a paper-thin whisper.

"Is something wrong?" Her voice quivered like a feather in the wind. "I didn't hear from you after I sent you the picture of that burner phone I found with Harper. That kid Scarlett is a trip." A weak laugh.

An idea struck Adrian like a mallet upside the head. An absurdly simple, excellent idea.

He mashed the button to start the Kia's engine.

"Adrian?" she asked again, her voice hitting a higher pitch.

"I've been busy, Steph."

"Something's wrong. I can tell. What happened?"

"They fired me."

Clutching the wheel, he gunned out of the parking space and veered out of the lot, tires squealing.

"They fired you? What?"

"It's not over."

"What're you talking about? What's not over? What're you doing?"

"Gotta go. I've got business to handle."

He clicked off the call. Steph called him again, but he didn't answer her, and when she followed up with a text—*please, talk to me, I'm worried about you*—he didn't respond.

He returned to the road after picking up an item from his apartment. Fifteen minutes later, he was in the strip mall that housed Barnes Investigations.

～

Raymond Barnes looked up from his laptop when Adrian entered the small office.

"Good morning, Mr. Wall. Have you reconsidered our offer?"

Adrian sat on one of the chairs facing the desk.

"I want to talk to your client," Adrian said. "Face-to-face. Today. I've got something he'll want."

Barnes leaned back and rapped his ballpoint pen against his finely trimmed goatee.

"You look agitated, Mr. Wall. What happened?"

"I woke up," Adrian said.

He placed the flash drive on the desk.

Earlier, Barnes and his client had offered compensation for their "assistance" against the Washingtons, but the offer hadn't crystallized in Adrian's mind as a viable step until FiPro fired him.

The detective plugged the stick into his laptop, tapped a few keys, and paused to study the screen. A sly grin crept across his face.

"How did you come across this information?" Barnes asked. "Surely it wasn't willingly provided to you?"

Adrian didn't have the stomach or clarity of mind to detail last night's sorry misadventure.

"Will your client be interested or not?"

Chuckling, Barnes picked up his smartphone and thumbed the screen.

"I'll set up a meeting," he said.

44

The detective's client, Arthur Calhoun, lived in Dawsonville, about thirty miles north of Alpharetta. As Adrian navigated the route with Google Maps, he could think only one thing, the phrase like a mantra in his mind: *It's not over yet.*

Trevor texted him while he was driving.

Yo, what's going on, bruh? I heard security walked you out the building! WTF?

Adrian grimaced. This would be the headline of the day at the company: "Adrian Wall escorted out of the building by security." There would be rumors circling about what he had done to earn his downfall, all of them completely wrong, but that moment would be memorialized as his legacy at FiPro: a head-hanging walk of shame.

A fresh rivet of anger bolted through him. He responded to Trevor: *It's not over yet.*

Trevor shot back another question, but Adrian couldn't allow himself to get bogged down in a back-and-forth while he was driving. His friend didn't know a tenth of what percolated beneath the surface.

Adrian neared the address that Barnes had given him: a property lay just ahead, the entrance obscured by thick shrubs on a winding country road on the outskirts of town. Slowing his SUV, Adrian peered at the dusty driveway on his right that led to Calhoun's home.

A banged-up mailbox that looked as if it had been run over by an eighteen-wheeler and posted back up stood at the end of the access path. Faded white letters at the top of the box stated: *Calhoun*.

Before embarking on his trip, Adrian had Googled Arthur Calhoun and found his LinkedIn profile, which included a photograph. He was a hale-looking White man with a lush mane of silver hair and striking aquamarine eyes. Calhoun was a bigwig in the logistics industry, one of those businesses Adrian knew little about. Still, Barnes had assured him that his client was "a man of means."

Searching Calhoun's name also yielded hits on the obituaries for his wife and daughter. Calhoun's wife, a Black woman, had been decades younger than him, the woman bearing him a child who had been young enough to be his granddaughter. All the same, they were gone, and Adrian felt sorry for the guy.

Adrian turned into the driveway. Elms and maples lined the bumpy, pothole-filled road, tossing him up and down in his SUV as he rode along.

After he had driven several hundred yards, the trees thinned, and the driveway broadened to reveal a dated ranch-style home. Painted pale blue, it was in dire need of repainting. It featured dusty ivory shutters and a roof that looked one bad storm away from collapsing, the gutters overflowing with debris. An enormous but diseased oak tree towered in the yard, kudzu vines clutching the lesioned trunk in a choke hold.

The newest thing there was a silver Ford F-150 parked in a carport beside the house, its rear panel caked with dust.

If Adrian hadn't seen the surname posted on the mailbox at the entrance, he would have assumed this was the wrong address. The detective had boasted that his client had money, but in Adrian's opinion, this didn't look like the home of a wealthy man.

I've come this far. I might as well go through with it.

He parked behind the pickup truck, got out, and went to the front door. A storm door served as the exterior entrance; a section of the glass pane was shattered, and a web of cracks spread across the surface.

Adrian looked for the doorbell, but the button was broken, too. He settled for knocking with his fist on the storm door. Calhoun ought to be expecting him.

He waited a minute, and no one responded.

Adrian stepped to one of the curtained windows beside the doorway, cupping his hands around his face to try to see inside the home. However, the heavy draperies blocked his view.

He knocked again. After waiting another minute, with no answer, he pulled out his phone, ready to call Barnes to ask if this guy knew he was coming, when he heard movement on the other side of the doorway.

Finally, the door creaked open.

A hunched-over man peered at Adrian through the storm door's broken glass. If this was Calhoun, he'd aged dramatically since he'd taken that LinkedIn portrait.

"Mr. Calhoun?" Adrian asked. "I'm Adrian Wall. Barnes should have told you I was coming."

Calhoun said something, but his voice was so thin Adrian couldn't hear him.

"Can I come in?" Adrian asked.

Calhoun waved him in with a shaky hand. Adrian opened the door and crossed the threshold.

Calhoun leaned on a cane, and a nasal cannula was attached to his nostrils, pumping supplemental oxygen into his lungs. Standing perhaps five feet six, he wore baggy gray sweatpants, threadbare house shoes that revealed socked feet, and an oversized blue T-shirt that hung on him like a gown. Calhoun's complexion was pale as sun-bleached bone. Brittle stringy white hair crowned his head like a ragged mop.

The only sign of vitality came from those blue eyes. They shone with vivid curiosity as he assessed Adrian.

Calhoun offered his frail, liver-spotted hand. To Adrian, shaking his hand was like exchanging a handshake with a cadaver.

"Thanks for agreeing to see me on short notice," Adrian said.

"You drove all the way up here, son," Calhoun said, his watery voice carrying a pronounced Georgia accent. "I hope you have something good to tell me."

Adrian pulled the USB drive out of his pocket and handed it to Calhoun, the man accepting it with trembling fingers. Calhoun looked at the device, his thin lips contorting into a scowl. He offered the drive back to Adrian.

"Come on back and talk to me," Calhoun said.

Calhoun shuffled deeper into the house with much effort, and Adrian followed.

∼

Although the exterior of the home was in shambles, Calhoun kept the interior spotless. Considering the man's fragile physical condition, Adrian assumed he employed a housekeeper.

The place was furnished with basic tables, chairs, and sofas, badly mismatched items that might have been acquired from a yard sale. Much of the flooring was glazed brick, a relic from the seventies; he saw beige shag carpeting in other areas. Lots of photographs hung on the walls and stood on tables, pictures of his wife and daughter in happier times.

The smell of disinfectant permeated the house, reminiscent of an ICU ward in a hospital. It masked any other odors that might have accumulated over time, leaving everything smelling artificially clean and sterile.

Calhoun led Adrian to a wooden deck attached to the back of the house. The sitting area was furnished with wrought iron patio furniture. A pitcher of iced tea stood on the table, paired with two glasses, one already full.

"Tea?" Calhoun asked with a slow gesture toward the pitcher.

"Sure, thanks."

Adrian poured himself a glass and, following Calhoun's lead, settled onto one of the chairs. The deck overlooked a rambling backyard with grass cut so low it looked as if the lawn had been scalped by a mad landscaper. A six-foot-high wooden fence, several of the planks sprung free from their foundation, encircled the vast space.

"This is my childhood home," Calhoun said in his watery voice, which strengthened as he warmed to his topic. "I came back here after I sold our house in Alpharetta last year. My folks have been living in Dawsonville for ages."

"I wondered why you were here," Adrian said. "It wasn't what I expected."

"My grandpa was a chicken farmer, but you want to know his real business? Making moonshine. He had his own moonshine still, and he'd run his whiskey down Thunder Road to sell it."

"Thunder Road?"

"Georgia State Highway 9, son." He smiled. "Alpharetta Highway."

"Oh, right."

"But me? I took my tail to college, started my business, and moved my family into Country Club of the South. Ever heard of it?"

Adrian nodded. The exclusive gated community was on par with St. Martin's, where the Washingtons resided.

"I know I can't afford a house there," Adrian said.

This brought a chuckle from Calhoun, an utterance that sounded like a hacking cough. "I'm happy to be rid of it. I was only there 'cause of Nadine." He sipped his tea, his hand trembling so badly that the ice cubes rattled like bones in the glass. "This place, my old home, suits me better these days. I ought to spruce up the joint a bit, but at my age, it doesn't seem to matter . . ."

As Calhoun trailed off, he placed his tea on the table, and shifted in his chair to study Adrian. Adrian sipped the tea and found it brewed as weak as Calhoun's voice.

"How did your daughter get hooked up with the girl?" Calhoun asked.

"At school. I hear you were behind her parents pulling her out of Queen's Academy?"

"Eh, done out of sheer spite. Benefiting nobody at all. And see—now the girl's become the mosquito feasting on your ass, so what did it help? I only passed on the problem to some other poor fool."

Listening, Adrian placed the USB drive on the table, a visual reminder to Calhoun of the purpose of this visit, but Calhoun didn't appear to notice. A mistiness came over the older man's eyes.

"I miss Nadine and our little girl," Calhoun said, his voice brittle. He dug a handkerchief out of his pocket and dabbed at his eyes. "You know when we got hitched, only my mama and a couple cousins came to our wedding? My daddy, some of my people, couldn't stomach the thought of me marrying a Black woman."

"Love is color blind," Adrian said.

"Yes," Calhoun said firmly. He tapped his index finger against the table, emphasizing the point. "But there's being *plain blind*, too, and that ain't so helpful. Look—the girl gained a reputation at the academy over the years. Smart, but sneaky—real sneaky. Folks talked. Everybody said, 'Oh, she's only a cute little kid—don't make nothin' of it.' I bought into that, too."

Adrian held the cold glass, waiting.

"Plain blind, like I said, it ain't so good," Calhoun said. "When my daughter and the girl got friendly, I had those blinders on despite what my gut told me." He tapped his sallow stomach. "Me being the old White guy, coming from a long line of moonshine-slingin' rednecks, most folks seeing me as out of touch, anyhow, I didn't want to say what I was feeling deep down and come off sounding too judgmental. Know what I mean?"

"I got it."

"Nadine knew straight off the girl was trouble, but I kept

wearing those blinders." He mimed putting on a pair of glasses. "Back then, I was trying to encourage the girls, saying they were only kids. Hell, most of the time, I was too busy working anyway to pay attention to what was happening. Then, my little girl started getting into trouble at school."

Adrian thought about Harper's cheating incident. "This sounds familiar."

"She got arrested after the school incidents. Shoplifting."

"Stealing?" Adrian said. "But you're rich; you could have bought her anything."

"*Would* have bought her anything she needed, yes. But, son, I understand this now: it wasn't about owning stuff, 'cause the girl's parents got plenty of money, too. Nope, it's about doing what you aren't supposed to do. No rules. No law. Do what you want, whenever you want."

Adrian heard Scarlett's voice echoing in his memory: *Whatever I want, whenever I want it.*

Calhoun continued: "Now, you pair that with a certain type of cunning, of knowing how to wear childhood like a kind of . . ." He frowned, straining for words. "Like a kind of mask, I reckon . . . and now, son, you have a very dangerous human being on your hands." He stared at Adrian, his gaze brighter than at any point in their conversation. "You've got someone who must be handled with extreme caution."

As Calhoun's words washed over him, Adrian picked up the USB drive from where he had placed it on the table.

"Barnes said you were willing to pay for information," Adrian said. "I've got what you want right here."

Calhoun inclined his head. "You got my attention, son."

"There's enough dirt on this drive to help you. It has inside details on things the Washingtons have worked with their attorneys and handlers to cover up."

A coughing fit overcame Calhoun, the man pressing the handkerchief to his mouth. Wincing, Adrian waited for him to compose himself.

"So, what you got there," Calhoun said, "does it include what happened to my Nadine and our little girl?"

"I haven't examined every document on it, but when I skimmed it, I saw several mentions of your names."

"I need more than mentions, son. I need something that can wrangle them into a courtroom."

"And I need ten grand up front," Adrian said. "If everything checks out and you have what you need to return to court, I want another hundred and fifty thousand dollars."

Calhoun didn't flinch at the demand, which told Adrian what he needed to know about this man's resources.

"You sound like a fella knows exactly what he wants," Calhoun said.

"It's what they owe me." He didn't intend to explain how his demand matched Lamont's job offer's compensation details, right down to the promised ten-thousand-dollar signing bonus. It was none of Calhoun's business.

"I'll talk to my man," Calhoun said with a slow nod. "I think we can do business."

Calhoun extended his hand. Adrian shook it, but Calhoun didn't immediately release his hold on him.

"What are you doing about the girl?" Calhoun asked. "Is your kid still friends with her?"

"We've cut off their friendship. It's being handled."

"No, son." Calhoun squeezed Adrian's hand so tightly that Adrian's knuckles cracked from the sudden pressure; Adrian tried to pull out of his grasp, but Calhoun held him fast, gaze burning. "Listen. Nadine and I believed that same foolishness. This girl is more cunning than a fox eyeing a henhouse. You need to gather up your family and leave town."

Leave town? Because of a child? Was this man's mind as frail as his body?

"Do you mind letting go of my hand now, sir?"

"Promise me you'll leave town."

"I'll talk to my wife about it, all right?"

Calhoun loosened his grip, and Adrian snatched his hand away and massaged his tingling fingers. The older man's surprisingly firm hold had drained the blood out of his hand.

"You got your eye on that money, but that's a mistake." Calhoun sipped his tea, grimacing as if he found the taste lacking. "What good will it do you to gain a small fortune but lose your entire world?"

45

Stuck at home alone, with no mobile phones, left only with her school laptop, Harper thought at first that she would go nuts with boredom. Because that day was technically the start of her in-school detention, her teachers had posted a bunch of assignments for her on their online learning platform. Without the distraction of going back and forth to class, Harper finished all the work before lunchtime, and then, with nothing left to do, she was bored.

Well, bored and seriously worried, too.

How could she stop being friends with Scarlett? It wasn't Scarlett's fault that she had been caught cheating. While Scarlett had shown her how to use the AI app to create essays ("It's a major timesaver, sis"), it had been Harper's decision to use the tool. Her mom punishing her by trying to destroy her friendship with Scarlett didn't make any sense.

But it was typical of Mom. Mom hadn't liked Scarlett from the beginning; Scarlett intimated that Mom was envious of Scarlett's family, and Harper tended to believe her. This cheating thing gave Mom an excuse to break up their friendship.

Sometimes, she really hated her mother.

Harper made a turkey sandwich for lunch and switched on the TV in the family room. She thought she would find something on Netflix while she nibbled on her meal (and wow, it *hurt* to chew because of her swollen face), but most of the YA shows that she enjoyed featuring teenage girls revolved around friendships. Such shows made Harper sad, and she tossed aside the remote control.

Restless, she returned upstairs to her bedroom.

A book lay on her desk: *Spin*, a YA mystery novel by Lamar Giles. Her cousin Willow had given it to her; the two of them used to share books all the time, but since Scarlett had entered Harper's life, Harper didn't bother reading anything that wasn't required for school.

She picked it up, stretched across her bed, and started reading. The story grabbed her on the first page, and she had lost track of time when she heard the doorbell chime.

Harper rose from the bed.

Since she was a much younger child, her parents had warned her against opening the door to strangers. But curiosity pulled Harper to her parents' bedroom, which had a big window that overlooked the driveway.

An unfamiliar black car was parked in front of their house.

The doorbell chimed again, twice more, and the visitor rapped hard against the door and yelled: "Harper, it's me!"

Harper grinned. She couldn't believe it.

She hurried downstairs to let Scarlett in.

Standing in the hallway, Scarlett lifted Harper's chin and turned her head sideways as she studied Harper's face.

"Jesus, it looks worse than it did in the pics you sent me, Harp," Scarlett said. Her jaw tightened. "Your mom ought to be arrested for child abuse."

"That's why she didn't let me go to school," Harper said.

"What a bitch. I had to cut class and come over, sis. When you didn't text me back, I got worried about what else your psycho mom might do."

Scarlett had taken an Uber to her house like she usually did when traveling. Her level of freedom always impressed Harper. Why couldn't her parents relax and allow her more independence?

"How'd you get out of school?" Harper asked, though she suspected she knew the answer.

"Lamont called me out sick." Giggling, Scarlett lifted her phone and played her dad's AI-cloned voice: *"This is Mr. Lamont Washington III. I regret to inform you that my dear daughter, Scarlett, will be absent from school today due to an unexpected illness. Her mother and I hope that she will return tomorrow."*

"I'll never get my phone back," Harper said. "My mom took the one you gave me, too. She came in and got it when I was sleeping."

"She's such a bitch! How do you deal with her?"

"What am I supposed to do about it? She's my mom."

"I could think of a few things, sis." Scarlett glowered. "This bullshit about us not being friends anymore has pissed me off. Do you know that a thirteen-year-old girl is considered an adult in some parts of the world?"

"Are you serious?"

Scarlett bobbed her head. "That's why my parents let me do whatever I want. I pick my friends. I go wherever I want. They don't get in the way."

"My mom would never go for that, ever."

"Anyway, we should get out of here. Aren't you sick of being home all day?"

The prospect of hanging out with Scarlett unsupervised was far more appealing than spending the rest of the day reading a book alone in the bedroom. Harper used to enjoy such simple, solitary pursuits, but when Scarlett entered her life, activities that had captivated her in the past failed to compare to the addictive highs of her friend's presence.

"What if my mom comes home?" Harper asked. "She'll kill me if I'm not here."

"At this point, sis, you probably aren't joking about your psycho mommy. All right, we'll go out for a little bit and then come back. Cool?"

"Only for a little while," Harper said, glancing at a wall clock.

"That's my girl." Scarlett snapped open her purse and withdrew a makeup compact; unlike Harper's parents, Scarlett's family allowed her to wear makeup. "Let's cover up that battered housewife bruise on your face, and then I'll grab us an Uber so we can get outta here."

46

Steph spent much of the day attempting to woo prospective home buyers to sign on the dotted line with a battery of residential properties, but it had little effect. Lately, she had been on a run of bad luck, plagued with fickle prospects who wanted to tour every house on the market. The showings rarely led to offers.

Since her separation from Adrian, the business had been shaky, as if her personal and professional lives were symbiotically connected in the worst way. She had managed to keep her head above water but nothing more. If her losing streak continued, she'd have to dip into her emergency fund to make ends meet, and she'd need to consider adding a side hustle. She'd seen folks driving far more luxurious vehicles than her Toyota Camry making DoorDash deliveries. You did whatever you had to do when your back was against the wall.

Around three in the afternoon, Steph returned home. Tension curdled her stomach as she parked in the driveway.

She didn't want to confront her child, didn't want to see that look of accusation on her daughter's beloved face. Seeing Harper pained her so much that Steph felt like someone had smacked her, too.

The house was silent; the television was off in the family room.

"Harper?" Steph said, raising her voice loudly enough for her child to hear her upstairs. Harper couldn't have been wearing earbuds to listen to her usual music because she was deprived of her iPhone.

No answer.

Upstairs, Steph found Harper's bedroom door half-open. The room was shadowed, the bed unmade and empty.

The bathrooms were vacant, too. She checked every other room, including the master bedroom, and didn't find her child.

"Harper?" Steph said again, though it was clear by then that her daughter was not in the house.

Unease plucked her heart. She hurried downstairs to get her phone out of her purse, planning to call Adrian and ask if he had picked up their daughter or some such thing.

Opening her bag, she heard car doors slam in the driveway. A few seconds later, the front door swung open.

Harper came inside, but she wasn't alone.

Scarlett was with her.

∽

Steph gaped at the two girls. After everything that had happened between her and Harper in the past twenty-four hours, she was at a loss for words.

Harper clapped a hand to her mouth, gaze darting to and fro as if she wanted to scurry into a corner and hide. But Scarlett smiled at Steph.

"Hey there, Mrs. Wall," the girl said. "How are you doing today? I took Harp out to get some fresh air. She was going nuts inside this house all by herself."

Steph finally regained her voice.

"You." She pointed a shaky finger at Harper. "Go. In. Your. Room. Now."

Harper started to bolt, but Scarlett touched her shoulder, stopping her.

"Hold on a second, Harp," Scarlett said. "I want you here for my little chitchat with your mom."

Scarlett was still beaming at her. Steph's mouth was dry. Had her ears deceived her? Had this teenager ordered Harper, Steph's child, to disobey her?

Harper balanced on the balls of her feet, her gaze swiveling back and forth between Steph and her friend.

"I want you out of my house," Steph told Scarlett. She pointed to the door. "I'm giving you three seconds."

"Or you'll do what?" Scarlett smirked. "Smack me, like you did my sister here? I almost convinced Harp to call Child Protective Services, you know. You're lucky, Mrs. Wall."

"Get out of my house!" Steph said.

"You're such an annoying bitch. All the screaming and stomping. You're like a toddler having a tantrum. Pipe down."

No one had ever talked to Steph like this in her life, much less a child. A *child*.

She's evil, Steph. You know what she's been accused of doing, remember? Do you have any doubt about what this girl is capable of?

While Harper gawked at her friend, Steph marched to the door and snatched it open. She put her hand on Scarlett's arm, but Scarlett shook off her touch.

"If you lay a finger on me, I'll sue your raggedy ass for every penny you've got." Scarlett glowered at her.

"I'll call the police!" Steph said.

Scarlett stood her ground in the hallway.

"Let me be clear, Mrs. Wall," she said. "If you touch my friend again, you're going to jail. I'll call CPS myself and give testimony of your abusive behavior. Do we understand each other?"

"Get the hell out of my house, you evil little bitch," Steph said. "If I ever see you in my home again, I'm calling the police."

"You pathetic little people and your empty threats." Scarlett clucked her tongue. "Remember what I said, child abuser." She glanced at Harper. "Harp, we'll talk soon, sis."

"Get out!" Steph screamed.

Scarlett pantomimed firing a pistol at Steph. Smiling, she sauntered out of the house, where the Uber driver waited in the driveway.

Steph slammed the door, locked it, and leaned against it. Her head pounded so hard it felt as if it would explode open like a dropped cantaloupe.

Behind her, Harper fled upstairs to her room. Steph couldn't summon the energy or will to chase after her, shout, and impose more punishments.

Because now, she was scared.

47

That evening, Adrian met Steph at his sister-in-law's townhouse in Roswell, as Steph requested via a text message. She didn't tell him why he was to meet her there; she said only that he needed to go there to talk to her.

When Adrian pulled into the driveway, parking behind Steph's Toyota, she came outside to meet him as if she had been looking out the window for his arrival. Her appearance struck him: though she wore her usual work ensemble, a blouse and business skirt, shadows darkened her eyes.

As soon as he got out of his SUV, she came into his arms and hugged him. Puzzled, he held her.

She was shaking.

"Babe, what's going on?" he asked. "Why are we here, and why do you look like someone died?" A terrible thought hit him. "Wait, is it Harp? Is she—"

"She's okay. She's inside." She stepped out of his embrace and dragged her fingers through her hair. "A lot's happened today. We needed to get some space in a safe place."

"A safe place?"

"I kept Harper out of school today for obvious reasons. Scarlett came to the house, and the girls went somewhere in an Uber while I was at work."

Once again, Scarlett had outmaneuvered them, he realized.

"I was home when they came back. Scarlett got in my face." Steph hugged herself. "I know you'll say she's only a kid, but knowing her history with her last so-called friend, and the things she said to me, and how she said them . . . that girl scares me, Adrian, she really does. I had to bring Harper somewhere safe."

"Is Harper in danger?"

"She's in danger so long as that little devil child knows where to find her. But Harper thinks *I'm* the enemy, the big baddie for keeping her away from her friend. She doesn't get it at all."

"God, what a mess." He leaned against his car. "It's been one helluva day."

"You got fired."

"I don't feel like talking about that right now." He glanced toward the townhouse. "Is Kellie okay with Harper staying here?"

"My sister's not a fan of Scarlett, either, remember? Kellie doesn't have a landline. We've taken both of Harper's phones, and Willow has strict instructions not to allow Harper to use her phone, either."

"We're treating our daughter like a prisoner," he said.

"I don't like it, but it's necessary until we get this under control. I want to file for a restraining order against Scarlett."

If Adrian hadn't studied the contents of the file he had copied from Gina, he might have scoffed at his wife's idea. But he knew better.

Steph watched him, jaw clenched as though anticipating his disagreement.

But he said, "Is it possible to get a restraining order against a minor? I've never heard of that before, Steph. I've heard only about adults getting restraining orders slapped on them."

"I plan to spend tomorrow calling lawyers to find out," she said.

"What about school?" he asked. "We can't send her to school, right? Scarlett's there."

"She can do her assignments online until we sort out everything. Maybe we'll have to transfer her to a new school. The school year just started. Moving her may not be as disruptive as we think."

"Turning our lives upside down because of a teenage girl." Adrian rubbed his temple; he was developing a fresh headache. "I'd be laughing at how ridiculous it all sounds if I didn't know what she's capable of."

"I'm surprised you're on board with everything now. I expected you to accuse me of overreacting, as usual. What changed?"

He took out the thumb drive, a duplicate of the device he had given Barnes after his visit with Arthur Calhoun, and pressed it into Steph's clammy palm.

"What's on this?" she asked.

"Confirmation."

"Confirmation? Of what?"

"That you're not overreacting. Not even a little bit."

48

Restless, though it was past midnight, Scarlett paced the floors of her family's mansion.

Sometimes, her mind worked so rapidly, like the gears of a ceaselessly churning motor, that she found it impossible to go to sleep, and she would spend the night wandering the lonely corridors of their enormous home. Usually, she eventually tired herself out and settled down to slumber somewhere outside her bedroom; on other nights, she wandered until she noticed the sun peeking through the windows.

This night felt like it would be of the latter kind.

Things had taken a turn with Harper, and she didn't like it.

Harper's bitch mother had discovered the burner phone Scarlett had given her, cutting off their backup communication channel. Although Scarlett could have acquired another phone during their adventure earlier in the afternoon, experience had taught her that the same trick never worked twice. Probably after Scarlett left their house, the whore had cavity-searched Harper for a *new* phone.

So, burner phones were out. Scarlett needed to formulate a new strategy. Something better.

Something bigger.

Ruminating, she paced and paced. Not having Harper available to communicate with whenever she wanted was driving her nuts. Harper adored and idolized her, and Scarlett craved that attention, basked in the sunshine of Harper's never-ending worship. Every time Harper gazed upon her with those adoring puppy dog eyes, Scarlett got a little charge of pleasure and felt more alive.

Other things charged up Scarlett, too, she had learned.

Lying.

Stealing—from people and from stores.

Sneaking into other people's houses. She had "explored" over a dozen homes in their own neighborhood and had never been caught once.

Planning pranks was fun, too.

Most fun of all? Planning "accidents."

Accidents were fun, fun, fun.

Like the one with her cousin a few years ago . . .

Her cousin's name was Addison, and everyone called her Addy. She was the daughter of her dad's brother, and she and Scarlett were the same age. Their matching ages and blood connection as first cousins should have sealed their bond, but Scarlett had despised Addy for as long as she could remember.

Addy was a little bitch who went out of her way to tell on Scarlett for *everything*. It was: "Aunt Gina, I saw Scarlett trying to steal a doll at Target." Or: "Uncle Lamont, Scarlett tried to make me drink some of your alcohol." Or: "Daddy, Scarlett says we should put sugar in your gas tank."

Such a little conniving bitch. Scarlett swore that one day, she would take care of her for good for her attempts to make Scarlett's life boring.

The opportunity presented itself when they were eleven years old, and Addy had come over to spend the weekend at their house. Knowing her cousin was planning to visit, Scarlett spent days plotting.

She found the answer in the swimming pool's drain cover.

Addy, like Scarlett, had taken swimming lessons and was a good swimmer, which meant that Scarlett's parents left them unsupervised in the pool (lousy parenting, Scarlett knew). But who would have suspected that the pool's drain cover was apparently "defective" and would become loose while Addy was swimming in the deep end—and that the powerful vacuum pump, exerting hundreds of pounds of sucking pressure, would snatch Addy right to the bottom and pin her down there until her face turned blue?

Scarlett waited until her cousin had been submerged underwater for a full minute, and then she shrieked for help.

By the time Gina ran outside and switched off the pool's power, it was over. The problem of the annoying cousin was solved permanently, and no one was the wiser. The police investigated, and Addy's mother (another bitch) dared to insinuate something nasty about Scarlett's behavior during the "accident," but Gina and Lamont protected her, as was their job.

That had been so much fun.

Almost as much fun, in fact, as how she had schemed to deal with her dead best friend's parents . . .

Zoey had been her best friend ever (until Harper came along). They were in the same grade at Queen's Academy, and they had always sort of been cool with each other, but in sixth grade, they attended several of the same classes, and that was when they got really tight as friends. Zoey's family was wealthy, too, but their bond had nothing to do with spending money.

Zoey was the perfect audience for Scarlett's deviant acts. She never snitched—the *number one trait* in a true friend, 'cause snitches get stitches—and she always went along with whatever Scarlett wanted to do, no matter how wild the suggestion.

Stealing clothes was a favorite activity of theirs. Once, at a local Target, store security nabbed Zoey, and the cops came and everything, and *still*, Zoey didn't snitch on Scarlett. That was a true sister.

Predictably, her parents became an issue. It was another case of the bitch mother who labeled Scarlett a bad influence, blah, blah, blah. Bitch mommy wanted to cut off their friendship, and Zoey's spineless dad went along with the idea.

"I hate them," Zoey had texted Scarlett before her mother confiscated her phone. "Sometimes, I want them to die."

The light bulb kicked on in Scarlett's mind, but she didn't say anything to Zoey immediately.

Scarlett had learned literally hundreds of ways to commit murders without getting caught. She was an avid fan of true crime books, television shows, blogs, and podcasts; it was a topic she studied, like some girls her age obsessed over makeup and clothes. Arranging accidents and using difficult-to-trace poisons were excellent means to dispatch someone who didn't deserve to draw another breath.

The real-life case of Marie Robards was instructive. She was a sixteen-year-old in Texas who poisoned her dad back in 1983. Robards used barium acetate, a chemical she had pilfered from her school's chemistry lab; she added it to her dad's taco dinner one night. Daddy had a fatal heart attack soon after that. Robards would have gotten away with it if she hadn't been dumb and told a friend what she did—the so-called friend snitched to the cops. (Another reason why snitches get stitches.)

Scarlett shared the story with Zoey, careful not to send her links or anything that could be traced back to her if Zoey lost her nerve. Scarlett also pointed out where their school's chemistry lab kept their supply of the deadly chemical—in an *unlocked* cabinet in a storage room, without a surveillance camera. (After all, they attended a private school, and surely, the well-behaved children of wealthy parents didn't require monitoring via closed-circuit cameras.)

With these details Scarlett had pointed out to her and a healthy dose of consistent encouragement, Zoey did the rest herself. Zoey even served up the poison in a taco dinner for her parents, a nod to the Robards girl.

Mommy died of a heart attack, but the dad survived, barely. One out of two wasn't so bad, Scarlett reasoned. She was proud of her handiwork until Zoey let guilt overwhelm her and took her own life. Disappointingly, Zoey had written about it all in a diary, and the bumbling cops came after Scarlett.

They had zip on her, though—and a dead girl couldn't testify . . .

It was around three o'clock in the morning when Scarlett had her light-bulb moment for her Harper conundrum. The epiphany brought her to a complete stop as she had been pacing through her family's fully equipped gymnasium.

It was perfect, she realized.

She turned the idea around and examined it from all angles, like a jeweler inspecting a diamond with a loupe.

Flawless, she thought.

Smiling to herself, she wandered back to her bedroom. She lay in bed, finally able to sleep now that she had discovered how to silence Harper's annoying parents forever.

49

"This is crazy," Steph said to Adrian.

Steph had plugged the USB drive he had given her into her laptop, which she had brought to her sister's house. She'd planned to spend the night to keep a close watch on Harper. So much had been happening lately that she didn't trust her daughter.

She was still rattled by her confrontation with Scarlett and the teenager's hypnotic hold over her daughter. Never in her years of parenting had she expected to be dealing with such a situation. Facing Harper when she got boy-crazy? Yes. But a toxic friendship with a malicious, murderous girl? Never.

They had set up her computer on the dining room table. She and Adrian sat side by side on chairs while she skimmed the drive's contents.

It was disturbing stuff, and proof of two things: the corruption she had long believed festered at the roots of the Washington family; and most of all, Scarlett's innate malice. She found correspondence with attorneys about Scarlett possibly rigging their swimming pool to drown her young cousin—a damaging allegation the lawyers put firmly to rest. She read inside details of how the family had shielded Scarlett from culpability in her friend's poisoning of her parents, an outrage that had driven Mr. Calhoun to seek retribution.

There were minor items, too, which served to paint a richer picture of Scarlett's pathology. Steph found evidence of several incidents between Scarlett and others at Queen's Academy, from outright bullying to her orchestrating cruel pranks; one faculty member had even threatened a lawsuit when he claimed Scarlett set him up for a child pornography accusation by installing damning photos on his computer. Scarlett had also faced numerous shoplifting charges at various retailers over the years, which the Washingtons' high-priced legal team had persuaded the stores to drop.

"Wow." Steph's head spun. She turned to Adrian. "How did you get all of this?"

Adrian cleared his throat. Whether he realized it or not, it was a known tell of his. What was he going to lie about this time?

"Does it matter how I got it?" he said. "Calhoun's gonna pay me good money for the information." Fire flashed in his gaze. "After everything I've been through, I deserve it, Steph."

He's still acting as if he's the only one affected by this situation, she thought. *What he's been through? What about what I've been through? What about our entire family?*

Her sister had already retained a lawyer to investigate what had happened on the Six Flags roller coaster. Her niece, Willow, was traumatized by the accident and scheduled to see a counselor. Harper was alternately furious at them and apologetic, trapped in a hurricane of conflicting emotions.

Yet Adrian sat here talking about what he deserved because of what *he* had been through.

She had been planning to ask if he wanted to spend the night, too—she'd already cleared it with Kellie—but she changed her mind. She needed another night away from him. Let him go back to his apartment.

Gina could keep him company.

Steph knew the woman was somehow connected to Adrian acquiring the dirt gathered on that thumb drive. She *knew* it.

"I've never been so humiliated," Adrian continued. "They walked me out of the building like I stole something after Lamont promised me a new job."

"You could start looking for a position elsewhere," she said. "FiPro isn't the only company in the world, Adrian."

He glared at her. "They owe me. It's not over."

Steph nodded toward the laptop. "Giving this info here to Calhoun for money will solve what? I haven't heard you say anything about ensuring justice is served."

"I need to get paid."

She made a dismissive gesture, unplugged the drive from her laptop, and placed it in front of him.

"You need to get your priorities straight," she said.

Rising from his chair, he swiped the drive off the table and shoved it into his pocket.

"You don't get it," he said. "As usual. I'm gonna check on Harp and then go home."

"You do that," she said.

Steph didn't try to stop him.

∼

Adrian found Harper in the guest room. Although it was only eight o'clock in the evening, she lay on the double bed, wrapped up in bedsheets.

Adrian tapped on the door. "Harp, are you awake?"

She stirred but kept her head covered. He entered the room and sat on the bed next to her.

"You've had a busy day," he said.

She pulled down the sheets. Her hair was tousled, her eyes

reddened from crying. The side of her face was an ugly purple, and the sight of it turned his stomach.

"I hate being here," she said. "I want to go home."

"You're here for a reason, Harp. Your mom and I don't agree on everything, but I agree that you need to be here for a while to let things cool off."

Her gaze dimmed a few more shades. "When can I get my phone back?"

"Believe it or not, life existed before smartphones, kid. The world went on fine without them."

"I need to talk to my sister."

"Your sister?"

She let out an exasperated sigh. "Scarlett."

"Do you know the things she's done, Harp?"

Harper's gaze tightened. "What things?"

"Her cousin drowned in their swimming pool. This happened a few years ago. It was ruled an accident, but some thought Scarlett schemed to cause it."

Harper didn't respond, but Adrian saw a glimmer in her gaze.

"That's not all," he said. "Her former best friend committed suicide—after she poisoned her parents. The girl's mother died, and the father hasn't fully recovered. I met him today, as a matter of fact. The girl wrote in her diary that Scarlett planned the poisoning, but her parents covered it up."

"Zoey?" Harper asked in a whisper.

"That's the girl's name. Did you know about this?"

Harper shook her head, but her lips were parted in a haunted expression.

"My sister would never hurt anyone," she said, as if trying to convince herself.

"Willow says she unbuttoned her seat belt on the roller coaster."

Harper squeezed her eyes shut in obstinate denial.

"We only want to keep you safe, honey." He squeezed her shoulder.

She looked at him. "Can I use your phone?"

"Use my phone? To contact Scarlett?"

She nodded.

He didn't understand her. Had she not grasped anything he'd said? It was as though she was literally addicted to Scarlett.

"No, Harp. You can't use my phone. Why would you ask me that?"

"Whatever."

Glowering at him, she snatched the covers back over her head.

50

Finally, Adrian received good news: Calhoun agreed to his terms for exchanging the data on the flash drive. He visited the investigator's office on Friday morning to pick up his first payment.

Barnes slid the manila, business-size envelope across his desk. Adrian picked it up, peeked inside, saw the ten-thousand-dollar check payable to him, and felt like doing a happy dance in the office.

I deserve this and then some. No matter what Steph says, I'm done apologizing for what I want.

"How long before I get the rest of it?" Adrian asked Barnes. His proposal was ten grand up front and a hundred and fifty thousand later.

"Give us a few weeks to review the details with Calhoun's attorneys. The intel you gathered may not be admissible in a criminal trial. Still, there are other things we can extract from these people."

"Like a fat settlement?"

Barnes lifted his chin but didn't answer.

"I should have negotiated a cut of the settlement instead," Adrian said. "They'll probably pay out millions to keep this quiet."

"Don't get greedy, Mr. Wall. Whatever you've been through with these folks, you've feathered a nice little nest for yourself."

"You can never have too much," he said.

Barnes scowled at him. Adrian didn't care; he didn't need this man's approval. He shook the guy's hand and returned to his car, where he slid the check out of the envelope and kissed it.

Although he had "feathered a little nest for himself," as Barnes said, he realized he needed to improve his negotiation skills. If he had played this situation with more savvy, he could have set himself up for a much more lucrative payday.

That was the downside of always dwelling near the bottom rungs of the ladder: you didn't know what you didn't know until it was too late. The main reason he craved mentorship with Lamont was so the man could share his insights on how to ascend to the top.

But that opportunity had blown up. Lamont hadn't returned any of his messages. He had fired him from afar as if those chummy discussions between them had never happened.

It still pissed off Adrian.

He drove back to his apartment and brewed a fresh pot of coffee. Despite the money funneling in his direction, he needed to apply for unemployment benefits and resume looking for a new job.

He popped open his laptop. His phone buzzed as he was sipping coffee and searching on a job board.

It was an unfamiliar number and possibly a spam call, but when you were job hunting, you learned to answer the phone anyway—it might be an HR recruiter calling to schedule an interview.

"Good morning, Adrian."

Adrian bolted upright in his chair, his sudden movement almost knocking over his coffee cup.

It was Lamont Washington.

51

"I owe you an apology, brother, for how things have deteriorated. I'd like to visit your home this evening and sit down with you and your wife to reach a mutually beneficial agreement on some crucial matters. I request that only you and your lovely wife attend; I will participate on behalf of my family. Can I visit at seven o'clock tonight?"

"He wants to bribe us," Steph said. She stood in their kitchen balancing a glass of wine. Her lips curved in a sardonic grin. "He's already got wind of what you gave to the detective and wants to throw a wrench into the works. Mark my words."

It was about ten minutes before Lamont was scheduled to arrive. Adrian paced their kitchen, his palms moist. He was as nervous as he usually felt before a job interview, and he kept reminding himself that Lamont had contacted *him* for the sit-down and that he held the advantage here.

The phone call earlier that day from Lamont had been such a shock to Adrian that he'd been unable to immediately summon any words in response, while Lamont's message sounded like a carefully prepared script. When Adrian managed to splutter, "Why'd you fire me?" Lamont paused for a few seconds as though cautiously choosing his words. He answered, "We'll discuss it this evening, brother. We'll mend all fences, I promise."

"I don't care how much money he throws at us," Steph said, sipping her wine. "I'm not agreeing to any arrangement that includes Harper and his devil child continuing to see each other. That is nonnegotiable, period."

"I know, Steph. You've only said it ten times already."

"Then I'm saying it eleven times." She swirled the wine in the glass, regarding him with what he interpreted as a skeptical look. "I know how you get when folks are talking about money. I still want that restraining order on Scarlett—whether she's a teenager or not, we can get it done."

"I know."

Adrian drained his can of club soda, grabbed another from the fridge, popped the tab, and took a long swallow.

He wished Lamont hadn't asked Steph to be included in their discussion so it could be just the two of them chatting, man to man. Steph's cynicism and general distrust of wealthy people could muck up the waters.

He circled to the living room, where the windows gave a view of the front of the house. Lamont hadn't yet arrived. Would he drive himself in one of those high-end luxury cars he owned? Did he use a chauffeur when traveling about town?

He wasn't sure what Lamont meant by "mend all fences," but Adrian doubted he would demand reinstatement at FiPro. Too much damage had been done to his reputation at the company for him to return without a cloud of suspicion hanging over him at every step.

Besides, what he craved most was a mentorship with Lamont. For the man to take him under his wing and illuminate the path to the gilded life that Adrian believed he deserved—that instruction was far more valuable than a mere job somewhere. As the saying went:

Give a man a fish, and you feed him for a day. Teach a man to fish, and you feed him for a lifetime.

He wanted Lamont to teach him how to fish. He didn't care about how Lamont had erected legal smoke screens to protect Scarlett from accountability for her crimes; he reasoned that any father with the means would have done the same thing; he surely would have if the positions had been reversed. To Adrian, this wasn't about morality or ethics.

This was about money.

Rubbing his damp palms together, he paced back to the kitchen.

"I'm glad he's not bringing Gina, though," Steph said. "That woman works my last nerve."

"Same," he said, but for different reasons that he'd never share with his wife.

He checked his phone. It was three minutes to seven. He expected Lamont would be precisely on time; a Black man hadn't scaled the heights Lamont had reached by arriving late to meetings.

His bladder was full from his gulping down almost two cans of club soda. Adrian hurried into the half bath off the house's main hallway for a final bathroom run and mirror check. After using the toilet, which seemed to take forever, he washed his hands thoroughly, careful not to splash water on his business casual clothing—a nice blue golf shirt and khakis—and last, he checked his reflection.

He had a bright red pimple in the center of his forehead, like a tiny, glistening third eye. When he was under stress, his diet went to crap, and greasy junk food triggered his acne breakouts, even though he was over forty.

He cursed and glared at the bulging bump.

To squeeze or not to squeeze?

In his back pocket, his phone vibrated. He had scheduled the meeting on his calendar (as if he could have possibly forgotten an upcoming chat with the CEO).

It was seven o'clock.

"Forget it," he said to himself.

He switched off the light and stepped into the hallway.

"It's time!" he called out to Steph, who was still in the kitchen.

"I know!" she answered.

Although he had washed and dried his hands, his palms were already dampening again.

He heard a grumbling vehicle nearby.

"I think he's here!" he said to Steph.

Putting on his best smile and smoothing over the front of his shirt, Adrian walked to the front door, his phone swinging in his hand.

The door exploded open, and the nightmare began.

52

The call had come in at twenty minutes to seven o'clock.

"This is nine-one-one. What's your emergency, please?"

The caller answered with a thin sob, and after a beat, a girl who sounded like a teenager composed herself enough to speak in a fragile voice.

"My mom, my daddy... they've both been drinkin'... they're fighting... he said he's gonna kill her this time!"

The operator, herself a frequent witness to domestic violence between her own parents when she was a child, felt her heart hum in empathy with the young girl.

"Okay, honey, I'm going to help you. First, I need you to get somewhere safe. Can you do that now?"

Another wail. "Daddy's got his gun!"

The operator strived to maintain her composure. From experience, both personal and professional, she understood these domestic violence situations could erupt into chaos with terrifying quickness.

"What's your name, honey? We're sending help."

"Harper... Harper Wall..."

"Can you give me your address, Harper? Tell me where you are."

The operator saw the mobile phone's location as a blue dot on her large flat-screen display, indicating a residential neighborhood in Alpharetta. Still, caller verification of the data was critical.

"851 Rosewood Drive . . . Oh God, I'm so scared. Please send somebody. Mommy has a knife, and Daddy has his gun and says he's gonna kill us all!"

Scarlett had taken an Uber to the Walls' crappy little neighborhood. Sitting on a swing on the community playground, with a perfect view of their house a hundred yards away, she used her burner phone to call 911.

She was so bright, she knew. She had an IQ of 135, smarter than most adults. Because she was only fourteen, though, they thought they could outwit her.

That evening, she would prove them wrong like she always did.

While sucking on a lollipop, she watched the cops pour into the subdivision and gather in front of the house, stealthily preparing for their operation.

She giggled and wriggled her legs as she swung up and down.

This was going to be so much fun.

Kill them all . . .

53

The SWAT team breached the house's door with a battering ram, the tool slamming against the door with a thunderous boom.

Dazed, Adrian staggered backward along the hallway. Steph screamed behind him, and something shattered.

Broken free from its hinges, the door tumbled inward and struck the floor with a bone-jarring crash. Dust, splinters, and debris spread everywhere, forming a hazy cloud. A squad of heavily armed police officers hustled through the doorway. Five, six, seven, eight—he couldn't count them all. In his confused state of mind, it seemed like a hundred.

Why were the cops in his house? He was supposed to be hosting Lamont, Mr. CEO, the wise man who would show him the path to the top. Not these menacing agents of swift and severe justice.

All the cops brandished guns. They aimed at him and barked orders.

"On the floor, motherfucker!"

"Hands up!"

"Drop the weapon!"

His mind reeled. If this was a dream, it was the worst nightmare he'd ever had. He was too terrified to speak, his mouth so dry he couldn't summon enough saliva to form words.

Raising his hands, weak-kneed and stumbling, he bumped into something in the hallway. Items crashed to the floor, and glass broke into tinkling shards.

"I said, drop the weapon!"

The gun barrel nearest him looked like a dark portal to eternity.

It's over, he thought. *The cops will blow me away in my own house, and I don't know why. It'll all be over. Everything is over.*

Although he had used the bathroom only minutes ago, he felt his bladder let go, warm liquid streaming down his thigh.

"Drop it!"

Was he still holding his phone? They thought it was a gun?

He let it fall from his grasp and collapsed to his knees.

The officers swarmed him, guns pointed in his face. One of them snarled and delivered an elbow to Adrian's chest, a blow that felt like a spear penetrating his heart.

"Get down!"

Gasping from the elbow strike, he fell backward. He hit the hardwood floor, pain shooting through him and warm blood filling his mouth—all of it far too real to be a dream, no matter how unimaginable it seemed.

Steph was sobbing. Where was she? He couldn't see her.

Rough hands flipped him over onto his stomach. Adrian turned his head to the side so he could still breathe, but a knee pressed into his back with the crushing weight of a truck.

"I . . . didn't . . . do . . . anything," Adrian said in a wheezing voice. "This . . . is . . . mistake . . ."

A framed photograph had shattered against the floor, inches from his face. It was a picture of him, Steph, and Harper, taken when their daughter was only two years old, in harmonious times when each day was so sweet it made his heart ache with happiness.

I threw it all away, he thought with sudden clarity. The realization was as painful as the agony in his chest. *Oh God, it's my fault. I had it all, and I threw it all away.*

An officer wrenched his arms behind him as if trying to rip them out of their sockets.

"I'm so sorry," Adrian whispered, tears trickling into his mouth.

He didn't know to whom he was apologizing, but in a flash, he saw all his mistakes, every selfish decision that had led to this tragic moment. He would have paid any price for one chance to turn back time and make things right.

"So sorry," he breathed.

They snapped cold metal handcuffs around his wrists.

When the SWAT team exploded through the door, Steph screamed and dropped her wineglass, where she stood at the end of the hallway. It smashed against the floor, glass shards and wine spraying over her feet.

Is this really happening? This can't be real.

Less than a minute ago, she had been preparing to put on a phony smile for Lamont Washington, her thoughts directed to sniffing out the lies she believed he was planning to deploy to manipulate them. She only agreed to this meeting because she felt guilty about Adrian losing his job. She had lost her temper (justifiably so, she reasoned) when she had called Gina and went on her tirade. She hadn't thought about the blowback that might hit Adrian, too.

But the sudden, inexplicable appearance of a team of gun-wielding cops was the most terrifying thing she had ever witnessed in her life.

This can't be happening.

She couldn't stop screaming.

Shouting commands, the officers trained their weapons on Adrian. She was convinced they were going to shoot him. She was going to see them gun down her husband only a few feet away from her.

Oh, sweet Jesus, Lord, please.

Adrian dropped his phone and got on his knees. Officers surrounded him, and one of them hit him in the chest. Adrian sobbed as they pinned him to the floor and cuffed him.

Two officers charged her next.

Instinctively, Steph raised her hands high above her head. Her knees wobbled.

"Are you armed?" one of them asked her. "Do you have a knife?"

A knife? What were they talking about?

"No!" Screaming, she whipped her head back and forth. "No, no, we didn't do anything. We haven't done anything!"

Roughly, one of the officers searched her.

"She's clean," the cop said. "Where's the girl?"

"What girl?" Tears tracked down Steph's cheeks.

"Harper Wall. Your daughter. Where is she?"

Steph's mind raced. "She's not here. She's staying at my sister's house in Roswell."

"Search the house," another officer barked to a colleague, and one of the cops set off to look.

Steph heard footsteps thundering up the stairs and doors slamming.

"What in the hell is going on?" Steph asked.

"Harper Wall reported a domestic dispute," the cop who had searched her said. "She reported that your husband was threatening you with a firearm, and you were armed with a knife."

"What?" Steph said. "That's a lie! Harper's not here! We're not arguing!"

The cop glanced at Adrian, cuffed on the floor, and cursed, anger smoldering in his gaze as some realization seemed to take hold.

The officer who had left to investigate their house returned.

"No one else is here," he said.

"Can I use my phone, please?" Steph asked. "I need to make sure my baby is okay."

"Go ahead," a cop muttered.

Trembling, Steph called Kellie, putting their call on speakerphone so the officers could listen. Kellie confirmed that she and the girls, Willow and Harper, were in the kitchen eating pizza and playing cards; afterward, they planned to watch a movie.

"Harp hasn't left the room in at least an hour, Sis," Kellie said. "What's going on over there?"

"I'll call you back."

Steph ended the call and turned to the police officers.

"It was a goddamn prank," one of the cops said with disgust.

A police officer (the same one who had elbowed him in the chest) removed Adrian's restraints and helped him to his feet. Adrian wobbled, his stomach churning. He propped his hand against the wall to keep his balance.

After taking a brief statement from each of them, the SWAT team cleared out of their house. Two of the cops picked up the front door and positioned it in the doorframe, but the battering ram had damaged it so badly that it would need to be replaced.

Adrian rubbed his teary eyes and looked around at the broken picture frames and overturned furniture. One of the cops had stepped on his phone, cracking the screen. He plucked it off the floor and examined the display.

"Lamont never came," he said dully, chest still throbbing. He dragged his hand down his face.

"It was a setup," Steph said. "It was that evil little monster, Scarlett. She did this to us."

"I heard Lamont's voice on the phone, Steph. It sounded *exactly* like him. Somehow, she must've faked it."

"Pure evil," Steph said.

Adrian touched his head. His temple had knocked against the hardwood floor when the cops had flipped him over to cuff him. A knot pulsed underneath his fingers.

"I'm sorry," he said to Steph. "I know she did it, but it all started with me, and I hope you can forgive me."

54

They packed suitcases and their most important valuables and went to Adrian's apartment to store most of them. After they finished, they took their overnight bags and headed to pick up Harper from Kellie's house.

Until they repaired the front door, they wouldn't be able to stay in their own place—and besides, it wasn't safe.

His apartment might not be safe, either. Scarlett had been there, too.

Even Kellie's home could be risky. The morning of that fateful incident at Six Flags, Adrian picked up Willow from there. Scarlett was in the car and could remember the location.

He didn't dare underestimate the girl anymore. At that point, the only haven was a hotel.

"Calhoun warned me to leave town," Adrian said to Steph. He drove his SUV, Steph riding beside him in the passenger seat; she had left her car behind in the parking garage at his apartment, underneath a mounted security camera. "At the time, I thought he was being too dramatic. Deserting my place because of a kid. It sounded nuts."

"We could have died back there," Steph said. "We could have been gunned down in our home because of her."

"They call it 'swatting,'" Adrian said. "I've heard about it on the news. It started out with guys playing video games, making prank calls to the cops to have a SWAT team sent to another player's house to get revenge. Since then, it's happened all over the country. People have been killed when police show up at a house expecting a shoot-out 'cause of a nasty lie someone tells."

"Lord." Steph hugged herself.

Adrian had to force his mind to stop replaying the memory of the front door erupting inward, the officers storming inside, guns pointed at his face. He shuddered. The incident was going to haunt him for a long time.

"We need to call the cops on *her*," he said.

"The devil probably hid her tracks."

"Harper's going to know how Scarlett pulled this off. I'm sure of it."

"If she'll tell us anything."

"I'll talk to her." He glanced away from the road to look at his wife. "The onus is on me to make this right. I put us in this situation."

Steph watched him, but she said nothing.

"I blew up our family," he said. "I wasn't satisfied with what I had with us—I couldn't see it. I was so stuck on climbing the damned ladder, upgrading or whatever, and I drove you away."

"It's not all on you. I played my part." She shrugged. "But yeah, it was mostly you."

"Glad to hear we agree on something." He made a turn. "Would Harper have gotten sucked into this toxic friendship with Scarlett if our marriage hadn't blown up? I doubt it, Steph."

"It might've still happened, anyway. We can't protect her from everything. She's gonna need to learn how to choose her own friends."

He continued driving, drumming his fingers on the steering wheel as thoughts percolated in his brain.

"I'm going to return Calhoun's money," he said.

She made a sound in her throat. "Are you serious?"

"It feels like dirty money. I don't want it."

"He was going to pay you how much? Another hundred and fifty thousand dollars?"

"All I want is justice," he said. "I want Calhoun to take that file, work with his lawyers to build their case, and take it to those guys and hold them accountable for enabling that kid all these years while she's destroyed people's lives. That's all I want."

"What about your job? FiPro?"

"Didn't you tell me earlier that it's not the only job in the world? I'll have to start over and find something else. I'll figure it out."

Kellie's townhouse was just ahead. He veered into the driveway and parked beside his sister-in-law's car.

"We'll figure it out together," Steph said, touching his hand.

55

Harper's parents came to Willow's house late that Friday night to pick her up. Harper realized something was wrong—something bad had happened.

But no one would tell her anything. The adults spoke in whispered tones, and her parents moved with haste, helping her pack her things.

"We'll explain it all as soon as we get settled in," Daddy said.

"Settled in where?" Harper asked.

"You'll see," Mom said.

Harper sensed that it had something to do with Scarlett. These days, everything that happened to them was connected to her best friend.

Not being able to talk to Scarlett was driving Harper insane. Willow refused to let Harper use her phone, even for a minute, and Aunt Kellie despised Scarlett. She would never agree to let Harper borrow her smartphone, and Harper didn't bother to ask her.

It felt as if she were cut off from her entire world. It was *killing* her.

Her daddy tossed her things into his car, and they drove away from Aunt Kellie's. Not long after, they swung into the Hampton Inn & Suites parking lot.

"We're staying at a hotel?" Harper asked.

"It's the safest place for us right now," Mom said. "It's only temporary, love."

"This is about Scarlett, isn't it?" Tears pushed at Harper's eyes, and she wiped her hand across her face to flick them away. "What happened? Why won't you tell me what's going on?"

Ignoring her, they got out of the car, checked in at the front desk, and went to their room on the second floor.

If Harper hadn't been stewing in anxiety, she might have found this an exciting adventure. Staying at a hotel in their city might have been a lot of fun. But the tension in the air was so thick that Harper felt her stomach looping into knots.

Her parents rented a room with two large beds and said one was for her. As Harper sat on her designated bed, Mom and Daddy settled on the bed across from her.

All of them faced each other. It struck Harper how battered her parents looked, as though they had been through a battle. She'd also noticed earlier that her father had a bruise on his head that must have been painful, and she was afraid to ask what had happened.

At last, Daddy started talking. His reddened eyes suddenly appeared moist, and Harper realized that her dad was about to cry. It alarmed her. She seldom saw her father cry—the last time was when her nana had died.

"I owe you an apology, Harper," he said.

"Why?" Harper asked.

Mom made a shushing sound. "Let your dad talk, honey."

Wringing his hands in his lap, Daddy said, "The last year has been difficult for our family, especially for you. It's because of me. I wasn't happy with how things were going in my life, with my career, with us. I wasn't satisfied. It was a midlife crisis, I guess." He laughed, but it was a sound that made Harper's heart swell with pain.

Daddy rubbed his palms against his jeans. "I had lost perspective on what was important. I took out those feelings on your mother. That's why we got separated."

Harper felt a knot in her throat that was as large as an apple. It hurt to swallow.

"The separation was hardest for you," Daddy said to her. "I realize that now. It's like we turned your entire world upside down."

Harper sniffled. "I hated both of you for it."

Daddy lowered his gaze to the carpet between them, and Mom pursed her lips, her eyes glassy with tears.

"Can you please sit next to me, baby?" Daddy patted the mattress.

Harper moved to the other bed, her knees wobbling as she did. She felt so fragile, like she might shatter into a million pieces.

Daddy took one of her hands in his and Mom's hand, too.

"I'm apologizing to you, Harper, and I ask that you forgive me for being a shitty father. I promise to do better by you."

Harper sucked in a deep breath, her lips quivering. Tears ran down her cheeks in fat rivulets, and she didn't bother to wipe them away this time.

"It's okay," she said. "I . . . I forgive you."

Her father kissed her hand.

"Thank you," he said.

He kissed her mother, put his arms around them, and drew them close in a tight embrace, and Harper held her father as tears poured out of her.

She wished the moment would never end.

But the next thing Daddy said changed everything.

"We came here because Scarlett tried to kill us."

56

Adrian rose from the bed and paced the carpet before Steph and Harper. He explained, as succinctly as he could, precisely what had happened, starting with the phone call from someone who claimed to be Lamont Washington.

Harper looked shell-shocked as he spoke, her lips parted, but he could see the machinery clicking in her mind as she processed his words.

"She did it with AI," Harper blurted after he recounted the day's events.

"AI?" Steph asked. "How?"

"She copies people's voices with some app on her phone," Harper said. Now that Adrian had punctured her usual veil of silence when it came to Scarlett, she seemed eager to speak, voice crackling with energy. "She did it with her dad's voice. She uses it when she wants to skip school—she calls the school and uses her dad's voice to say she's sick or whatever."

"Too damned clever," Adrian said.

He couldn't help but admire the kid's cunning. Christ, she had made a fool out of him. The voice on the phone sounded exactly like Lamont's.

"She cloned my voice, too," Harper said. "When we had our sleepover, she copied my voice. It was supposed to be only for fun."

"Only for fun," Adrian said, the word sour in his mouth as he flashed back on those cops knocking down the door and pointing guns in his face.

"I'm willing to bet she used your voice when she called the police today," Steph said. "I'm convinced that's what she did."

"I understand the nine-one-one system tracks the location of people who make calls," he said.

"She takes Uber everywhere," Harper said.

"The kid came to our neighborhood then to do it," Steph said. "Hell, she did it when she picked up Harper."

"Yeah," Harper said in a mumble. "But how do you know she did it? You don't have any real proof, right? Someone else could've been playing a prank."

"Don't play the fool," Steph said. "You know damn well she did it, Harper."

Harper lowered her head and wouldn't look at either of them.

"We're going to the police with this information," Adrian said. "We're filing a report. This is a crime, and we're not letting this go until she's held accountable—for *everything*."

"Wait, what?" Harper's head snapped up. She looked from Adrian to Steph. "The police?"

"Damn right. The little devil is going to be charged with a crime," Steph said. "We're gonna take the info you gave us to the Alpharetta police station tomorrow morning."

"Until she's arrested, it's not safe for us," Adrian said. "Do you understand, Harper? Your friend is dangerous."

"Snitches get stitches," Harper whispered.

"What?" Adrian and Steph said in unison.

"I can't snitch on my sister," Harper said. "That's the rule. *Never snitch*. Snitches get stitches and wind up in ditches."

Adrian looked at his wife. He saw Steph's jaw tighten as she struggled to maintain patience.

"It's the right thing to do for our family," Adrian said. "Scarlett will be angry with you; she'll probably want revenge, but you'll be safe. As long as we stay united, we're going to be fine."

"I never should have told you guys anything!" Harper shouted.

She shot up from the bed and ran into the bathroom, slamming the door behind her.

Adrian dragged his hand down his sweat-filmed face and plopped onto the bed next to Steph.

"Did you get all that?" he asked her.

"Every word."

She showed him her phone; she had recorded Harper's disclosure of Scarlett's methods. Knowing Harper's continued obsession with her friend, they had anticipated that she would balk at saying anything or refuse to testify later. They wanted to be prepared for either event.

Adrian hated that they needed to resort to covert measures with their child, but they couldn't trust Harper to make judicious decisions regarding Scarlett. The girl had a dangerous hold on their child.

"When this is over, she's going to need counseling," Adrian said.

"Whatever it takes," Steph said. "But until our lives are back to normal, we're keeping total control. The next time our kid sees that little bitch, she'll be wearing an orange jumpsuit."

57

After a while, Harper emerged from the bathroom, but she didn't look at Adrian or Steph or utter a word. She climbed onto her bed and snatched the sheets over her head.

Adrian didn't push it and was relieved that Steph let it go, too. Harper would be salty with them, and that was to be expected. In time, she would come around.

Despite Harper's sullenness, he was encouraged. Confessing his failures to his wife and then his daughter had been one of the hardest things he'd ever done, but for an instant, he'd glimpsed the light that awaited them on the other side of this present darkness, and it gave him hope.

Later in the morning, they would visit the police station and file their report. He anticipated extreme pushback from Gina and Lamont, a team of high-priced attorneys fighting on Scarlett's behalf, and that was where Calhoun's involvement would help, too—especially when Adrian dropped his financial demands.

In the end, justice would prevail. But in the meantime, he had never been so exhausted and craved rest.

He took a perfunctory shower, dressed in fresh pajamas, and brushed his teeth. When he opened the bathroom door, he found Steph standing outside.

"I feel like I could sleep twenty hours straight," he said.

"No kidding. I'm gonna rinse off and crash, too."

She came in and brushed against him as he stepped forward to leave. He felt an almost crippling surge of desire for her. He reached for her waist.

Steph turned to him.

They kissed—a long, deep, tender kiss that left behind electric sensations on Adrian's lips.

"If we had the room to ourselves . . ." he said.

Steph's gaze was warm. "Soon."

Shortly after, she joined him in the queen-size bed, and they switched off the lamps. The only light in the room filtered from the bathroom; they had left the door ajar, and a night-light glowed within.

He fell asleep within a couple minutes of his head hitting the pillow.

Despite his fatigue, he woke in the middle of the night with an urgent need to urinate—an unfortunate and frequent occurrence as he progressed into middle age. He checked his phone, which he had placed on the nightstand.

It was a few minutes past two o'clock. Steph snored softly beside him.

As he shuffled to the bathroom, he passed Harper's bed. His daughter was bundled under the sheets, her form barely visible in the faint light streaming from the restroom.

Something's off.

He stepped to the bed. Slowly, he peeled back the covers.

A pair of pillows lay on the mattress, aligned end to end lengthwise, mimicking a slumbering body.

58

Steph had been dreaming about the evil child. In her dream, she was at home with Adrian, and the cops kicked in the door, and Scarlett led the charge inside. The girl held a gun so large it looked like a cannon, and she screamed at Steph to come toward her, after which she jammed the barrel into Steph's mouth and pulled the trigger—

"Steph." Adrian was shaking her shoulder. "Steph!"

Steph blinked. Harsh light seared her eyes, and for a moment she had no idea where they were.

"Harper's gone," Adrian said. He sounded out of breath.

The comment brought Steph upright on the bed, and her brain fog evaporated. She glanced at the other bed and saw the peeled-back sheets and pillows arranged to appear like a slumbering figure.

"Maybe she went exploring," Adrian said. "Maybe she's downstairs in the lobby or something, but it doesn't *feel* like that to me."

Steph had hidden her purse underneath the bed, worried that Harper would go for it. It was what she would have done if the roles had been reversed. In many ways, she and Harper thought alike.

While Adrian watched her, she got on her knees beside the bed.

The purse lay in the shadows, but Steph knew it had been disturbed while she had been sleeping.

She grabbed and unzipped it, knowing what she would discover before looking.

"She took her phone," Steph said.

59

Snitches get stitches and wind up in ditches.

While her parents slept, Harper lay underneath the bedsheets, wide awake, though it was late at night. The rule that governed her friendship with Scarlett blared like a bullhorn in her mind.

Snitches get stitches and wind up in ditches.

It was the one rule of their sisterhood that neither could ever break without facing dire consequences.

How could she have been so stupid? Why had she told her parents about Scarlett's voice-cloning app?

Maybe because Daddy had apologized for a lot of stuff, she had felt weak right then, and she hadn't been thinking clearly when they told her about what happened.

Sure, Scarlett had *probably* pranked her parents by setting up the fake meeting using her dad's voice and then called the police with some made-up story about them fighting. That was a Scarlett thing to do, and it could have gone very badly for her family.

But no one got hurt, right?

Her parents obviously would never agree, and they were set on going to the police. Scarlett would know Harper had broken their sisterhood rule. She would know Harper had snitched.

The thought was unbearable.

She had to make things right with Scarlett before it blew up in her face.

When she was positive her parents were asleep, she eased out of the bed. She hadn't put on her pajamas earlier; she still wore a T-shirt and pants, so all she needed to do was slide into her Crocs, lying on the floor across the room.

Mom had been keeping her iPhone in her purse. Harper had seen it there several times.

Her father kept his phone on the nightstand on his side of the bed, plugged into an outlet to charge it. Harper moved quietly and picked it up.

His device was locked, but the flashlight app worked without unlocking it. She searched around the room using her hand to block some of the light and avoid waking her parents.

Mom's purse was not on her nightstand.

Where would I hide my purse, if I were my mom?

Harper found it under the bed.

Harper rummaged through Mom's bag, retrieved her phone, and slid the purse back where she had found it.

Finally.

She returned her dad's phone to where it had been on the table. The last thing was to make up her bed so it would look like she was sleeping. Carefully, she put together the pillows and pulled the sheets over them.

She exited the room, quietly closing the door behind her.

Her parents would be furious about what she was doing. They would doubtless ground her for the next five years, but Harper was more worried about Scarlett discovering she had snitched.

Your friend is dangerous.

Daddy claimed to have evidence of crimes Scarlett had committed—actual murders. Yeah, right. Drowning her cousin in the swimming pool. Planning the poisoning of her dead friend's parents. If Scarlett had done those terrible things, why hadn't she ever gotten in trouble for them?

What Harper was sure of: Scarlett would never hurt her. They were sisters.

So long as she didn't snitch.

Harper turned on her phone and felt a wave of relief. Thankfully, the battery was at fifty percent.

At night, the hotel corridor was quiet, lit with soft overhead lighting, and she didn't see anyone as she hurried to the bank of elevators.

She fired off a text message to her friend.

I'm back.

It was late at night, but Harper expected a quick response, and she got it.

Howdy, stranger. Where the hell are you, sis?

Harper opened the map app and sent the location to Scarlett.

We really need to talk, Harper typed. *Now. Major trouble is coming.*

I'm coming to get you. Be there in fifteen.

60

They had dressed, left their room, and taken the elevator to the hotel lobby.

Adrian had opened the FindMyPhone app on his phone to track Harper. Although he had been exhausted when he had fallen asleep, adrenaline had awakened him as effectively as if he'd drunk an entire pot of coffee.

"She's not far from the hotel," he told Steph. "Looks like she's about a mile away but on the move."

"Jesus." Steph's bloodshot eyes looked like they were on fire. "Where the hell is she going?"

"You know where. Scarlett might already be with her."

"God."

The lobby was vacant and quiet at that late hour. The only occupant was a bored-looking desk clerk playing games on his smartphone and absently digging in his ear. He frowned at their approach.

"Something you need?" he asked. He took his finger out of his ear and glanced at it to check what he had found.

"Did you see a teenage girl enter the lobby a little while ago?" Adrian asked.

"She's our daughter," Steph said.

"She left." He glanced at his phone. "Like ten minutes ago?"

"You didn't question her about where she was going?" Steph asked. "She's only thirteen!"

"She ain't my kid."

"Was she with anyone?" Adrian asked. "Did anyone come in to greet her or something?"

"I saw her get in a blue Porsche. Sweet ride."

"You see a kid get in a strange car in the middle of the night, and you don't lift a finger," Steph said, glowering at the man.

"I only work here, lady. You ought to work on your parenting."

While Steph cursed, Adrian pulled her away from the counter.

"Gina and Lamont have a blue Porsche," he said.

"One of that demon child's parents picked up our daughter in the middle of the night? What's the matter with them?"

Adrian called Harper. Predictably, she didn't answer, so he texted her the simple question: *Where are you?*

She didn't reply.

He expanded the map to indicate Harper's location.

"She's at a Taco Bell on Haynes Bridge," he said.

"Then we're going, too."

They rushed out of the lobby. Adrian scrambled behind the wheel of his SUV and racked the phone in the dashboard holder so he could reference it while he drove.

He started the engine and slammed the gearshift into Reverse.

"The dot's gone," Steph said.

Adrian looked at the display. Steph was right.

Location tracking for Harper's phone had been disabled.

61

When Harper saw the sleek, shiny blue sports car veer in front of the hotel, she thought one of Scarlett's parents had come to pick her up. But then the passenger-side window slid down, revealing Scarlett behind the wheel.

Uh-oh. The last time she'd gone joyriding with Scar, her friend's reckless driving had terrified her. They had almost crashed into a tree.

"Get in, sis," Scarlett said. The car's engine growled.

Her hand resting on the door handle, Harper chewed on her bottom lip. She looked over her shoulder at the night-darkened hotel behind her. Her parents would lose their minds if they discovered what she was doing.

"Sis, are you coming or not?" Scarlett asked. "I drove all the way over here to see you. Get in!"

Scarlett revved the engine. If she had driven all the way to the hotel from her house without winding up in a wreck, Harper reasoned, she must've known how to drive the car.

Most important was the warning that looped in her thoughts: *Snitches get stitches . . .*

Going back inside to her parents was out of the question.

Harper opened the door and slid onto the soft leather seat. After closing the door, she snapped on the seat harness.

Like her, Scarlett wore a T-shirt, sweatpants, and Crocs. She had pulled her long auburn hair into a ponytail. But crimson webbed her hyperalert gaze, stress lines bracketing her usually jovial features.

Scarlett raked her gaze over Harper, her slender fingers clenching the steering wheel.

"Why're you guys staying here?" Scarlett asked.

"They said you called the police on them, Scar. That the cops came and knocked down the door and were gonna shoot them."

"That's what they told you, huh? Do you believe that, sis?"

Scarlett mashed the gas pedal. The sudden acceleration flung Harper back against the seat.

She wheeled out of the parking lot, zooming onto the road like a race car driver. Harper's stomach flip-flopped.

The car's sunroof was wide open. Cool air gusted inside, thrashing their hair.

"Can you slow down, please?" Harper asked.

"I promised I'd take you for a ride in Lamont's Porsche, remember? I know what I'm doing. We're gonna have fun."

They screeched to a halt at a red light. Harper exhaled, forcing herself to breathe.

"Your parents keep lying to you about everything, sis," Scarlett said. "Don't you hate that? Why can't they be honest with you, for once?"

"They're scared of you," Harper said.

"They should be." She grinned.

As the light switched to green, Scarlett floored the accelerator.

Oh God, Harper thought. *She's gonna kill us.*

At that time of night, the roads were mostly empty, which was good for them because Scarlett's wild driving otherwise undoubtedly would have led to a collision with another vehicle. She swung through twists and turns with abandon.

"I'm hungry," Harper said. She wasn't really; she merely wanted Scarlett to pull over somewhere so she could catch her breath.

"Me, too. Let's go here."

A Taco Bell was ahead. Scarlett whipped the Porsche into the parking lot, turning so rapidly that Harper's head rapped against the passenger window.

"Ouch!" Harper cried.

Scarlett giggled. She pulled into the drive-thru lane.

They ordered food and drinks. Harper worried that the food service worker would look at them, see how young they were, and call the police, but the guy at the window tried to flirt with Scarlett, and Scarlett, being Scarlett, blew a kiss at him and flicked her tongue suggestively, and he gave them extra tacos for free.

This was the excitement of hanging out with her friend. You never knew what would happen because she might do anything, and because she was so pretty and lively, people craved her attention and approval. Around her, Harper felt like a drab planet orbiting a giant sun—but she got to bask in her light.

Scarlett parked in a corner of the nearly empty lot, and they tore open the bags of food.

"I'm so hungry I can eat crap food like this," Scarlett said. She swiped a strand of lettuce away from her lips. "I've been sick worrying about you, sis. It was tearing me up to be unable to talk to you."

"Blame my folks," Harper said. She bit into a taco.

As if on cue, Harper's phone buzzed. It was Daddy calling.

"They're onto you now," Scarlett said.

Harper didn't answer, but Daddy sent her a message: *Where are you?*

"They're gonna track us," Harper said.

"Gimme that." Scarlett swiped her iPhone. "Let me show you how to turn off location tracking. Do you know your PIN?"

Harper gave her the number. Scarlett tapped the screen while Harper watched the process she followed.

"Done." Scarlett gave her back the phone. "They can't track shit now. Lying asses."

They ate their food and slurped their sodas.

"I believed their story," Harper said in a low voice.

Scarlett had been raising a straw to her lips. She cut a sideways gaze at Harper.

"What did you say?" Scarlett said.

Her voice had an edge, like a knife.

Harper's words poured out of her in a breathless torrent: "I sort of told them about the voice cloning thing you do, 'cause Daddy said your dad called him, but it wasn't really him, and then they said the police told them that *I* called the cops on them to say they were fighting, but it wasn't really me, and I remember you copied my voice and you could've done it and I was worried, Scar, my mom and dad could have died, and I'm sorry, I'm sorry I shouldn't have said anything, but now they're gonna go to the police and report you and they'll take my words and use them, and I'm sorry, I'm sorry, I'm so sorry!"

Harper finally stopped talking, her chest heaving, fresh tears wetting her cheeks.

Scarlett only stared at her for a heart-stopping moment without saying a word.

Then she started laughing.

62

Adrian drove to the Taco Bell because it was the last location the app had registered before Harper had disabled tracking on her phone. When they arrived, he saw only one vehicle in the parking lot, which wasn't a Porsche.

"We must've just missed them," Steph said through clenched teeth. "What now? Should we call the police?"

Adrian didn't answer, his thoughts racing. On impulse, he pulled into the drive-thru lane.

"You want to eat?" Steph asked, incredulous.

He edged past the order station and pulled up to the drive-thru window. A twenty-something guy slid it open.

"The order board is working," he said. "Whatever, what do you need?"

"Did you see a blue Porsche pull through here only a few minutes ago?" Adrian asked.

Recognition brightened the man's gaze. "Why?"

"Our daughter was in the car. We're trying to find her."

"She's only thirteen," Steph said, leaning across Adrian.

"Oh." The man's face reddened. "Crap, I knew the hottie driving was kinda young, but not, like, jailbait."

Adrian and Steph locked gazes at the same instant.

"That crazy little bitch is *driving*," Steph said, voicing his exact thoughts. "Jesus, I don't believe it."

Adrian thanked the guy and veered out of the lane, nosed into a nearby parking spot.

"I think she's done this before," he said. "Scarlett made a crack about joyriding in Gina's SUV when I picked them up to go to Six Flags. I thought she was only joking."

"Please, God." Steph steepled her hands together in a prayer gesture. "Please, Lord, keep our baby safe."

Adrian didn't want to make his next move, but he saw no alternative. He called Gina, allowing the call to be broadcast on speakerphone mode.

She didn't pick up. He called her twice more. On his third try, she finally answered in a throaty, tired voice.

"You tryin' to hit me up for another booty call, boo? Since we *both* know you didn't finish the job last time. Your little text message didn't fool me."

Steph swiveled in her seat to glare at Adrian. Adrian felt blood warm his cheeks, but he couldn't get sidetracked.

"Listen, Harper is gone," he said. "She's in your Porsche. *Scarlett is driving.*"

"She's only fourteen!" Steph said. "Do you crazy-ass people let her drive your cars, too?"

"Well, damn." Gina groaned. "My baby girl is gonna be the death of me. She sure is."

"I can't track Harper's phone anymore," Adrian said. "We know they were at a Taco Bell on Haynes Bridge a few minutes ago. Can you track Scarlett?"

"Please?" Steph said, hands clasped.

"We can see where the car is on our app," Gina said. "But listen, y'all, *no police*. If you call the cops, I'm not telling you a damn thing."

"Fine," he said. "Where are they now?"

A few seconds later, his phone buzzed. Gina had pinged him the vehicle's location on a map.

They weren't far, but the vehicle was on the move.

"Keep texting me, please, all right?" he said. "We'll be in touch."

"No cops," Gina said again. "We're coming."

As he ended the call and shifted into Drive, he felt Steph scrutinizing him.

"Booty call?" she asked.

"Nothing happened, like she said. But she wanted it to."

"And you didn't?"

"No."

He wasn't sure she believed him, but he didn't have the mental bandwidth to entertain the discussion.

Turning away from him, Steph took her phone out of her purse.

"Who're you calling?" he asked.

"The police. These people don't get to dictate what we do. I'm trying to save our daughter."

63

Still caught up in a manic laughing fit, Scarlett sped out of the restaurant parking lot and swerved back onto the road, the car bouncing over a curb. Food spilled out of the bags and onto the seats and floor.

Harper's heart thrashed like a frightened bird banging against a cage. She'd never seen Scarlett act like this before—like she had slid full tilt into a frightening state of mania.

She wished she hadn't told Scarlett what she had done, but what choice did she have?

Scarlett ran a red traffic light without slowing at all, and if it hadn't been for the late hour and the empty roads, they surely would have gotten into a wreck just then.

I've gotta get away from her, or she's gonna kill us.

"You, you, you, you, you!" Scarlett said, shifting from laughter to an eerie, screeching voice. "You, you, you, you, you!"

"I'm sorry, but I had to tell you—"

"Aargh!" Scarlett shrieked.

Harper reared back in her seat as Scarlett pounded her fists against the steering wheel.

"Zoomie, zoom, zoom, zoom!" Scarlett cried. "It's fun, fun, fun, fun, motherfuckin' fun!"

She whipped the Porsche from one lane to the next. Harper cried out, bracing herself for a collision.

"Wheeee!" Scarlett shouted. "Wheeeeee!"

"Please stop!" Harper said, her breath hitching in her chest. "Please, we're gonna die."

"I'm not afraid to die, are you? Huh? Dying would be fun, fun, fun!"

They ran through another red light. Someone honked at them.

"Oh God." Harper felt the food she had eaten churning in her stomach.

Madness flashed in Scarlett's eyes as she ranted.

"I kill people, sis, I fuckin' kill people, and you know why? You wanna know why? 'Cause it's fun! It feels so good! It makes me feel alive! Alive! I wanted to see your stupid parents gunned down, and I was gonna walk by and take a fuckin' picture of the carnage. I drowned my little annoying bitch cousin and I basically poisoned Zoey's parents. I pushed a crusty old bitch down the stairs in her house and killed her, too—nobody knows about that one! It was fun! Why can't you all see how much fun I'm having, huh? You and your boring and fuckin' normal stupid lives! I'm the goddamn queen of the universe, bitches! Woohoo!"

Harper was shaking her head, tears streaming down her face.

"Please, Scarlett," she said. "Please, stop."

"But we're having fun!"

Scarlett grinned, showing so many teeth that Harper was convinced the girl would leap toward her and bite her.

Harper spotted a gas station ahead, the store well-lit.

"I've gotta pee, super bad," Harper said. *Maybe I need to throw up, too.* "Please, I'll be really quick."

Without a reply, Scarlett veered into the gas station parking lot, clipping the curb with the edge of the sports car. She zoomed into a parking spot and slammed to a stop.

"Three minutes," Scarlett said. She added: "I'm timing you, *snitch*."

Her glower sent ice spinning through Harper's veins. Dramatically, Scarlett picked up her own phone and set the timer.

Harper climbed out of the car, her legs limp as spaghetti. Steeling herself, she hurried inside the station.

A middle-aged woman with a pierced nose and a giant butterfly tattoo on her neck stood behind the counter. She frowned at Harper's entrance.

"Are you all right, honey?" she asked.

No, I'm not all right. I'm with my friend, and she's scaring me to death.

"I need to use the ladies' room," Harper said.

The woman pointed, her brow creased. Harper felt the woman watching her as she made her way to the back of the store.

She didn't see anyone else inside, but that wasn't surprising. It was past two o'clock in the morning.

Inside the restroom, Harper sat on the toilet—she really did need to pee, she discovered—and as she sat there, she studied her phone.

I've gotta get away from her.

She called her dad.

"Where are you?" he asked, and she heard panic in his voice. "We've been trying to catch up to you."

Hearing her father triggered another wave of tears.

"We're at a gas station; I'm in the bathroom." She sobbed. "Daddy, I'm scared. She's gonna do something to me."

"Wait there, baby," Mom said. "Stay away from that little demon and try to stall as long as you can. We're coming, and so are the police."

"Okay."

"Can you turn on the location tracking again?" Daddy said.

"I'll try. I have to go, or she's going to come get me; she's timing me."

"Ask someone there for help," he said. "They'll call the police, too."

"Okay, I'm sorry."

"We love you," Mom said.

Hearing those words from her mom, despite every disobedient and stupid thing she had done to infuriate her parents, gave Harper strength.

Harper ended the call. She remembered how Scarlett had disabled location tracking, and she followed the steps to switch the feature on again.

Now, get help.

Harper washed her hands and bolted out of the restroom.

Scarlett stood right outside the door.

"I was going to come in there and get you," Scarlett said. She showed Harper the pocketknife she carried in her right hand; it was the pink-handled blade she kept in her purse. "Snitches get stitches."

Harper swallowed.

Stall, get help.

"I want to buy some candy," Harper said.

Scarlett rolled her eyes. "Do it."

Scarlett followed her closely as she went to a rack of chips and other snacks and selected a bag of some random candy. They headed to the counter.

The clerk's gaze bounced between the two of them.

"Aren't you girls too young to be out driving?" she asked.

"Mind your business, skank," Scarlett said.

The woman blinked at this unexpected insolence. Harper put the item on the counter.

"I don't have any money," she said to Scarlett.

"Seriously?" Scarlett reached toward her purse.

While Scarlett was distracted, Harper looked at the clerk and lip-synched: *Help me. Help me. Please.*

The clerk's face tightened, and she nodded, one of her hands slipping beneath the counter.

"What was that?" Scarlett spun toward the woman. "I caught something there. What're you doing with your hand, huh? Are you pushing a security button to call the cops?"

"Pay for your things and be on your way, miss," the clerk said.

Scarlett glanced from Harper to the clerk, and Harper got a sinking feeling, but she still wasn't prepared for what happened next.

"I told you, snitches get stitches, sis," Scarlett said.

With a quick swipe of her hand, Scarlett flicked her knife across the clerk's throat.

64

With Harper's reactivation of the phone's location tracking function, Adrian could see her location without Gina's assistance.

"They're at a gas station like she said. A couple miles ahead of us."

"Hurry," Steph said.

"We'll get there." He clutched the steering wheel in his clammy hands. "I'm driving as fast as I can without killing us."

Daddy, I'm scared. She's gonna do something to me.

Adrian hadn't believed he could be any more afraid, but his fear had topped new levels. Steph had already called the police and reported the incident, resisting the operator's assumption that this was a minor case of teens out joyriding. *This girl is a murderer, and she's going to kill our daughter.*

Unfortunately, they didn't have the license plate number to provide to the police, but how many blue Porsches were barreling around the area at this time of night?

They rocketed down the road, getting closer, while Steph called

911 again and told the operator what Harper had said and gave her location.

Please, God, Adrian prayed. *Please, help us save our child.*

65

Blood spouted from the clerk's throat like water from a broken pipe, spraying the counter, the cash register, and a tower of snacks standing nearby. Hands scrabbling at her neck, the woman collapsed to the floor.

Harper screamed.

"Come on!" Scarlett grabbed her hand like an impatient parent.

This can't be happening. It can't be happening...

Harper felt like she had exited her body and was floating somewhere above herself, watching events unfold. She saw Scarlett drag her out of the gas station and throw her into the passenger seat of the car; she saw her body rip the seat harness across her chest. Watched Scarlett slam the car into Reverse and screech backward, the bumper clipping the front of an SUV that had pulled into the parking lot, the collision jostling her body in the seat. Witnessed Scarlett howling with glee and then flooring the gas pedal, sending the car roaring forward and her body popping backward against the seat...

In a rush, Harper snapped back into herself.

Scarlett was shrieking.

"We're going down, bitches! Sisters to the end!"

She swerved back and forth across the two dark lanes unfurling ahead of them. The engine bellowed like thunder.

She's gonna kill us, Harper thought. It was her first clear, conscious thought since Scarlett had slashed the clerk's throat.

No, I won't let her. I don't wanna die.

Harper launched across the seats to wrestle the steering wheel out of Scarlett's grasp.

Fighting against her, Scarlett cackled and howled, wordless cries of glee and madness.

The car plunged across the road's shoulder like a cannon shot. It plummeted down a steep embankment, tossing Harper's stomach into her throat.

The vehicle tumbled end over end down the hill with a clamorous series of bangs and thuds. Jostled about roughly, Harper tasted blood as she bit her tongue. Airbags deployed with a *pop*, smacking against her face with enough force to nearly knock her out.

As if from a great distance, she heard the splash of the car landing in a creek.

Cold water gurgled into the vehicle.

They started to sink.

66

Driving fast, Adrian spotted the gas station ahead on the right. The blue dot on the map indicated that Harper had already departed and traveled elsewhere.

He didn't slow down but saw a black Tahoe angled across the parking lot near the station, the driver's-side door hanging open. A man wearing a hoodie paced near the store's entrance, phone pressed to his ear.

"Something's going on there." Steph peered out her passenger window.

"We keep going till we find our kid."

He blasted through a red light. The speedometer hung at eighty miles an hour.

We're coming, Harp. Hang on. We're coming.

The two-lane road twisted, rose, and dropped.

The dot on the map stopped moving.

"We're close," Steph said in between prayers.

The SUV's headlamps revealed a ragged, mowed-down line of shrubs along the road's shoulder.

Purely on instinct, Adrian hit the brakes. They shuddered to a stop at the mangled bushes.

"Calling the police again," Steph said.

Adrian threw open his door and ran around the front of his vehicle. He peered beyond the arc of the headlamps, searching the weed-choked embankment.

A nearby streetlamp offered only weak illumination of the area. But brighter lights glowed farther down, in a creek: a pair of glowing orbs.

A car . . .

Adrian shouted.

He started running.

67

We're sinking.

Harper didn't black out when the car landed in the water, but she sure felt like she was dreaming. The puffy airbags in her face. The seat belt like a strip of fire across her chest. The warm blood in her mouth.

It was surreal.

Cold, dark water poured inside through the open windows and sunroof. The rear of the car was sinking first, the front end pointed toward the sky, headlights shining, showing an owl perched on tree branches above them, the bird peering down at them.

It's like we're on a submarine, descending into the ocean...

Beside her, Scarlett's head lolled, lips parted. In the eerie glow of the dashboard lights, Harper saw blood trickling down the girl's face.

Was she dead or only unconscious?

Get out, Harper!

That voice, the wise part of herself always waiting on standby to advise her of the right thing to do if only she bothered to listen, shouted like a loudspeaker in her thoughts.

The cold water rose up to her waist, fast, like the massive mouth of a subterranean beast that wanted to swallow her forever.

Shivering, she unsnapped the seat harness and pushed it away, the belt sloshing through the encroaching water.

She heard a soft, whimpering sound and realized it was coming from her.

The passenger window was only partially open, and she didn't know where the controls were to lower it. She had never been in this car before.

But the sunroof yawned open, a portal to life.

She reached up with both hands and grabbed the edges of the sunroof. Icy, foul water poured over her face and into her mouth, making her gag.

She pulled herself up, grateful for PE class and the teacher's insistence on making them do pull-ups. But her sodden clothes added extra weight, and the steadily invading water fought to pull her back into the car.

Groaning and straining, she dragged herself up through the sunroof.

Scarlett seized her left leg.

"*Snitch!*" Scarlett's eyes smoked. "*Snitch bitch!*"

"No!" Harper screamed.

Scarlett pulled her down.

Harper pedaled her legs in a frenzy, water splashing. Scarlett lost hold of her. Thrusting herself upward again, Harper popped through the sunroof and broke free from the sinking car.

The water surrounding her was so cold, so deep. Deeper than any pool she had ever encountered. She kicked and batted her arms, the muddy water obscuring her vision.

"Help!" she gasped.

Strong, familiar arms encircled her.

"I've got you, Harp," Daddy said.

68

Adrian clutched his daughter against him, her shivering body feeling as frail as it had on the day she was born when he held her for the first time.

He didn't know what had become of Scarlett. Had she drowned in the sinking Porsche? Had she already escaped?

He didn't care. All that mattered was saving Harper.

Keeping one arm underneath Harper to hold her aloft in the water, he swam toward the creek's shore. He wasn't the greatest swimmer and was thankful to find Steph, stronger in the water than he was, waiting nearby to assist.

"We've got you, baby," Steph said, taking her from him.

Harper coughed and spluttered, but it sounded as if she were breathing. Steph had called the police and given their location. Help would soon arrive.

Behind them, water splashed.

Adrian was about to spin around, expecting the worst, but he was too late. Scarlett roped her arm around his neck, strangling him from behind.

She's still alive. Shit.

She screeched and howled in his ear, a vicious stream of unintelligible curses.

He struggled to break her grip, but she was unexpectedly strong. She twisted her legs around his waist, entangling him in her long limbs.

It was like fighting off an octopus. Water sprayed and splattered as he flailed.

Sharp metal flashed in the moonlight. He felt a fiery, stabbing sensation in his chest.

She had flayed him with a knife.

He gasped and gulped in dirty water.

Screaming, she slashed him again and again. Crippling pain tore through him.

She's gonna kill me.

She shrieked in his ear with malicious laughter, chanting: "Die, die, die, die, die!"

No . . . didn't come this far to let this kid kill me.

He roared: "Get. Off. Me!"

As a wave of desperate adrenaline flooded him, he grabbed fistfuls of her long, wet hair. He ripped at it, determined to tear it out at the roots.

Scarlett wailed in pain, her grip loosening.

He hammered his fist into her nose.

The girl's head snapped backward, her eyes rolling back to expose the whites. Unconscious, she floated away on the creek currents like a piece of driftwood.

Wheezing, Adrian swam toward the shore. Blood seeped from the gashes in his chest, and a cold, numbing weakness spread through him.

Keep going. You can make it.

Ahead, he saw Steph had safely pulled Harper out of the creek. Harper sat against a gnarled tree, alive.

The sight of her forced Adrian to swim harder. His feet finally met a firm surface, and he staggered out of the murky waters.

Steph rushed to him.

"Oh God, you're bleeding all over," she said.

His vision blurred, but he made out two other figures hurrying down the embankment to the creek: Gina and Lamont.

He flipped his middle finger at them and collapsed into Steph's arms.

A chorus of warbling sirens echoed in his ears as he sank into blackness.

AFTER

Nine years later.

Adrian and Steph hosted a party on the eve of Harper's college graduation. Over forty family and friends crowded into their home to celebrate.

To Adrian, his daughter's achievement felt like the culmination of a long journey that had begun the day she was born. He could still see her as a child, taking her first steps and saying her first words. The years passed by so quickly, and every day was precious.

As he strolled around their home, sipping a club soda and chatting with guests, he reflected on the life-shattering events that might have made this day impossible.

Fortunately, he had recovered from Scarlett's attack—the blade had missed his heart and vital arteries. But Scarlett, too, had survived that fateful night, and at last, due to overwhelming evidence, she was held responsible for her crimes. She was serving time in prison for several felonies despite her parents' best attempts to free her via multiple appeals; Adrian had lost track of the cases and her status since their efforts had failed so many times.

After much counseling, many tears, and a generous dose of

unconditional love from Adrian and Steph, Harper had moved on from that traumatic period, grown up, and developed genuine, healthy friendships. Many of those friends had come to the party.

"We did it," Adrian said during a private moment in the kitchen with Steph.

He could see in her clear-eyed gaze that she knew what he meant. No explanation was needed.

They exchanged a tender kiss.

"Time for the college girl to open her gifts," Steph said.

Adrian asked everyone to gather in the family room, where they had set up a small gift table. A collection of colorful bags, envelopes, and wrapped presents waited to be opened.

Harper gushed excitedly as she opened each one and thanked the givers. The last item she chose to open was a box adorned in polka-dot wrapping paper, about the size of a package that might contain a basketball.

"There's no tag on this one," Harper said. "Hmm. A secret gift?"

"Go on and open it, sweetie," Steph said.

Harper tore off the wrapping, exposing a cardboard box. She peeled open the flaps.

As she looked inside, her smile crumbled into an expression of horror.

And then she screamed.

Alarmed, guests rose from their seats. Adrian hurried across the room, seized the box, and looked inside.

It held a rag doll designed to resemble a young Black girl, but the face had been slashed with a razor, stuffing leaking from the multiple tears. A typewritten note had been nailed to the doll's chest.

Happy graduation, sis.
Snitches still get stitches.

HEAR MORE FROM BRANDON

Did you enjoy this novel? Visit www.brandonmassey.com now to sign up for Brandon Massey's free mailing list. Mailing list members get advance news on the latest releases, the chance to win autographed copies in exclusive contests, and much more. Your email address will never be shared and you can unsubscribe at any time.

ABOUT BRANDON MASSEY

Brandon Massey was born June 9, 1973, and grew up in Zion, Illinois. He lives with his family near Atlanta, Georgia, where he is at work on his next novel. Visit his web site at www.brandon-massey.com for the latest news on his upcoming books.